Deadlier than the Rest

MacLarens of Fire Mountain

SHIRLEEN DAVIES

Book Five in the MacLarens of Fire Mountain Series

Other Books by Shirleen Davies

Historical Western Romance Series

MacLarens of Fire Mountain

Tougher than the Rest, Book One

Faster than the Rest, Book Two

Harder than the Rest, Book Three

Stronger than the Rest, Book Four

Deadlier than the Rest, Book Five

Redemption Mountain

Redemption's Edge, Book One
Coming fall of 2014

MacLarens of Boundary Mountain

Colin's Quest, Book One
Coming in 2015

Contemporary Romance Series

MacLarens of Fire Mountain

Second Summer, Book One

Hard Landing, Book Two

One More Day, Book Three – Coming summer of 2014

For more information about Shirleen Davies and her books visit: www.shirleendavies.com

For permission requests, contact the publisher.
Avalanche Ranch Press, LLC
PO Box 12618
Prescott, AZ 86304

Cover artwork by idrewdesign
Book design and conversions by Joseph Murray at 3rdplanetpublishing.com

ISBN-10: 0989677354

ISBN-13: 978-0-9896773-5-6

Description

"A passionate, heartwarming story of the iconic MacLarens of Fire Mountain. This captivating historical western romance grabs your attention from the start with an engrossing story encompassing two romances set against the rugged backdrop of the burgeoning western frontier."

Connor MacLaren's search has already stolen eight years of his life. Now he close to finding what he seeks—Meggie, his missing sister. His quest leads him to the growing city of Salt Lake and an encounter with the most captivating woman he has ever met.

Grace is the third wife of a Mormon farmer, forced into a life far different from what she'd have chosen. Her independent spirit longs for choices governed only by her own heart and mind. To achieve her dreams, she must hide behind secrets and half-truths, even as her heart pulls her towards the ruggedly handsome Connor.

Known as cool and uncompromising, Connor MacLaren lives by a few, firm rules that have served him well and kept him alive. However, danger stalks Connor, even to the front range of the beautiful Wasatch Mountains, threatening those he cares about and impacting his ability to find his sister.

Can Connor protect himself from those who seek his death? Will his eight year search lead him to his sister while unlocking the secrets he knows are held tight within Grace, the woman who has captured his heart?

Read this heartening story of duty, honor, passion, and love in book five of the MacLarens of Fire Mountain series.

"If you're a reader who wants to discover an entire family of characters you can fall in love with, this is the series for you." – Authors to Watch

Dedication

This book is dedicated to some of my readers who have taken the time to send messages of praise and encouragement. Without you I would have little insight on how well I am meeting your expectations. My sincerest thanks to Patty, Nancy, Barbara, Amber, Kim, Amy, Daniel, and all those who have watched this journey unfold. Your enthusiasm and support has been a true blessing.

Acknowledgements

I want to thank my editor, Danielle Gavin, who offered insights and expertise.

Many thanks also go out to my wonderful resources, including Diane Lebow, an expert at guiding my social media endeavors, Joseph Murray who is fabulous at formatting my books for both print and electronic versions, and idrewdesign, the talent behind the wonderful book covers. Your work is greatly appreciated.

Deadlier than the Rest

DEADLIER than the REST

Prologue

Red Hook, Brooklyn

The combination of sea air and early evening drizzle blanketed the walkway in a sheet of slippery, wet slime. It was late afternoon and already the sky was as black as pitch. Meggie shifted from one foot to the other waiting for her brother. He was seldom late. She'd already waited an hour.

Her lower back ached almost as much as the muscles between her shoulder blades. She bent down to stretch the tired muscles, then stood to lift both arms above her head. Ten hour days as a cleaning woman and cook at the boarding house were taking a toll.

Meggie turned at the sound of footsteps, sure it was her oldest brother, Connor. He worked at the harbor in Red Hook, Brooklyn. Although many found it hard to find a job, Connor had always been able to find something at the bustling shipping port.

She looked up when the sound stopped, then turned in a circle. *Was he playing a game, sneaking up to scare her?* That would be just like him, trying to get her to laugh after making her wait.

The footsteps started again, becoming louder as they grew closer. Whoever it was made no attempt to conceal their approach.

"You alone, Missy?"

She heard the voice before she could make out the silhouette of the man who'd emerged from a nearby alley. He wasn't tall, perhaps five-feet-six, and his girth extreme. Dirty, ragged, damp clothing clung to his arms and legs.

Meggie stepped away at his approach. "No, I'm not alone. My brother is inside," she indicated the brick building next to her.

The stranger looked at the building and scoffed. "Ain't no one in there, Missy. Everyone knows the place is abandoned." He looked her over as if he were making some kind of decision.

Fear rippled through her. She'd never been approached before—Connor was always here to make sure of it. Meggie looked one direction, then another in a frantic attempt to find help.

She took another step back, then another, planning to turn and run. From out of nowhere a strong arm wrapped around her waist, pulling her close, and clamping a hand over her mouth. It belonged to someone taller than the stranger before her. She could feel his breath, smell the stench at his whispered command.

"Now don't you try to fight us. You understand what I'm say'n?"

Instead of complying, Meggie pushed hard against him, trying to kick backwards at his legs.

He swung her around. The slap snapped her head back. He pulled out a dirty rag and stuffed the gag in her mouth. Tears stung her eyes but the defiance remained. He swung her over his shoulder, then disappeared down the narrow alley, the other man on his heels.

****

He'd looked everywhere. Up and down the main street as well as every alley. The panic he felt closed in on him. Connor was late but he'd expected her to wait. Meggie knew how dangerous it was to walk home alone. Either he or their other brother, Pierce, accompanied her everywhere. But maybe...

Connor broke into a run, increasing his speed with each block. His arms pumped in a frantic attempt to increase his speed. The old, crumbling building where they lived was one block further. He hit the door hard, pushing it open, and dashed up the stairs. Connor fumbled for the key. Pierce pulled it open and stood back, allowing him to enter.

"Is Meggie here?" His breath came out in labored gasps. He bent at the waist and placed his hands on his knees trying to calm his breathing.

"She's not with you?" Pierce responded, his eyes wide. He poked his head out the door, then walked to the stairwell and looked down. No one.

"No. She wasn't there when I arrived. I looked everywhere." Connor stopped to think. Was there someplace else she'd go? Her closest friend lived blocks away. No, Meggie wouldn't go there alone he decided. "We've got to find her." He grabbed a tattered coat from a hook and slipped into it while Pierce did the same. "But we keep each other in sight. I don't intend to lose you, also."

They searched for hours, stopped everyone they saw to ask if they'd seen her. It was after midnight when the brothers walked into the police station—all other options exhausted.

The police did what they could, at first, but with little evidence, they gave up within a few days. There was no body, nothing suspicious other than the fact she was gone. The station captain had more than once insinuated she was just a runaway.

Connor continued to leave each morning for his job at the docks but each night he searched, never giving up, and never believing Meggie had run away.

Days passed, then weeks, without word. On the anniversary of her disappearance one year later, Connor quit his job, packed what little belongings Pierce and he owned, and began what would become his life's work—finding Meggie MacLaren.

Chapter One

Salt Lake City, Utah Territory

Eight Years Later

Connor sat in the back of a large room, listening to the newest measures the United States Congress had taken against members of the Mormon Church. It was well known that the Edmunds Act prohibited polygamy several years before, making it a federal crime. Many plural marriage families went into hiding or seclusion, living just ahead of prosecution.

An underground of displaced polygamists existed within the city and the surrounding area. Most tended to live within the law, except for continuing their practice of keeping multiple wives. There was a fanatical minority, however, who refused to abide by the legislation. These families were committed to their polygamist lifestyle, and were known to protect their own.

Today's discussion centered on the newly enacted Edmunds-Tucker Act, which disincorporated the Mormon Church and effectively destroyed the cultural system that had guided it for years. There was little doubt the residents of the city, the entire region, were under the complete authority of the federal government. Utah was a territory and under federal control.

Connor didn't care at all about the church or its troubles. He was here for one purpose—to discover information about the man who held his sister, Meggie.

The last telegram from private investigators his former employer, Louis Dunnigan, had hired said Meggie was spotted in Salt Lake City. She had been in a wagon with two other women, three children, and one man. The men Dunnigan had hired were certain it was her. He needed to find the name of this man and his location.

Connor met with the two detectives, Fred Helms and Roy Crowley, when he'd arrived. They provided a decent description and a drawing of the man's face. From what Connor could tell, there wasn't much to distinguish him from many average looking men with brown hair and eyes.

The most critical information involved the man's association with the Mormon Church. The fact that he traveled with three women, none young enough to be his children, indicated he was a polygamist, living underground. That he had brought the women with him into the city was intriguing. The man was either bold or stupid given the penalties for multiple wives.

"Have you seen any of them since?" Connor had asked.

"No, and we lost them in the crowded streets. That's why we recommend the meeting tomorrow night. The Mormons are a tight-knit group. Don't expect much. But you just need one person who recognizes the man to give you what you need."

Connor stared at the black and white sketch. "You said he's tall?"

"He was seated in the wagon, but yes, he appeared to be tall with thick arms and large hands. The man towered over the others in the wagon," Fred replied. "You know you don't have to go in there alone. Roy and I can tag along, talk to some of them."

MacLaren thought about Fred's offer, deciding it was best to go on his own. "Thanks, but I think I should go alone. I'll probably stand out anyway, no sense drawing too much attention and scaring someone off."

The following night, Connor sat at the back of the meeting room, staring at the drawing with the hope that someone would recognize the face.

"I noticed you sitting alone. I'm Parley Smith. I don't believe we've met." Parley was a tall, slim man, with a graying beard, and slight stoop. "May I join you?"

Connor indicated the seat next to him and stuck out his hand, which the other man accepted. "Connor MacLaren."

Parley looked over his shoulder, surveying the scene, then took the empty seat next to Connor. "You're not a member of our church, are you?"

"No."

"Are you an enemy of our beliefs?"

"No. Just curious, nothing more."

Smith sat back and crossed his legs, becoming engrossed in the debate.

"It's a hard decision," Smith said after a few moments.

"What's that?"

"Giving up the old ways, even though most agree it's the right decision." He paused to listen to the speaker, then continued. "It's not easy having more than one wife." Parley sent Connor a thin smile.

"I can't imagine."

"You're married, then?"

"No. That's why I can't imagine what it'd be like."

Parley chuckled at the comment, deciding he liked this man even if he wasn't one of them.

"What brings you here?"

Connor needed to start with someone and Parley seemed like the best choice. He pulled out the drawing, holding it so the man could get a good look. "I'm trying to find this man. You recognize him?"

Parley held a corner of the paper to steady it. Connor noticed his eyes widen for an instant, then his face went blank. "No. I'm sorry, but I've never seen the man. Why are you looking for him?"

Connor knew the man was lying. He chose his next words with care. "I'm told he has several women with him. There is one who might choose to leave."

Parley didn't respond right away, but considered Connor's words. "It is a serious issue. To make a woman stay without her consent."

"Yes, it is."

Connor noticed the meeting had adjourned. Men broke into groups. Some already engaged in heated discussions, others spoke in quiet voices about their future. Parley stood and turned toward him.

"It was my pleasure to meet you, Connor MacLaren. Perhaps we will see each other again."

Connor watched Parley walk away to join one of the groups. He stood, selected some men a couple of aisles away and showed them the drawing he'd shown Parley. He received much the same reaction. No one had seen him—at least that's what they said. Again, Connor believed they were holding back. Someone in this room knew the man, where he lived, and the women with him. He wouldn't stop asking until he found that one person who was willing to talk.

******

Frustration ate at Connor as he rested his arms on the bar and sipped his whiskey. The saloon near his hotel was crowded with men playing poker, women plying their trade, and patrons just looking for an escape. He'd decided to stop for one drink before meeting the two detectives for dinner at a small restaurant around the corner.

"Hello, mister. Can I order you another drink?"

Connor glanced at the woman with dark hair and bright red lipstick. She smelled of tobacco, alcohol, and stale perfume.

"No thanks, I'm good."

"See anything else that may interest you?"

He knew she was trying to earn a buck, just like everyone else, but those activities held no interest tonight.

"Maybe a card game." It was blunt but the truth. That was the only thing that called to him and even that had little appeal.

"Suit yourself, honey."

As she turned to walk away shouting erupted from a table near the window. One man was standing, holding a gun which he pointed at a man across the table.

"I won't be cheated out of a week's earnings," he bellowed.

Another man from the table stood. "Put the gun down, mister. This here's a friendly game. No one else saw any cheating going on."

"That's only 'cause you weren't looking. This fellow's been cheating all night and getting away with it."

"Enough." The deep voice came from the bartender who held a shotgun pointed at the angry patron. "Put your gun away, or get out. Now."

A shot rang out, ricocheted off the bartender's arm before crashing into the mirror behind the bar. Another shot split the air. Those in the saloon watched as the angry patron looked down at his shirt to find it soaked in blood. The pistol fell from his hand as his body slumped to the ground.

"You'd better get the sheriff," Connor told the bartender before holstering his still smoking gun.

An hour later, Connor strolled out of the saloon having answered numerous questions about the shooting. Not one of the patrons could find a reason the killing wasn't justified. In their minds, the man had tried to kill the bartender. It was a righteous kill.

******

"Meggie, would you get some water while you're outside?" At thirty-one, Nina was several years older than Meggie. She was Jeremiah Moser's first wife, had borne him two children, both girls. He'd taken a second wife, Ada, who'd borne him another daughter. In his quest for a boy, Jeremiah married Grace but she'd never conceived. He'd bought Meggie from a drifter. They'd married within days. Only his first two wives were of the Mormon faith, but that hadn't seemed to matter to Moser.

Unlike Meggie, Nina was content with her life and wouldn't consider leaving the man who'd provided a home and food for her and their daughters.

"Of course. I'll be back in a few minutes." Meggie slipped outside. They lived a considerable distance from the city, isolated from neighbors, and miles from any means of escape.

It was a clear night. She could make out several constellations. Her brothers used to point them out to her when they crept up to the roof of their boarding house and watched stars shoot across the sky. She thought of Connor and Pierce every day, wondering how they were and if they ever thought of her.

Meggie filled two buckets of water from the pump, then started for the house. Jeremiah kept telling them he would install plumbing for the kitchen, but so far, he'd made no progress. The women still hauled water in buckets and heated it on the wood burning stove. At least there was a roof over their heads. There'd been many times when there wasn't.

"You sure are taking your time, girl."

Meggie cringed at the grating voice behind her. She hated it when he snuck up behind her, as he often did. She didn't respond, ignoring him as she continued toward the kitchen.

Jeremiah picked up his pace, coming alongside her, but didn't say another word or offer to take one of the buckets. Instead, he pulled out a small cigar, lit it, and looked through the window at the women inside. His women.

"I'll get the door, Meggie," Ada said from her seat at the kitchen table. She was five years older than Meggie, and trapped. Although Ada was of the Mormon faith, she didn't believe in plural marriages. She wanted away from Moser, despised her life, but didn't have the courage or money to make a run for it—not with a young daughter.

Grace was Meggie's closest friend. At least she had been before she'd snuck out late one night, leaving Meggie behind. She'd been gone for months. It still hurt to wake up each morning knowing Gracie wouldn't be there to talk with, share their mutual disgust of Jeremiah, and plot their escape.

The door opened and slammed shut indicating Jeremiah had entered the house. He walked up behind Meggie, slipping his hands around her waist, pulling her against him. "When's supper?"

Meggie jerked, trying to pull away. His grip tightened.

"Not long. Why don't you wash up?" Nina attempted to draw his attention to her. She knew the young woman didn't appreciate Jeremiah's attentions the way Nina did. She didn't hold it against Meggie. Her husband believed in the plural marriage doctrine. His brother was a leader in the church and encouraged Jeremiah to take more wives. It was the way of it.

"Hold off a little on it. Meggie and I have some things to discuss." Jeremiah wrapped a hand around Meggie's arm, pulling her behind him out of the kitchen, and up the steps to his room. He was a big man, over six feet tall, with muscled shoulders, and thick arms. Grace once said his hands were as large as bear paws—beefy, and rough. He wasn't unattractive with his square jaw, straight nose, and brown eyes. Jeremiah was fastidious in his appearance and well-read. Educated enough that he knew just how to make a woman do what he wanted without leaving a bruise or mark of any kind.

He pushed Meggie ahead of him into the room and closed the door. He pulled his suspenders off his shoulders, unbuttoned his trousers, and let them fall as he walked up to the bed. "Now, girl. You know what to do."

******

Grace wiped her hands on the already dirty apron, grabbed more dishes, and began to scrape off dried food. Work at the busy restaurant was hard but it included a small room, food, and a few coins each week. If she did really well, the owner, Jasper Bing, would slip her an extra coin once in a while. He was a nice man in his fifties, a widower, and he treated everyone with respect.

"Another order," Jasper called to the cook. "Three of the specials."

The hour was late, Grace was exhausted, and hoped her day was over. It appeared not.

"Grace, I need to step outside. Would you mind serving the men when their food's ready?" Jasper asked.

"Yes, I can do that." She was a mess and the last thing she wanted to do was go out front to deliver food.

Her arms filled with plates, Grace walked into the dining area. It wasn't hard to spot who the food belonged to—there was only one occupied table. Three men were huddled, talking in quiet tones even though the place was empty.

"Your food, gentlemen." Grace placed the meals in front of them and waited as the men continued their conversation, ignoring their supper and oblivious to her presence.

One noticed her and looked up. "You want something, sweetheart?" His eyes roamed over her—from her dirt-encrusted shoes, to her dirty apron, and back up to her face—a slow perusal, not truly suggestive, but it made her squirm regardless. His gaze locked with hers and held.

Grace was surprised at the intensity of his stare. His eyes were moss green with small flecks of golden brown. They were beautiful, captivating. She felt her skin warm and noticed the beginning of a smile on the man's face. She forced herself to look away.

"Um, no. I didn't know if you wanted anything else."

The man stared at her another moment, as if making a decision of some kind. Thankfully, another man broke the silence. "No, ma'am, we're fine for now."

She looked at the three again, nodded, and returned to the kitchen. When she peered back through the door, the man with green eyes was still watching.

"So no one offered any information on the man at all?" Roy Crowley asked drawing everyone's attention to the reason they met. He was in his thirties, had been in law enforcement his whole life, and now worked for Louis Dunnigan, a businessman out of Denver.

"Not in so many words, but I swear five or six recognized the drawing. They know him. I'm certain of it." Connor was frustrated but understood this was a long process. He knew those of the Mormon faith were loyal to their own. At the same time, they were good people—given time, someone would come forward.

"Anyone in particular you got a sense knows the man?" Fred Helms was in his mid-forties, with dark hair greying at the temples. He'd planned to retire a couple of years ago, but everything changed when his wife died.

"A couple, but one in particular." Connor thought of Parley Smith and the way the man had been so open, until he'd seen the drawing. "Smith's his last name."

Fred let out a slight chuckle. "Son, most everyone around here's named Smith, is a Smith relation, or knows a Smith. You got a first name?"

"Parley."

"All right, so Parley Smith might know the man. Did you get the name of any others?" Roy asked as he scribbled on a pad of paper.

"No. They were all tight-lipped. I'm going back in a few days to another meeting. Maybe I'll have better luck." Connor ate in silence but kept his eyes on the kitchen door, hoping she'd walk out. Something about the woman caught his interest. There was no obvious reason why she should. Although pretty, the woman wasn't anything remarkable, not like some of the beauties from his past. But damned if he didn't want to get another look at her.

"The new U.S. Marshal just got to town. He doesn't know many people yet, but he'll keep an eye out for us. He's got his hands full with the new legislation about plural marriage. Don't know if he'll be much help."

"You know him, Fred?" Roy asked.

"Nah, he's way too young for me to have known him," Fred grumbled and finished off the last bite of supper.

Connor pushed back from the table and threw some bills down for the food. Fred grabbed his wrist.

"Put it away, MacLaren. All this is on Dunnigan. Will be until you find your sister."

Connor looked at Fred and picked up the money. Dunnigan sure was paying on their agreement. Much more than Connor had ever expected.

Chapter Two

Grace sat on the bed trying to work out the kinks in her back and shoulders. She'd waited in the kitchen until all three men had left. Thankfully, they hadn't requested anything else which saved her from dealing with the handsome stranger whose eyes drew her in. She'd never experienced anything like it—disturbing yet exciting.

It was a blessing that no one else came in because she was spent. She'd started at six that morning and it was now eleven at night. Too long of a day, and she had plans that needed her attention.

Grace laid her head on the pillow. She had nowhere near enough money saved up for a new start in a different town. South somewhere seemed the best—New Mexico or, maybe, Arizona. She could get lost in either state. Just not California. No, that's where her family had moved to years ago.

She'd loved her mother and older sister, but her father was a cruel man, and not in the same way as Jeremiah Moser, her husband. Moser was Mormon by birth, not by choice. He used to tell her the only thing he got from his faith was the right to marry and bed more than one woman.

Grace placed an arm over her eyes and tried to relax. She hated when thoughts of her father or husband stormed her mind. Her father had married Grace off to Jeremiah when they moved from Salt Lake to Stockton, saying he didn't have enough money for another mouth. She was the youngest of two children, and in her father's mind, the weakest. Grace knew better.

Her mother and sister had fought for her, but he'd been adamant. Once Father made up his mind there was no changing it.

At first she'd thought her father had provided her the freedom she craved, that he had done her a favor. That is until the first night in Jeremiah's bed when he laid down the rules and instructed her in what he wanted.

She'd never been with a man, other than the few kisses she'd shared with a young farmer before her father had decided to move on. Her mother had told her what to expect just before Grace's father had pulled her mother away and pushed her into their wagon.

Grace did as he asked but found him repulsive. There was no love and she didn't believe in his ways, his faith. She wanted to live her own life, on her own terms, not under the thumb of a man who repelled her. Grace rebelled at the physical contact. It had taken days to recover from the painful experience. She didn't rebel again. Instead, she spent all of her time preparing for her escape. Now she had another plan in mind—one that would be much more dangerous to her and others.

******

Meggie lay in bed, sick and disgusted. Jeremiah had been rough tonight, more so than normal. She'd been so sore she missed supper, telling Nina that she didn't feel well. Nina and Ada knew the cause. Their common husband didn't take out his particular needs on his first or second wife, or on Grace. No, he saved them all for Meggie. Grace had been his preferred bedmate before she'd run away. Now he fixated on Meggie.

It was a cold night. She pulled the thin blanket around her, lay on her side, and drew her knees up, wrapping her arms around her legs. Her body was tired but her mind wouldn't still. At least she had a private room. Jeremiah made sure each wife had her own quarters, that way he could visit whichever one he wanted without disturbing the others.

She stared out her window at the clear sky, remembering the night Carter's men had grabbed her. It had been a long journey to where Carter had ordered them to take her. They'd stopped several times, but she never saw anything familiar. Her hope of being discovered in the back of the wagon decreased as night turned to day, then day back to night. Early the next morning they'd arrived at their destination.

Herm Carter had been a surprise. His men were rough, dirty, and unpleasant. Carter was well dressed, a businessman who lived in Philadelphia and dealt in people. He'd taken one look at Meggie and decided to hold onto her until the time was right. She was beautiful, he'd said, and a virgin, which meant he could get more money for her.

However, he had another client in mind. One who preferred a woman with experience. Carter had chuckled. Well, she did have experience.

Meggie had cleaned and cooked in Carter's home for months while he waited for the client to visit Philadelphia. Her birthday had come and gone—she was now seventeen. If she'd been with her brothers there would have been a celebration. Not much, but something to remember. This time it passed without a thought.

It was rare that she saw the man who held her prisoner. Someone was assigned to her each day, from the time she woke until she crawled into bed. No one touched or threatened her. It was a constant state of limbo, one that caused more confusion than worry.

One evening there was a knock on her door. She opened it to find Carter.

"Hello, Meggie. If you'll come with me, there is a gentleman I'd like you to meet."

She knew the time had come and, with all the courage she possessed, followed him downstairs. Carter opened the door to his study and stood aside for Meggie to enter. She walked in and stopped. Two men sat in large leather chairs, smoking cheroots, and sipping what she assumed was whiskey. They turned at the sight of her and stood.

"Mr. Jackson, Mr. Delaney, I'd like you to meet Meggie." That was all Carter said before he left her alone with them and closed the door.

The one introduced as Mr. Jackson walked up to stand a foot away. His eyes roamed over her, from top to bottom. "Turn around please, Meggie," he said. She turned her back to him, and heard a soft chuckle. "No, turn all the way around, in a circle."

Once the circle was complete he turned to his friend, Mr. Delaney, to whisper in his ear, then looked back at her.

"Please, have a seat. I have some questions for you."

She sat on the window seat, as far from both men as she could get without leaving the room.

Eugene Jackson and Dodge Delaney looked at Meggie, then each other. With her back ramrod straight and hands folded in her lap, she looked more like a school girl than the experienced woman Carter had described.

"How old are you, Meggie?" Eugene asked.

"I'm seventeen."

"Are you from here?"

"No, Red Hook. Is that near here?" she asked. Neither men could miss the hope in her voice.

"No, it's a long ways from here," Eugene replied, puzzled by her question.

"Oh. I wasn't sure but thought it might be far. I can't see the ocean like from home." The sadness in her voice cut through both men.

Eugene had acquired women from Carter before, but all were older than seventeen. He'd set them up in a small house near his estate until he tired of them, then he'd provided each with an allowance and freedom. The women were experienced, knew the rules, if you could call them that. This one didn't look like she knew a damn thing.

The door opened and Herm Carter strode back into the room. "Well, Mr. Jackson, do we have a deal?"

"Are you quite sure she's experienced, Carter? You know my thoughts on this." Neither Eugene nor Dodge had ever taken up with a married woman or an innocent. They led simple lives. Ran their estates down south, or what was left of them, gambled, drank, took care of their people, and each kept a paramour. No wives and no commitments. Neither had the slightest interest in love.

"Would I say so if it was otherwise?" Carter replied then looked at Meggie. "Would you call yourself experienced?"

She looked from one man to the next before her eyes settled back on Carter. "Yes sir. I have experience."

"You see, gentlemen, it's as I said." He sat down behind his desk. "So, do we have a deal?"

Eugene still felt uncomfortable, but she'd said herself she had experience. Who was he to call the lady a liar? Besides, she was one of the most beautiful young women he'd ever seen. Breathtaking would be the word he'd use. And she'd be more so once he took her home and bought her new clothes.

"Yes, we have a deal."

Meggie had listened to the conversation but instead of her eyes following Eugene Jackson, they stayed fixed on Dodge Delaney. She'd never had a beau, but if she had, she'd want him to look just like Delaney.

******

The sound came from a long ways off. Meggie curled up tighter in the covers. The noise persisted. "Meggie, you up?"

Meggie's eyes flew open. Bright light streamed into her room indicating the morning was half over. She jumped out of bed and grabbed her dress. "Yes, I'm up, Ada. I'll be right down." She'd fallen asleep on thoughts of Dodge. Such a long time for the memories to remain so fresh.

She dashed into the kitchen, thankful not to see Jeremiah. "Where is he?" she asked Nina.

"Still in bed. Should be down anytime."

"Be grateful for it while you can, Meggie," Ada said.

"The girls?" Meggie asked.

"Oh, they're fine. They finished breakfast a couple of hours ago and have been outside ever since." Ada continued drying dishes as she spoke.

It was Meggie's job to roust and feed the three girls each morning. After that they'd play until she was done with her other chores and had time to school them. Jeremiah didn't like the school in town—he wanted to keep everyone close to home, and now that Grace was gone, Meggie was the only one with much education. She was also the only one, besides Jeremiah, who could read.

“Thank you.” Meggie placed a hand on Ada’s arm and squeezed. “He would be furious with you if he knew I wasn’t up to take care of them.”

Ada smiled as she handed Meggie a plate with eggs and bacon. “Eat up. I have a feeling the day’s going to be real long.”

******

“Coffee, mister?” Grace asked, then took another look at the man who’d just taken a seat. Her heart picked up a beat and she found herself taking a small step away.

“Yes, please,” Connor said. “Ah, the lady from last night, correct?”

“Yes, sir, I was here last night. I’m usually here each morning and night,” she answered, filling his cup quickly before moving on.

Connor watched her walk from table to table, talking to each customer, smiling and laughing. She had a beautiful smile, one that lit her face, crinkling her eyes. And her hair. He’d noticed it last night—fiery red, with streaks of gold. It was the kind of hair made for running your hands through. Connor shook his head and turned his attention back to the drawing he’d placed in front of him. He’d eat, then start showing it to anyone who’d look. Connor folded the paper and placed it in his pocket.

“Here you go.” Grace placed a plate filled with eggs and ham in front of him.

“I didn’t order anything yet, sweetheart.”

She bristled at the endearment. “We only have two choices—this and flapjacks. You look like an eggs and ham kind of man to me, sir.” Grace looked down at him, not for a moment showing her smile.

She was right, but he wasn’t going to tell her that. He sure wasn’t used to people making choices for him—even if it was just eggs and ham.

“Fine. But I’ll take flapjacks, too. And more coffee,” Connor muttered.

She strolled into the kitchen and let loose with the smile she’d been holding.

“What you grinning at, girl?” Jasper asked.

“Oh, nothing, Jasper. Just something a customer said.”

Half an hour later the kitchen door slammed open. Grace looked over her shoulder to see her customer filling the doorway, glaring at her. She dropped the dirty dish back into the sudsy water, dried her hands, and faced him. Whatever he had to say, she probably deserved it.

Connor walked up and grabbed one of her hands. “Open it,” he ordered.

She wanted to pull loose but something in his eyes made her comply. Her palm opened, and he dropped one twenty dollar gold coin in the center. “You were right. I am an eggs and ham man.” He pinned her with his eyes but there was no hint of humor in his voice or his face. She stared into her palm to confirm what he’d done was real. When she looked back up all she saw was his back as he sauntered out of the restaurant.

******

"I'm looking for Parley Smith. You know him?" Connor had ridden to the other side of Salt Lake. He'd been told that Parley was an attorney with an office a few blocks from the Temple. It was a two-story house with the downstairs divided between a large sitting area opposite a room filled with books, and a rectangular conference table. The woman who greeted him stood when he entered.

"Elder Smith isn't in right now, but I expect him later today. Would you like to leave a message for him?"

"My name is Connor MacLaren. Elder Smith and I met last night at the meeting."

She wrote down his name. "Will you come by later, Mr. MacLaren?"

"Yes, I'll be back today." He started to leave then had a thought. Connor pulled out the sketch. "You wouldn't happen to know this man, would you?"

The woman's eyes opened wide at the drawing, but she said nothing.

"Does he look at all familiar?"

"Well, he does hold a slight resemblance to one of Elder Smith's relatives." She focused on the drawing once more. "I'm just not sure, but it does look a little like him."

"Do you know his name?"

"Well, I..." The door opening and closing stopped her.

"Good morning, Mary." Parley Smith entered the office and set his hat on the rack. He recognized Connor right off. “Mr. MacLaren. It’s good to see you again.” He noticed the drawing in Mary’s hand and took the paper from her. “I see you’ve shown the drawing to Mary. Unfortunately, I’m sure that she’s never seen the man. Isn’t that right?” He glanced at his secretary.

“Well, I was just taking a look when you walked in Elder Smith.”

“And?” Smith asked.

She looked at Connor then averted her eyes. “Uh, no. I don’t know who he is. I’m sorry.”

Satisfied, Smith looked back at his visitor. “So, what may I help you with, Mr. MacLaren?”

Connor’s eyes narrowed as his head tilted. He knew for certain the man was lying, but didn’t know why. He wondered how far he could push him, and if now was the time, or if he should wait until later, when the man was alone. Connor slid the paper from Smith’s fingers, folded it, and replaced the drawing in his coat pocket.

“I thought we could meet for dinner today. That is, if you have the time.”

Smith took out his pocket watch, looked, and then snapped it shut. “I’m afraid today won’t be possible. Perhaps another time?”

“Of course.” Connor tipped his hat. “Another time then.”

Chapter Three

"I tell you, Jeremiah, the man has a sketch that looks like you, and he's persistent. He won't leave until he's sure you're not the man he wants." Parley Smith had taken his buggy to his half-brother's farm. It was a long drive from his office, but the matter couldn't wait. "What could he want with you? What have you done?"

"Nothing. I've done nothing," Jeremiah insisted. He kept his private life with his wives sealed inside the walls of his house. The women would not speak of it to anyone, he made certain of it.

"Then why would he have the drawing? You must be honest with me." Smith was an elder in their church and couldn't afford to be tainted by any type of scandal. There was enough upheaval and dissension from the new law. He didn't want to add to that burden. Besides, it was crucial that those who still believed in the doctrine of plural marriages, like the other church leaders and their families, be protected and allowed to continue their faith in the way stipulated by church leaders. Jeremiah was a devout Mormon and adhered to the plural marriage doctrine. He no longer spent long hours in saloons with whores. He had ceased being an embarrassment to the family years ago.

"There is nothing, Parley, I swear it. I am not the man I was years ago. Nina, Ada, and Meggie take care of me and the children. Our farm is good. There is nothing to worry about." Jeremiah searched his memory for anything he may have done that would cause a man to come looking for him. Nothing came to him. People may not like the way he treated Meggie, but that was between his wife and him. What happened in his house was his business only.

"And you treat your wives well? They are not unhappy or want to leave, like Grace?"

"Grace was crazy, you knew that. She never showed restraint, would not bow to my will, and talked of me to the others. It is good she is gone. The house is better for it." Just the thought of Grace still sent ripples of anger through Jeremiah's body. One day he would find her, bring her home, and punish her in a way that fit her transgression.

"You must stay away from town until this man leaves. Whatever he thinks you've done, I'm sure he is mistaken, but others might not be so sure. They don't know how you've changed, settled down, since your marriages." Parley strolled to his wagon and pulled up onto the seat. "You be careful, Jeremiah."

Jeremiah watched his half-brother leave and wondered what he might have done to come to the attention of an outsider. If the man was here to arrest him for his plural marriages, then he would work with the marshal. No, that couldn't be the reason.

He knew he was sometimes rough on Meggie, but that was his right as her husband. Moser understood his needs were different from most men. The whores he frequented had always satisfied those desires. They knew what he liked—rough, hard, with violent force when needed. He did nothing that would permanently hurt a woman or leave lasting scars. After all, he was the one who had to look at them. He didn't see anything wrong with being physical if it brought him satisfaction. Besides, his methods were nobody's business but his.

The only thing that he could come up with was that Grace was still in the area and complained to the marshal. Or that somehow Meggie had gotten word out about his methods. He was determined to find the reason the stranger sought him out.

Jeremiah fumed as he walked to the house. "Meggie!"

"What is it, Jeremiah? Why are you yelling?" Nina had stopped her work and rushed into the kitchen at the sound of his voice.

"Where is Meggie?" His voice was harsh, demanding.

"I believe she's out back with the children. They're playing a game of some kind. Why?"

Jeremiah didn't answer. He stormed from the house, the door slamming behind him.

He stood a hundred feet from the house and scanned the area. He saw no one. He stalked toward a small barn and saw movement from the back. A minute later one of his daughters came running around the side, giggling as she made her way to him. She wrapped her arms around his legs and looked up.

"Hello, Papa," she smiled.

For an instant her father softened and placed a hand on her head, stroking her hair. "Where is Meggie?"

The young girl turned and pointed. "She's back there, Papa."

"Good. Now you go to the house and help your Mama."

"Yes, Papa."

He followed the continued laughter until he saw his other two daughters playing jump rope. His oldest held one end and Meggie held the other. The middle girl jumped up and down, laughing while she tried not to stumble. The girls stopped when they saw him approach.

"Go inside, girls," their father said in a soft voice, but his eyes were fixed on Meggie.

The moment his daughters were out of sight he grabbed Meggie by the arm and yanked her behind the family wagon. "What have you been telling people, girl?"

"I...I don't know what you mean," she stammered. He could already see the fear in her eyes. Good, she should be afraid.

"Who have you talked to about us—you and me?" he demanded.

His questions confused her. Jeremiah never let her out of his sight on the few visits to town and he never let her speak with anyone.

"No one. I haven't spoken with anyone," Meggie said and tried to pull her arm from his grasp.

He squeezed hard before releasing his grip. "You better be telling me the truth because if I discover different, you know what will happen. You understand me?"

"Yes, of course, I understand." She rubbed her arm knowing a bruise would show by suppertime.

Jeremiah glared at her another moment then turned back toward the house. She watched him leave, grateful he'd only hurt her arm and nothing more. If only she could run and hide like Grace. But she couldn't. Besides, where would she go? Without Grace, she was utterly alone.

******

"What are you planning, Gracie?" Jasper asked. He'd watched her for an hour, sitting by the lake, alone. Still, he could almost feel the wheels turning in her head. The girl had something she was working through, he was sure.

She smiled. Jasper was the only person who called her Gracie. Except, once in a while, Meggie would call her by the nickname. Grace liked it.

"Why, nothing. Just enjoying the day off and being away from the restaurant." Grace returned to her daydreaming. Jasper had offered to drive her to the lake, more of a marshland really, that was fed by one of the tributaries of the Great Salt Lake. It was Sunday and Jasper Bing did not believe in working on the Lord's Day. It had taken most of the morning to reach the water, and it would take several hours to return, but it was heaven in Grace's mind. She caught a shadow out of the corner of her eye and saw that Jasper was crouching next to her, looking for small stones to throw in the water. He didn't speak for several minutes, just absorbed the quiet of being out of the city.

"What's eating at you, Gracie? And don't tell me nothing 'cause I know better."

She'd never tell him the truth. It wouldn't be right to pull a nice man like Jasper into her plan to somehow go after Meggie and free her. She wasn't certain Jeremiah would come after them. If he did there were no guarantees he wouldn't resort to violence. No, if she was going to talk to anyone about what she intended it would be someone who wouldn't be hurt were she caught.

She'd been thinking about how to go about it all morning and felt she'd come up with something that might work. If she succeeded, the two of them would flee south, maybe to Arizona or New Mexico, but away from Salt Lake Valley, and the reach of Jeremiah Moser.

"It's nothing really. Just thinking about my family and how much I miss them. Especially my Pa." May God save her from burning in hell for such a lie.

He wrapped an arm around her shoulders. "I know it must be hard, no family nearby to visit with and talk. My daughter's in Denver with my three grandchildren. I miss them every day but I know her husband's a good man. At least they visit every couple of years." Jasper thought for a minute. "You know, they're due for a visit this year. When they come, I want you to meet them. You'd like my daughter, she's about your age."

"If they're at all like you, then I know I'd like them." Grace leaned back into Jasper's solid body and relaxed. In her heart, she knew she wouldn't be in Utah when his family arrived. She'd be long gone, and so would Meggie.

******

It was late, cold, and dark, but Meggie grabbed her robe and a small blanket, then crept down the stairs. She needed air, a walk, and to clear her head. Jeremiah's accusations had plagued her all evening. He'd confronted her just after Elder Smith visited and she intended to discover why. What had his half-brother said that made Jeremiah rage at her?

The moon was full, providing plenty of light for her walk through the fields. They were between planting seasons. It was easy to see where she walked but also made her location clear to Jeremiah if he woke and found her gone. She kept low and made a path toward the trees that lined their property. Her spot wasn't far. Meggie had only shared it with one other person. Grace had thought it was where they did their best thinking.

Meggie found their tree and spread out the quilt she'd brought. She looked around once more to be sure Jeremiah hadn't followed her. When she was certain she was alone, she sat, then laid down on the soft fabric.

She loved this spot. There was a small brook not far away and she could just make out the sound of moving water. Meggie closed her eyes as memories washed over her.

Charleston, South Carolina, several years before

Eugene Jackson had taken her to his small estate outside Charleston, South Carolina. It was north of the city but near the water. The harbor and boats reminded her of Red Hook. She remembered her first day at Eugene's home. He and Dodge Delaney had escorted her up the wide steps and into the large entry.

"Benjamin and Nettie, I'd like you to meet Meggie. She'll be staying with us a few days until I get her settled." By settled, both his butler and cook knew Eugene meant that he'd move her into a small house a few miles away. They knew his routine—this was the fourth woman in as many years. He'd visit her a few times a week for several months then tire of her. Eugene was a generous man. The first three were experienced, sophisticated women, and he'd made provisions for each. This one was different, not at all the same as the others. Poor girl, she'd be alone and lonely most of the time, and in the end, he'd set her free.

To everyone's shock, Meggie made a slight curtsy, then stood erect, just like Connor had taught her to do around people of means.

"Meggie, there's no need to curtsy to Ben and Nettie. They work here."

"Oh, like me," Meggie said in a solemn voice and turned to the butler and cook, "I have experience as a maid and cook at Mr. Carter's home. Just tell me what you want me to do..." She stopped when she noticed the look on all their faces.

Eugene's eyes flew open and his jaw dropped. Son of God, was that what she'd meant at Carter's when she said she was experienced? Carter had lied to him. What the hell was he going to do with her now?

Dodge Delaney let loose with the most robust laugh she'd ever heard. Instead of subsiding after a few moments, the laugh grew until he was bent over, wiping tears from his eyes. "Sorry, Eugene, but you must admit, this is a gem. Experienced..." he tried to continue but fell into more fits of laughter.

Eugene looked at Dodge in disgust then turned to Ben and Nettie. "Please take Meggie to the kitchen and provide her with a meal. I need to have a word with Mr. Delaney."

Dodge just made it to a chair in the study before the humor of Eugene's situation hit him again. He'd never seen his friend so dumbstruck.

"What am I to do with her now, Dodge? My God, she's an innocent."

"Damn if I know, but you can't just throw her out." He stood and walked over to the small bar to pour a drink for himself and one for his agitated friend. "Perhaps you could find another unsuspecting soul and use the same trick on him," he suggested and worked to suppress a chuckle.

"Ah, hell. You know as well as I that I can't do that."

Dodge took pity on his friend. "Well, she could stay. With her experience she might be a big help to Nettie. After all, your cook is getting older. I'm sure she'd welcome the help."

"I can't."

"And why not? She's a fine girl. You could train her to be a lady's maid, Nettie could teach her to sew. Once the girl's ready you can find her a position in Charleston."

"No."

Dodge was confused by his friend's reluctance to even consider allowing Meggie to stay, but kept his questions to himself. "All right then, you tell me what you'll do with her." Dodge strolled to his chair, sat down, and lit a cheroot, taking a long drag.

Eugene paced back and forth, mumbling a few words, and shaking his head. Dodge didn't interrupt. He knew this was his friend's way of working through a hard decision. He looked to Dodge, his eyes locking on his friend.

Dodge knew that look and shot from his chair. "No. Absolutely not. I will not take Meggie off your hands. She's your problem, you deal with her."

"She's perfect for you. You've always had a way with young women."

"Not virgins," Dodge's voice rose.

"You could teach her. You've said you want someone you can talk with, trust more than our normal women. Someone you could keep but who wouldn't push for marriage." Eugene looked to his study door then back at a face that had turned hard as stone. "She's a beauty as well as being closer to your age than mine."

"I'm only three years younger than you."

"Yes, but she's seventeen. At twenty-two, you're a mere five years her senior. I'm almost an old man compared to you."

"Oh for pity's sake, you just turned twenty-five." Dodge shot back the rest of his whiskey. "And again, if I wasn't clear the first time, the answer is no." He grabbed his hat and gloves. "I'm already late for an appointment. I know you'll make the right decision, Eugene. You always do."

Eugene had let her stay, instructing Nettie to let her help in the kitchen and garden. She had her own small room. One day Eugene had returned from Charleston and placed a package on her bed. Meggie stared at it before ripping the paper open to expose three dresses. She pulled one out, holding it to herself, and turning in a circle. It was the loveliest thing she'd ever seen.

She ran out of her room looking for Eugene, spotting him in his study. Breathless, she walked into the room. "Thank you, Mr. Jackson. It is the most wonderful gift I've ever received." Her smile lit the room, her joy at his small token so much more than he'd imagined.

He didn't answer, just stared behind her. Meggie made an abrupt turn to see Dodge Delaney leaning against the wall, his arms crossed. She stared at the impression he made—confident, knowing, as if he understood something no one else did. Her heart beat faster and a swallow lodged in her throat. His effect on her was unnerving.

"Oh, Mr. Delaney, I didn't see you there." She looked back at Eugene. "Well, thank you, sir. They're wonderful." She dashed out the door as fast as she'd entered, leaving Dodge to stare after the beautiful young woman.

******

Present day

Meggie felt something tickle her face and swatted at it with her hand. A moment later it happened again. This time she opened her eyes to the first light of dawn. *Morning!*

She jumped up, grabbed her quilt, and ran for the house, trying to get into the kitchen before anyone saw her. Her pace slowed when it was apparent that no one was up. The house was quiet. She crept into the kitchen, built a fire in the cook stove, and began preparing oatmeal. Moments later Nina and Ada joined her, surprised to see Meggie still in her sleeping dress.

Ada walked up and took the spoon from Meggie's hand. "I'll take this. You dash upstairs and change before Jeremiah sees you."

Meggie didn't waste a moment, taking the stairs two at time. Within minutes she was back in the kitchen, waiting for their husband and the girls to appear. That had been close. Her heart pounded in fear. Her disobedience hadn't been discovered—at least not this time.

Chapter Four

Salt Lake City

Connor skirted the throngs of people standing outside talking, waiting to enter the meeting hall. He knew it would be the same discussion as a few days ago, but it was the one place where numerous men of the Mormon faith gathered where he was allowed to attend. As an outsider he wasn't allowed in their Temple.

Unlike last time, he took a seat in the middle of the room on an outside aisle. It gave him a good viewpoint without being as obvious as he felt the week before. He spotted Parley Smith as he entered and took a seat near the front. Smith hadn't noticed Connor. MacLaren's eyes wandered over the other men but none fit the sketch or were as tall and muscular as the detectives had described.

"So what would you have us do, Elder Snow, divorce our wives and push them aside?"

"And what of the children, Elder Snow? Would they still carry our name, live in our homes?"

The questions brought Connor's attention back to the front. The men had genuine concerns about the new law against plural marriages, how they could abide by them and still handle the responsibilities they'd accepted with more than one wife. Most of the men in the gathering held leadership positions of some form in their church. They'd accepted the doctrine of polygamy as part of their faith, but they also understood the need to comply with the laws of the other states. Utah aspired to statehood and it would never be achieved as long as plural marriages were accepted.

"I have three wives, Elder Snow. If I divorce my second and third wives, where will they live—how will they live?"

Elder Snow held up both hands, palms out. "Please my friends, let us discuss your concerns and what we might do."

The discussions that followed were heartfelt and difficult, resulting in high emotions, confusion, and anxiety. Connor watched it all play out. Most understood the need to go along with the new law, which had the potential of garnering support for their faith from a public who'd scorned their beliefs for decades.

There were some, however, who scorned the new law and were determined to continue the lifestyle endorsed by their leaders for years. Connor could pick out the men he thought would go deeper underground to protect their way of life. These were the ones who'd know the man he sought.

He kept his eyes on the men he viewed as dissenters—those who'd refuse to give up their additional wives. Two groups formed. One near the front consisted of seven men. The group of eight at the back tucked into an alcove with one member peering over his shoulder to be sure they weren't overheard. Both groups spoke in quiet tones, formulating their next steps.

Connor stepped near one group, pretending to read the document in his hand while listening to their hushed voices.

"We will move farther out, Robert, away from those who would persecute us."

"How far away can we go, David? We must travel to town for supplies and we need to have neighbors for protection." Robert replied.

"We can form our own community. Share trips to town and protect those left in the homes. It is better than divorce and watching our wives and children being raised by others," the one named David replied.

"We will speak with Moser. He lives several miles out with three wives and their children. Few settle out that far. He once said there is much more land around him that is available to farm. We will seek his counsel," Robert suggested.

"Ah, Mr. MacLaren. I see you have joined us again tonight."

Connor's head snapped up to see Parley Smith standing beside him. He hadn't even noticed the man's approach. His first inclination was to ignore the man and continue eavesdropping, but he knew that would be impossible.

"Mr. Smith, it is good to see you again," Connor replied, still trying to listen to the conversation a few feet away.

"I've been thinking about your invitation. Would you have time tomorrow? It seems it would be good if we got to know each other a little better."

"Tomorrow would be fine. You name the place."

"Shall we say Beaton's at noon?" Parley suggested.

"I'll see you then, Mr. Smith." Connor watched the man walk away then turned his head toward the group of men, but they'd vanished. He wondered if it had anything to do with Parley being so close. Smith didn't seem like the kind of man to go underground but perhaps he knew those who did.

******

Grace was late. Even though she lived just above the restaurant, she'd over slept and now hurried down the outside steps while fastening the last of the buttons on her dress. She hoped no one spotted her in the early morning light. Head down and concentrating on her task, she rounded the corner and plowed smack into an immovable object.

"Whoa there, sweetheart, before you hurt yourself." Strong hands gripped her upper arms, keeping her upright. Without his help she would've bounced back and off the wooden walkway.

"Let go of me," she snapped and tried to pull away, but his grip held.

"Well, I can do that but not until you apologize for almost running me down," Connor replied.

He'd recognized her in an instant with her red hair and violet blue eyes.

"Apologize? Are you daft? You're the one who ran into me," she stormed, twisting her body from one side to the other, trying to free herself.

"Is that so?" His deep, soft voice floated over her just as it had in her dreams of him last night. He stared at her another moment then loosened his hold and stepped back.

She took a steadying breath and brushed stray hairs from her face. Grace knew she'd turned red—heat radiated in waves off her cheeks.

She lifted her gaze to his and licked her lips.

Connor watched her attempts to compose herself as her skin faded from deep red to a soft, blush pink. He had to adjust his previous thoughts on her—she was a beauty. Then she licked her lips. The small movement hit him like a kick to his gut.

"You're right," Grace mumbled.

He tried to focus on her words. "I am?"

She took a calming breath before glancing up. "Yes. I ran into you, and, well, I'm sorry. I was late for work. Actually, I am late and need to leave, now." She hurried around the corner and in through the front door of the restaurant. Passing the waiting customers, Grace dashed into the kitchen to hang up her coat, then rested her back against a wall. She took another deep breath. He was even more handsome when a mere six inches away.

The man was tall, with broad shoulders, and a muscular frame. He wore almost all black, with a white shirt opened at the collar. His hair was dark and wavy, falling onto his forehead. Her fingers had itched to touch it and she'd found herself fisting both hands in her pockets to stop herself from acting on the impulse.

"Gracie, you ready to work yet?" Jasper asked as he poked his head around the corner. "You all right?"

"Yes, I'm fine. Just overslept. I'll head out front right now." She grabbed an apron, tied the knot, and pushed through the door to the front. Connor was just hanging up his hat when she walked in, a grin still played on his lips.

"Hello again." Connor looked her up and down before taking a seat. "No injuries I hope."

"No injuries," she glanced at the other waiting customers. "Do you want the special?"

"Sure, as long as it's eggs, ham, flapjacks, and coffee." He kept his voice low. Connor leaned back in the chair and watched her blush. God, she was pretty when she blushed.

"I'll get it right to you." Grace's voice was just above a whisper. She turned, sucked in another breath, and stepped to the next table.

He sat, watching her, how at ease she seemed around everyone—except him. Truth was, he felt the same around her. A little off, like he was somehow disconnected from his body. It wasn't a comfortable feeling and one he meant to shake. He had no business wanting anyone, especially someone as sweet as her.

Chapter Five

"Meggie! Where are you?" the girls squealed as they ran through the barn trying to find her. She'd found a great spot this time, in a pile of hay just outside the small storage closet. The girls stopped, whispering to each other, then she heard them take off again. Sometimes she'd move, to throw them off, but this time Meggie decided to stay beneath the hay. Eventually they'd find her, then the game would start again.

Jeremiah had left before noon, taking Nina and Ada with him to a neighboring farm. A man had ridden up a couple of days ago saying they needed him at a meeting. Afterwards the women would be providing supper for everyone. Meggie had been instructed to watch the girls and not go beyond the bounds of the immediate house area.

It had been a wonderful day, just she and the children. The chores were done, a chicken stew warmed on the stove, and the knowledge that her husband wouldn't return for a few more hours filled her with a peace she hadn't known for a long time.

Meggie could hear the children in the distance, still yelling her name. She closed her eyes and relaxed under the warmth of the hay. She thought of another glorious day, years ago when she still lived in Eugene's house.

Charles, South Carolina, several years before

There'd been a stream on his property. He'd escorted Meggie there several times after her work was done, asking questions, and coaxing her to talk about herself. She'd been a scared, pitiful creature when Eugene had introduced her to Ben and Nettie. Now, weeks later, she'd gained more confidence, and believed she'd found a place in his house.

"Do you have family, Meggie?" he'd asked on one stroll.

"Yes, I have two brothers. One is five years older and the other just a year. We lived in a small boarding house in Red Hook." She glanced up at him and added, "That's in Brooklyn."

"Yes, I've heard of it. A shipping harbor, as I recall."

"My oldest brother worked at the docks, the other apprenticed with a tool maker."

"You miss them?" Eugene had asked.

"I do, but I'm sure they've forgotten all about me. It's been so long since Carter's men took me." She stared at the rolling stream and wondered where the water stopped, if it had a destination or continued to flow in circles, like her.

Eugene winced at her comment. He'd been told that Meggie had come to Carter willingly. That she'd run away. "So, you didn't run away from your brothers? They didn't harm you?"

Meggie's head snapped around. "Why, no. Is that what Mr. Carter told you?" Her eyes searched his. She needed the truth.

"Yes, he did. Foolishly, I believed him."

They stood in silence for a long time before Eugene broke the silence.

"Would you like me to hire someone to find them?"

"You'd do that?"

"Of course, Meggie. It's not my intent to hold you here against your will. Just tell me their names, and I'll do the rest."

Before she realized what she was doing, Meggie had launched herself into his arms. "Thank you," she'd whispered as tears formed in her eyes.

Eugene gently moved her away and offered a folded handkerchief. "Don't thank me yet. I don't know what luck we'll have, but at least we'll give it a try."

******

Present day

"Hah! We found you," the girls sang over and over.

She'd lost track of time as the memories rolled through her, but now she had to get the children fed and in bed before the others returned.

"Yes, you did find me. You are all so clever." The girls skipped back to the house, holding hands and laughing.

Meggie watched them lead the way and wondered how she could escape from Jeremiah's clutches, and start a new life. She couldn't do that without money, and she had none. Then an idea hit. Jeremiah kept money in a tin box in his study. He didn't realize she knew what it was, but Meggie had seen him drop money into the tin a few times. Could she take the chance? What if he'd counted it before he left and checked it again when he came home? She'd make sure the tin was still where he'd hidden it, count the money, and decide if she'd take some tonight or wait.

The girls had finished dinner and were tucked in bed. She came downstairs, lantern in hand, and checked outside. No one. The moon was still bright enough that Jeremiah would definitely come home and not stay at the gathering. Sometimes he did stay, but only when Nina was at the house, not just Meggie. She knew he didn't trust her, and in that, he was right.

The tin was on the third shelf up, behind his desk where he could reach it by twisting in his chair. She set it on the desk and opened it. There were coins and silver certificates, plus some other currency she didn't recognize. Meggie counted what she could and was stunned at the amount—almost three hundred dollars. She'd just placed the lid on the tin when she heard the kitchen door fly open. She returned the tin to its place, grabbed the lantern, and ran to the foot of the stairs just as Nina and Ada walked around the corner.

"How was it? Did you have a good time?" Meggie asked, trying to calm her racing nerves.

"Oh, yes, it was wonderful. There must have been fifteen men and close to forty women." Ada walked to the hall tree to hang up her bonnet. "I so wish you could've been with us." She gave Meggie a brief hug before walking up the stairs to check on the children.

While Jeremiah was occupied outside, Meggie said her goodnights to Nina and followed Ada up the stairs. Her husband would almost always leave her alone if she were already asleep.

Except sleep didn't come. Her mind was occupied with schemes that would lead her away from Moser. The one that kept popping back into her head involved waiting until Jeremiah was gone. Most times he'd take either Nina or Ada to worship services with the children, leaving two wives at home. Meggie was always one of them. The only time he'd taken everyone was several weeks ago. They'd gone to services, then driven straight back to the farm, not staying for dinner as most of the members did.

If Nina stayed, she'd have no problem getting away without her noticing. She paid little attention to Meggie, focusing on the children and her chores. It was different with Ada.

Meggie was close to Ada. When it was the two of them they spent their time together with the girls, doing their work and playing. It would be too difficult to leave if Ada was the one who stayed with her. Even though Jeremiah's second wife had never been treated in the same way as Meggie, she sympathized with the younger woman, and wished there was something she could do to help. Of course there wasn't. Ada was pleased that Grace had gotten away.

It was an easy decision. Wait until Jeremiah took Ada to temple with the children, grab the money, and leave.

******

Jeremiah unharnessed the horses from his wagon and groomed them, all the while replaying the discussions he'd had tonight with the other men. They wanted his advice—how he managed to live so far from town with three wives, continue to buy supplies, go to temple, and not draw attention. Could it be done if they formed an organized community of those who wished to continue the principle of plural marriage that Joseph Smith introduced into the church? Could they erect their own Temple, eliminating the need for all of the men to travel to town each week?

He knew he wasn't like most of the men who believed in the practice because it was a principle of their faith. Jeremiah also realized that the majority of those who practiced polygamy were church leaders or had relatives in a leadership position. He practiced the principle for two reasons—his half-brother was a church leader and encouraged the practice, and Jeremiah could indulge in his particular needs without drawing attention. He'd kept those needs hidden until he'd paid money to a stranger for Meggie. He expected little from her other than she bow to his wishes.

Jeremiah finished putting the horses away and pulled out a thin cigar. He liked the ideas of a society outside the normal community. A group of like-minded men who were willing to live a quiet life away from the interference of those who didn't understand their ways. Plus, he liked the fact that these men looked to him for guidance and leadership. He could help mold the group in a manner most beneficial to him. They planned to meet again in another week. There was much to think about before then.

******

Connor took a seat at the only empty table, ordering his usual from the man who walked out from the kitchen. The food was good but he returned for one reason, to see the red haired woman who worked there. He didn't even know her name, yet she drew him like no woman he'd known in a long time. It was just a way to pass the time while he searched for his sister—at least that's what he told himself.

"You've been coming in pretty regular the last week. Thought I'd better introduce myself." The older man wearing a well-used apron stuck out his hand. "I'm Jasper Bing. I own this place."

"Pleased to meet you, Mr. Bing. I'm Connor MacLaren."

"Call me Jasper." He watched as two customers dropped money on their table and left. "You like the food or is there some other reason you keep coming back?"

The man was direct. Connor liked that. "Both. Food's good and your help is easy on the eyes." He took a sip of coffee and eyed Jasper over the rim of his cup.

"I see. Well, I got to tell you that Grace is a nice girl and works hard. She's been a real good addition to the restaurant. Customers like her and she's dependable."

Grace, huh. At least he had a name. "I can see that, Jasper." Connor wondered if there was some hidden meaning in Jasper's words. Jasper didn't let him wonder for long.

"Lots of men come in here and watch her. A few have asked about her. I can tell you she's got no use for men. Don't know her reasons, it's just the way it is. That girl keeps to herself more than any woman I know."

Connor sat back and eyed the man. He wasn't used to anyone questioning him about his actions or motives. Most people stayed away. He'd been told he had a look about him that warned people off, made them wary. Maybe that was true, he didn't know. But one thing for certain, he didn't like being cautioned off anyone.

"Thanks for the advice, Jasper. Tell you what, if I get to the point that I can't resist your pretty little server, I'll be sure to let you know." Connor didn't smile, just drank the remainder of his coffee and placed the empty cup on the table. "Nice to meet you." He threw some coins down and walked out, leaving Jasper to wonder what had just happened.

Connor was becoming more and more frustrated with his search, and the conversation with Jasper had increased his irritation. Not only had Grace not been at the restaurant but the owner had warned him off. Hell, all he wanted was to look. Connor enjoyed watching her and the way he made her uncomfortable. Whatever the reason, making her blush brought some sunshine to his otherwise grim life.

The dinner he'd had with Smith the day after the men's gathering brought him nothing. Although Parley listened to Connor's story, the man was adamant he didn't recognize the person in the sketch. He offered to pass it around if a copy was made. Connor had been a range detective and lawman before that. The man was lying, he knew it. That left him with one choice. He knew where Parley worked and he'd find where the man lived. Then he'd have him followed. Fred Helms and Roy Crowley were itching to make something happen. At some point Parley would make contact with the man in the sketch, Connor was convinced of it.

He rode to a small general store several blocks from the restaurant. He'd learned that one of the men from the meeting owned the place. He was a staunch opponent to the new law and was the one who'd mentioned a name—Moser. Connor had no reason to believe that Moser was the man he sought, but it was a start. And he was desperate for anything that would lead him to Meggie.

There was a bell over the door that chimed as Connor entered, announcing his presence. "Be right with you," a man called from the back room.

Connor busied himself looking at some of the items. It was basic, as stores went, with none of the luxury items you'd expect in the fancier emporiums. He picked up a woman's hat with an emerald green ribbon. As he held it an image of Grace crossed his mind and the hat fell from his hand. He stared at it and shook his head as if to erase the image.

"May I help you?"

Connor looked at the same man he remembered from the meeting—medium height with thinning brown hair and a thin mustache. "I need some shave cream and a couple of boxes of forty-fives."

The man set the shaving cream on the counter. "The ammunition is in the back." He was gone a minute then placed the two boxes down. "Anything else?"

"That's it."

The man named a price and Connor counted out the money before grabbing his purchases. "Oh, I almost forgot." He placed the items down and pulled the sketch from his pocket. "Wonder if you recognize this man."

The moment the man's eyes focused on the paper they widened. He was unable to hide the surprise that registered on his face. "Uh, what do you want him for?"

"So you know him?"

"Didn't say that, mister. Just wondered why you'd be looking for him." The man was flustered. That was a good sign.

"Nothing much. Just want to speak with him." Connor settled his hip against the counter and waited.

The man's eyes shifted to the image.

Connor could see sweat form on the man's forehead. *Got you*, Connor thought.

"Uh, no, sorry. I don't know the man."

"You're sure? There's no possible way you've ever seen this man?"

"No, I'm quite sure. Now, if you'll excuse me, I've got some work in the back I need to finish." The man disappeared behind a curtain.

Connor tucked the drawing back in his pocket and left. He turned his horse away from the store, then a block later circled around to the alley, and waited. Within ten minutes, the man emerged, slipped on his coat, and climbed into a wagon. Connor stayed close enough to follow but far enough back so the man wouldn't notice him. It didn't take long before the man stopped in front of a jewelry store on a main street. He jumped down and rushed into the building, not noticing that Connor sat atop his horse a few yards away.

He peered through the window to see three men speaking near the back counter, the one from the general store waving his hands, and the others listening, their faces etched with concern. An older, tall man walked away, then rejoined the other two. They continued speaking for a few minutes before the owner of the general store walked out.

Connor stepped away a few yards and waited. Half an hour, then an hour passed, but no one else left the jeweler's. He stayed a little longer, then left, heading to his meeting with Roy and Fred.

He rode Crusader toward the hotel, where the two detectives would be waiting. It was early afternoon and the streets were crowded. The hotel was just a block away, a few doors down from another saloon and a small bank. As he passed the bank he saw a man trying to conceal the gun at his side while closing the entry doors. Connor watched as the shades were closed. He checked the large clock above the bank's entrance. Two o'clock. Too early for them to close. Something wasn't right.

He guided his horse down the adjacent alley and slid off, pulling his Colt from its holster. Three horses were positioned a few yards away. He guessed they belonged to the robbers.

Connor made his way to a side window. Inside were three men, all with guns pointed at the teller, a man who Connor guessed to be the bank manager, and two customers, both women. The teller was pulling money from a drawer and placing it inside a sack.

Connor dashed over to a back entrance. He turned the knob and the door popped open. Instead of leading him into the bank lobby it opened into a hallway with additional doors. One he presumed would open into the bank. He knelt before one, then another, looking through the keyhole. The door he sought was the third one. Again, the door opened with one turn. He slid through the opening.

"Hurry up, old man," one of the robbers shouted at the teller.

"Yes, sir."

Connor could hear the voices as he inched his way along a back wall, trying to get a better view. He rounded a corner and found he was five feet from one of the robbers—the one who held his gun on the two women.

"Maybe we should take one of these women with us, as a hostage," the man yelled over to the others.

"Shut up, Del," one replied.

"Here," the teller said and pushed the sack toward the outlaw holding a gun on him.

The three started toward the back door. They'd have to walk right past where Connor stood.

He moved back to the hallway, pulled open a door, and ducked out of sight. The three robbers ran from the bank, into the hall, and outside toward their horses. Connor followed, but stayed behind the alley door. Before the men could mount, Connor aimed and fired, then fired once more. Two of the outlaws lay on the ground.

The third skirted around his horse, using it as a shield.

"Put your gun down. There's just one way out of here and that's right past me. You'll never make it," Connor shouted.

The answer was a gunshot that split the wood above his head. Connor held. He could wait the man out until the sheriff arrived.

"You got them?" a voice said from behind Connor.

He looked to see the sheriff standing a few feet away. The same person he'd met the night he'd killed the angry saloon patron.

"Yeah. Got two of them, but the third is still out there."

"I have a deputy at the entrance to the alley. Even if he makes it on his horse, he can't get past my man."

Just then the robber threw himself over his horse, stayed low, and tried to ride out. Connor raised his gun and fired. The last outlaw fell to the ground. He walked with the sheriff to check the bodies. All dead. The lawman glanced up at Connor.

"How long you in town for, MacLaren?"

"As long as it takes to find my sister."

"Not that I'm not obliged for your help today, but we haven't had this many killings in months. Now there's been four in a week, all by you. Might be best if you finished your business and left."

Connor nodded, mounted Crusader, and rode down the street to the hotel.

Chapter Six

Fred and Roy waited for Connor at a corner table in the hotel dining room. They'd been meeting with the marshal and the few town leaders who weren't Mormon, passing around the sketch, and pressing for information.

"What do you make of it?" Roy asked as he scanned the lists of names he'd compiled. They checked each man off the list once he'd seen the drawing. "Out of all these people there's only two who think he looks familiar. Neither knew a name."

"I think the man stays to himself, lives outside of town, and frequents only establishments owned by people he knows well." Fred stopped as Connor approached their table and took a seat.

"Anything?" Roy asked.

"Maybe. I'll need your help." Connor ordered dinner from the server who'd walked up. Once she'd left, he continued explaining his experience at the general store and what he'd observed at the jeweler's. He'd gotten the store owner's name from the millinery next door and provided it to the two men. "One of the three will get in touch with the man in the drawing, I don't believe they'll wait long. Seeing the face in the sketch shook up the owner of the general store. It wasn't more than ten minutes before he left to meet the others."

"Roy and I'll work out following the owner of the general store and Smith. They've both seen you, so it's better if we follow them. What about the jeweler? You said his name's Wallace?" Fred asked.

"Yeah. I'll stay on him. What about the others you were meeting with, Roy?"

"Two men thought they recognized the face but didn't have a name. Appears our man stays within a small circle."

"Anyone mention the name, Moser?"

"No. They've heard of Parley Smith, though. Apparently the man's pretty high up in the local leadership. He's friendly with those outside the church, but no one knows much else about him, except he practices law. Smith is one of the Mormon leaders trying to work out how to divide families. Rumor is he has three wives of his own." Fred threw his napkin down and leaned back in his chair. "Interesting dilemma for these folks."

"Yeah, the marshal's in the thick of it. Arrested two men this week on charges of polygamy. The government sent in about a dozen more lawmen to help out. Guess they expect more arrests of those who refuse to go along with the new regulation. One man we spoke with expects their church will hunker down to protect their own for as long as they can," Roy said.

"From what I heard at the meeting, there are those who plan to defy the order and go underground. Our man will be part of that faction." Connor pushed back from the table. "If there's nothing else, I'll head out to watch Wallace. I'll be in touch."

******

Grace had gotten up early. She'd made friends with one of the customers at the restaurant. She was an older widow who owned a good-sized ranch outside of town, but also kept a place not far from where Grace lived. Grace figured the woman was in her late fifties, but you wouldn't know it from watching her. She preferred to ride her horse and wore pants instead of a skirt. Ruth Dix was a woman who knew her own mind and lived life the way she wanted. Grace admired her a great deal.

Ruth had offered to let Grace borrow of one of the horses the woman kept in town. Her small house was on a half-acre, fenced all around, with a corral and stable in the back. There was room for a wagon, but not much else. Her husband had set it up years ago so they'd have a place in town when he needed to come in for business. His ranch was too far out to travel back and forth in a day and it had become their getaway when they wanted privacy. With five children, all grown and living around the ranch property, Ruth now stayed in town a week or two each month and always made it a point to visit Grace.

The morning had gone by fast. She rode through the countryside recalling the numerous trips to town the wives and children had made with Jeremiah before he'd decided that isolation was the best way to keep them safe. At least that's how he'd phrased it. It was late morning when she spotted the farmhouse indicating she'd made it to Moser's property. Grace spotted a couple of horses grazing, about half a dozen cows, and the pigpen. He kept three or four pigs plus a few dozen chickens for the family's use. The animals and the garden provided most of their food.

She dismounted and tied her horse to a nearby branch. The rest of the way would be on foot. Grace knew the place by heart, every bush and tree, the stream, and how the pastures were laid out. She'd come today for one reason—to see Meggie and make sure she was all right. The memory of the morning she'd left, snuck out without her friend, still caused a ball to form in her gut. At the time, it had been the only way to break free. Now she wished she'd taken Meggie with her.

Jeremiah had always treated the youngest wife in a different manner than the rest. Although he'd never beaten or purposely inflicted pain on Grace, she knew he'd been rough on Meggie. He'd always seen her as different—more of a throwaway than the other three. Grace had left to get away from the absolute control he exerted over the family. Meggie needed to leave for her own safety. Someday Jeremiah would go too far and Grace was determined to get her friend away before that day came.

She hid in the trees and waited. When she continued to see no activity she crept forward, staying low but moving as fast as she could. A door slammed. She looked up to see the three girls storm out of the house and run toward the back of the barn. They must have just broken from their morning lesson with Meggie. Now it was time to play.

Grace hunkered down. She knew Meggie would be out within minutes of the children leaving. It was her job to keep them schooled, entertained, bathed, and clothed. Nina and Ada tended to the household needs and garden, while Jeremiah took care of the animals.

Within a couple of minutes Grace spotted her friend open the back door. She held it ajar a moment before stepping out and closing it behind her. She followed the same path as the children, disappearing behind the barn.

Not a minute later Jeremiah appeared at the door with Ada. "Meggie, come back here. Ada's going to watch the girls."

Meggie walked from behind the barn to see Ada strolling toward her. "No need, Jeremiah. I can watch them. I have a new game I'd like to teach them." Grace could hear the combination of hope and fear in Meggie's voice.

"I said Ada will watch them. You come into the house. Now." Jeremiah's command and meaning were clear.

Meggie left the children, passing Ada who looked at her with sympathy. There was nothing anyone could do when Jeremiah gave an order. The youngest wife walked up the steps, ignoring her husband who held the door open. It slammed behind her like a death knell.

Grace's gut clenched. She knew why Jeremiah had called Meggie to the house, and could almost imagine what was happening right now in his upstairs bedroom. She closed her eyes and took a deep breath. Grace looked down to see both hands clutching her dress in tight fists. She said a silent prayer and made up her mind—this would be the last week Meggie spent in that house with that man.

******

"You go to your room now. Clean up then come down to help Nina with supper." Jeremiah's voice was curt as he buttoned his trousers and pulled his suspenders back up over his shoulders. He looked at the girl, his youngest wife, and shook his head. She sure wasn't strong. Not like the women at the brothel he used to frequent. But she was what God had provided and he was going to take advantage of it. "You hear me?" he glared at her.

"Yes, I hear you. Give me a minute and I'll get dressed." Meggie didn't mean to leave the security of the covers until her husband had left the room. She heard the door close and looked up. He was gone. She reached for her dress and chemise, quickly put each on, then silently walked to her room a couple of doors away.

Meggie knew he wouldn't expect her down for at least an hour. She sat down by her window and looked out, remembering the day she'd lost all hope of ever seeing her brothers again.

Charleston, South Carolina, several years before

Eugene called her into his study. "Do you remember a few weeks ago when I told you I'd look for your brothers?"

Her eyes flew open and Eugene could see the anticipation in them. "Yes, I remember."

He hated to dash that hope but knew his next words would wipe it from her, leaving her with few options. "My men found where you lived." It was a hovel, they'd told him. "But they're gone, Meggie. Left months ago, and no one's heard from either since."

Her whole body deflated at his words. Gone. They'd moved away without her. She bent her head, not wanting Eugene to see the tears that formed.

"I'm sorry, Meggie. I can continue to search, but..." his voice trailed off.

She looked up at him, swiping away the moisture from her cheeks. "No, you've done everything you can. There's no way of telling where they've gone. I just need to forget them, as they've forgotten me." She stood and walked up so that she touched the edge of his desk with her dress. "Thank you. You did more than I ever expected." She turned for the door.

"Meggie?" Eugene's voice was soft and full of regret.

"It's all right. I'll be all right," she said without turning and closed the door behind her.

He sat for a long time, feeling miserable for the young woman he'd come to care about. She wasn't for him, never would be, but he'd grown to respect her. Meggie never complained, worked hard, and accepted the miserable circumstances life had delivered. Eugene needed to make a decision about her. He could keep Meggie here, perhaps train her as Dodge had suggested, which would mean she'd leave once he'd found her a position elsewhere. Somehow that didn't seem quite right to him. He poured a drink and pondered her future.

Another option was for him to take a wife. Meggie could then stay as a maid to the new Mrs. Jackson. The problem was he had no one in mind and no plans to marry. He'd sworn himself to a bachelor's life without the commitments a relationship involved. However, he hadn't ever considered a marriage of convenience. The more he thought of it, the more he warmed to the idea. Someone accepted by the Charleston society, who'd bear him an heir, and take care of his household while he remained free to pursue his private interests. It just might work.

He tossed down the last of his drink and headed out.

"Ben!"

"Yes, Mr. Jackson?"

"I'm riding over to Mr. Delaney's. Don't hold supper, I'll dine with him."

"But, Mr. Jackson, there's a storm coming. Perhaps you should wait?"

"What I have to tell Delaney won't wait I'm afraid. If I have to I'll stay over, but I need to speak with him this evening."

Sprinkles of rain had just started as he dashed from the house to his stables, saddling his big stallion. Within minutes he was riding toward Charleston, and Dodge's estate. Halfway there the storm broke in full and pummeled him and his horse. The sounds of thunder rumbled near, but he pressed on. Just when he thought the rain might be letting up, a large crack of lightning hit a nearby tree, spooking his horse. He tried to calm the animal, but another crack sent the animal into a panic. The horse bucked wildly, sending Eugene flying, smashing his body against a large tree, and rendering him unconscious. His broken body slid to the ground.

Chapter Seven

New York City

"You're sure of what you heard, Mayfield? All three, Newell, Swain, and Proctor?" Alexander McCann asked Chester Mayfield, one of his lead investigators.

"Yes, sir. I'm quite positive the men are being released. Something about a new witness coming forward with an alibi for the night of the murders."

Alex McCann owned one of the most prestigious private investigation and security firms in New York. He catered to wealthy, elite clientele, but also helped longtime friends when the need arose. One of these was Connor MacLaren. He'd known Connor when both were young and worked the docks of Red Hook. They'd helped each other out of various jams until Connor and Pierce had moved away in search of Meggie.

Not long after the MacLarens had moved, Alex had found a sponsor who sent him to school and fronted the money to start his business. He'd paid off the sponsor years ago and was now free to help others. At one point, both Connor and Pierce had worked for him. He wished he could lure them back, but that wouldn't happen until Meggie was found. Mayfield was assigned to help them. Now they handled the search alongside Louis Dunnigan who'd hired his own men to investigate. Alex was of the opinion that the more help the better.

"When will they be let loose?" Alex couldn't believe the men Connor and he had caught at the murder site with the weapons still in their hands would be released. They were cold-blooded killers. They'd vowed during their trial that they were innocent and when they got out would come after Connor and Alex. All three should have hung, but a deal had been made and they'd been sent to Auburn Prison instead.

"Three days."

"Shit," Alex muttered. "That's Friday. I'll get messages off to Dunnigan and Connor. You grab two other men and keep watch when the prisoners are released—one man on each. I want to know where they go, who helps them, and what they do each day. If you need more men just let me know. Understand?"

"Yes, but what about you?" Mayfield knew that Alex would now be a target. "Even though we'll keep watch, you need someone with you at all times."

Alex was taken aback. It hadn't registered that his life was in danger also. "So you think I need a body guard? Are you implying I can't take care of myself, Chester?"

"Well, no, sir. But you need to consider it. These men are killers and they blame you and MacLaren for putting them in prison. You aren't safe." Mayfield wiped a handkerchief across his damp brow. "What about Mr. Jericho?"

"I just dispatched him to Salt Lake to keep an eye on Connor." Alex needed to think about Mayfield's suggestion. His home and office were secure, but he moved in elite circles that could endanger others. "Get me Hatcher."

"Yes, sir." Chester left with a sense of accomplishment. Lee Hatcher was the perfect choice—unobtrusive, professional, and dead accurate when the need arose. Besides, he owed Alex his life.

******

Salt Lake City

The pitch black afternoon clouds moved from the west. It would soon cover Salt Lake, blocking the sun and unleashing a pounding thunderstorm. Grace watched as the darkness crept over the farm. She didn't want to leave, preferring to watch for Meggie, and confirm that Jeremiah hadn't mistreated her. Guilt plagued Grace every day at the thought she'd left her friend to defend herself from the disgusting creature who was their husband. She'd snuck out without a word. Meggie must hate her.

Grace pulled her eyes from the growing storm, then glanced at the farmhouse back door when she heard a shout. It was Ada, calling the girls inside.

She had to leave if she was going to make it back in time for the evening customers. Jasper had been good to give her most of the day off. People who didn't appreciate his kind nature or generous heart would sometimes take advantage of the man. Grace didn't want to be one of those. She slipped through the bushes to return to her horse. Before she had gone far, the sound of men's voices drifted through the air. Grace crouched low and listened. She was glad the horse was still hidden a good distance away. The sound increased until it seemed the voices were right on top of her.

Grace ventured a look around a dense stand of trees and froze. Jeremiah and another man moved toward her. She had seen a man ride up earlier, but hadn't noticed Jeremiah leaving the house to meet him. She'd been too busy worrying over Meggie and watching the clouds.

But now they had moved within several yards of her. The other man waved his arms back and forth in front of Jeremiah, but her husband just ignored them. Once or twice Jeremiah attempted to placate the other man, but gave up when it became apparent his words didn't help.

"The picture was you, Jeremiah. There was no mistaking the likeness. Why is this man here and looking for you?" Ezra Thomas, the owner of the general store had ridden to the farm. "This could not come at a worse time. We have all agreed to meet again to discuss the establishment of a new community. But now, with this man looking for you, it may be unwise to take the chance that he will be watching."

"Were you followed?" Jeremiah asked.

"I watched but saw no one."

"Then he does not know you are here, that you know me, or that there will be a gathering this week, correct?"

"I suppose." Ezra spoke the words but the tone and hesitancy of his voice told Jeremiah that the man was frightened.

"You are worried over nothing, my friend. Go home. Tell the others that the stranger does not seek me as I have done nothing. My conscious is clean." Jeremiah's eyes panned the countryside, a clear sign that he, too, was agitated at the stranger's persistence in locating the man in the drawing. "The gathering will take place as planned." He clapped Ezra on the shoulder as the two men turned toward the house.

Grace's heart had slammed into her chest as the men approached. They'd stopped perhaps fifteen feet away before finishing their conversation. Her feet seemed frozen in place and she'd developed chills—more from the fear of being discovered than the cold breeze.

The conversation replayed in her mind. Someone was looking for Jeremiah, but who, and why? Although he was a despicable, disgusting man, who had no respect for women and saw them only as vessels to fulfill his needs, he had not broken any laws, at least none that Grace knew about. The church allowed men to rule their households in the manner needed to attain discipline. She'd never heard of a man being punished for mistreating his wife. No, there must be another reason for the search.

Grace hurried to her horse. She glanced at the farm house in time to see Meggie step off the back stoop. At least she knew her friend was okay. There was much to do before coming back for Meggie. That would be her last time on the farm. It would be the day she took Meggie away.

******

Roy Crowley had followed Ezra out of Salt Lake only to lose him when a large herd of sheep blocked the road. There had been no way to ride around. He hadn't been able to catch-up to the store owner and accepted that he'd have to wait.

He'd watched from a distance as Ezra rode toward him a couple of hours later. The detective hadn't discovered who Thomas had gone to meet. As Ezra guided his horse toward Salt Lake, Roy noticed another figure riding low but in the same direction several hundred yards behind Thomas. When the rider sat up he noticed it was a woman. Roy backed further into the bushes, allowing her to pass within several yards before he reined his horse around to follow.

He didn't follow Ezra, confident the man was riding back to his store. Instead, he stayed on the woman, curious as to who she was and why she'd be riding from the farm alone.

The afternoon sky had turned to ebony. Flashes of lightning preceded loud cracks of thunder, while the wind continued to whip her dress around her legs. Grace looked up and caught a fat drop of water on her face before brushing it off and continuing down the almost deserted street. She was just a couple of blocks from the restaurant, but turned into the entrance of Ruth's property to return the horse. Grace still couldn't believe her good fortune at finding a friend such as Mrs. Dix. Of course, if Grace called her that Ruth would scold her. She preferred Ruth, insisted on it if they were to remain friends.

Grace rode into the stable, dismounted, and removed the saddle. By the time she'd started to groom the horse, Ruth had joined her, offering a hot cup of coffee and biscuits.

"Did you find what you were after, Grace?"

"Yes, and no," Grace replied. "It's complicated."

"I have no place to go if you want to talk about it." Ruth sat down on a bale of hay and waited. She held her cup in both hands, warming from the chill of the storm.

Grace finished with the horse, threw in some clean hay, and stretched. She hadn't ridden that far or fast in a long time. It felt good. Her parents had a horse, but Jeremiah wouldn't allow his horses to be used for anything except farm work and pulling their wagon.

"I rode out to check on a friend. She's isolated and I needed to be sure she is all right."

"And is she?"

"No, not really." Grace stopped to decide how much more she could tell Ruth. She needed someone to confide in and knew Ruth wouldn't betray her. "She's the youngest of four wives."

Ruth took that in a moment. "I see. Does she want to leave?"

"Yes. She doesn't know I've come to see her, or that I plan to help her leave. No one knows, except you."

Ruth stood and took Grace by the arm. "Come on inside. This is going to take some time."

"I really should leave for the restaurant." Although voiced, Grace's protest was weak.

"Don't worry about Jasper. There won't be much business in this weather, and if need be, I'll speak to him." Ruth tightened her grip on Grace's arm just enough to lead her in the right direction as the rain pounded down around them.

Roy watched from a distance as the two women dashed through the storm and into the house. He'd heard of this woman. Ruth Dix. She and her late husband were almost legends in Salt Lake. It wouldn't be hard to find out more about her, or about Ruth's relationship with the young woman.

Something about the younger woman nagged at him. She looked familiar but he couldn't place the face. By the time he'd gotten a good look at her she was drenched, but the feeling he'd met her before remained. Well, Roy knew he'd figure it out in time. He decided his time was now better spent following Ezra and learning more about the man on the farm.

******

It was late by the time Roy joined Fred and Connor at the little restaurant where they'd met a few nights earlier. He was beat, and by the looks of the others, they were as well.

"Coffee, gentlemen?" Jasper asked as he set down three cups.

"All around," Fred said and picked up his cup. "Plus a steak for me, if you've got one."

"Same here," Roy said before letting the owner leave for the kitchen.

"And you?" Jasper asked Connor.

"Same." Connor looked around the restaurant. It was about half full but no sign of Grace. It appeared Jasper was the only one working the front. It annoyed him that he felt disappointment at her absence.

"Got some bad news, Connor." Fred reached in his pocket and took out the telegram from Alex McCann. "You need to read this."

Connor took the message and read it through. His face didn't change, nor did he speak—just folded the paper and placed it in his pocket.

"That's it?" Fred asked.

"What else is there? Swain, Newell, and Proctor are being released. Nothing can change that."

"And if they come this way to find you and make good on their threats?"

"They're dead."

Roy and Fred looked at each other but neither spoke. Connor was right. If those men came to Salt Lake to find him, neither man believed for a moment that the three would leave alive.

Their conversation was interrupted as Jasper placed their food down and refilled their coffee.

"The message mentions something about Jericho. You know the man?" Fred cut into his steak and took a bite.

Connor didn't understand why Alex had sent their long-time friend, Jericho, to Salt Lake. He should be in New York, protecting Alex and his family. Connor didn't want to place any others in danger if the three did show up in Utah.

Alex and he had met Jericho, or Mr. Jericho as he liked to be called, when they were working the docs in Red Hook. He and Alex had been about seventeen. Jericho was the owner of a bar near the harbor and didn't take to water rats who didn't treat his customers with respect.

Alex and Connor were minding their own business, drinking beers after a long day, when three men walked up and grabbed their drinks, tossing the liquid on the floor. "We don't allow no Irish trash in this place," one man bellowed and slammed his fist on their table.

Alex leaned back in his chair and grinned. "That's good then as we're Scots."

The man glared at Alex, gripped his shirt, and hauled him up. If Jericho hadn't interrupted the scene, Alex would have ended with at least a broken nose and maybe more. Connor would've been treated to the same. Instead, Jericho grabbed the man by his collar and belt, walked him to the entrance, and threw him out, then turned to the bloke's companions. "You two want the same, or can you make it outside under your own steam?"

he'd asked them. They'd fled and never returned to the small bar.

Jericho had been a fixture in both their lives, as well as Connor's brother Pierce, ever since. He worked for Alex most of the time but had also worked for Louis Dunnigan, helping Drew MacLaren overcome his injury. Now he was being sent to help Connor. The man was at least fifty. Connor wondered if Jericho would ever slow down.

"Hey, MacLaren, you still with us?" Fred asked when Connor hadn't responded to his question about Jericho.

"Yes, I know Mr. Jericho. Alex and I've known him for years. You can trust him." Connor finished his steak and looked around the room. No sign of the pretty young woman who normally served him.

Just then the door flew open and Grace raced toward the kitchen, soaking wet, and shivering.

Roy's head snapped up at the sight of her. "It is her," he said and started to rise.

Connor stopped him with a hand on his arm. "What are you talking about?"

Roy filled Fred and Connor in about following Ezra Thomas, then losing him. He explained about following the young woman to Ruth Dix's home. "She appeared to be following Thomas. I'd like to know why."

"Who's Ruth Dix?" Connor asked.

"She and her family are longtime residents. They own a ranch several miles outside of town and a house a couple of blocks from here. I spoke with her when we first arrived—thought she might recognize the drawing. Well, guess I'd better to speak with the woman." Roy started to rise again.

"I'll speak with her," Connor strode to the kitchen before Roy could respond. He spotted Jasper at a large work table. "Where's Grace?"

"I already told you..." Jasper began before Connor cut him off.

"Where is she?"

"I'm right here. What do you need?" Grace walked from behind a corner, still trying to do something with her wet, unruly hair. She came to an abrupt stop when she saw who had asked about her.

"We need to talk," Connor said.

"And what would we need to talk about, Mr...?"

"You can call me Connor."

"All right, Connor. What do we need to talk about?"

"It's private."

She pursed her lips trying to decide if she wanted to be alone with this man. "Maybe after I'm finished..."

"Now, Grace. We have to speak now." Connor turned to Jasper. "Do you have an office or someplace private?"

"Storage room's about the only place."

Connor turned back to Grace. "You lead the way."

Chapter Eight

Auburn Prison, New York

"Your belongings," the guard told the prisoner who stood before him. Other guards were doing the same with two other prisoners. Ex-prisoners as of fifteen minutes earlier. The three had changed into their own clothes and been walked to another room to collect their personal gear before a last stop at the exit room.

"My gun?" Len Proctor asked as he shoved some loose coins into a pocket. A tobacco pouch followed.

"Don't have any guns. You'll have to figure out how to get it back once you leave here."

"Horses?"

"Same. There's a wagon that'll take you to town. From there you're on your own." The guard walked the few feet to anther door and unlocked it. "Through here."

Len walked into another small room and waited. Earl Swain and Bert Newell joined him a few minutes later, followed by another guard with another set of keys. He opened one last door and threw it open. "Out there boys. Hope we never see any of you again," the guard said and stood aside.

It didn't take long to reach their destination. It was a gray, bleary day. Rain came down in soft waves, not hard, but enough to soak through their clothes if outside long enough. They only had what was on their backs. At least each owned a coat to curb the chill.

Len climbed from the wagon and looked around for the person who was to meet them. It didn't take long. A tall, lean man, with a thin face, and blank expression stood under the shelter of an overhang about fifteen feet away. His posture, hat, and thick, wool rain coat indicated he was a man of wealth.

Roscoe Vance had pulled the strings that got the three released and exonerated of the murder charges brought against them by Alex McCann and Connor MacLaren. Now he'd provide them with what they needed to hunt down the two men and eliminate them. After that they'd be free to pursue the gold they'd gone after several years before. Gold they'd killed for, gold they should have been spending instead of wasting away in Auburn. McCann and MacLaren would pay for those squandered years.

The three men walked toward Vance. It was Len who spoke. "Glad to see you. I assume you have what we need."

"Horses, train tickets, gear, guns, and money are ready. You'll stay here tonight and travel to New York City in the morning." Vance handed Proctor keys. "For your rooms tonight." He then passed over a thick envelope.

Len tore it open to find a hand written note and money.

"That's McCann's office and home. A man named Lee Hatcher works for him. Appears he's acting as a body guard. Handle it any way you want, just don't fail on this." Vance's tone was hard, unbending.

"What about MacLaren?"

Vance handed Len a second envelope. "This is where MacLaren is staying in Salt Lake. Again, take care of him however you want."

"And the gold?" Len asked.

"Bring me MacLaren's gun and you'll get the rest of the information." Vance buttoned his top coat. "Don't contact me until both jobs are finished. Do you understand?"

"Yes. Just be sure you have the information on the gold when we return. I expect it won't take long to kill off McCann and MacLaren. There's three of us. They won't last the month."

Len's bravado was lost on Roscoe Vance. He knew the outlaws for what they were—lowlife murderers, nothing more. He just hoped they'd kill the two men who'd cost him his business and marriage years ago. At least he hadn't gone to prison like the three men standing in front of him. He'd had enough money to ensure that, but now he wanted payback, and these men were going to give it to him.

******

Salt Lake City

Connor pushed Grace into the small storage room and closed the door behind him. "Now, I want some straight answers."

"Answers to what?"

"Why were you following Ezra Thomas today and meeting with Ruth Dix?"

"I don't know what you're talking about. And if I did, I certainly owe you no explanation for what I do. Now, I want out of here." Grace's eyes had grown wide and color crept up her neck at Connor's questions.

"Not until you tell me your connection to Ezra and Mrs. Dix." He kept his voice low, measured.

"It's none of your business." Her eyes narrowed to slits as the words came out. *Who was this man to question her?*

"Not good enough." Connor was losing patience, not just with Grace but with his close proximity to her in the tiny storage room. His body tightened and it was all he could do to stop himself from running his fingers along her cheek and down her long, slender neck. He needed to get the information, then get out of this room, and away from Grace.

They glared at each other, neither budging.

Grace finally broke the silence. "What do you care what I did or who I met with?"

Connor scrubbed a hand over his stubbled face, then rested his hands on his hips. "Look, I just need to know why you were following Ezra."

"If I tell you will you let me out of here?"

"It depends on the answers."

She let out an exasperated breath. "Fine. I was looking for a friend, not following Mr. Thomas. I recognized him, but didn't want him to see me. That's all. I don't know why he rode out that way."

"And Ruth Dix?"

"She comes in here sometimes. Ruth lets me use one of her horses."

"Is the friend a man?"

"No. She's a wife of a Mormon man. No one of consequence."

"You rode a long way. Did you see her?"

"Yes, I saw her but she didn't see me. Her husband would never allow it, he doesn't approve of me. I just wanted to be sure she was safe." Grace's voice had softened, turning wistful.

"And is she?" Connor moved a little closer, his voice low. He was almost brushing up against Grace. He could smell the soap from her still damp hair.

Grace looked up, startled to see how close he'd gotten. "Yes. She seems all right." Her whispered response drew Connor even closer. He lifted a finger and moved an errant strand of hair behind her ear.

"And you weren't following Ezra Thomas?" Connor's voice had grown thick, husky.

"Uh, no." Grace couldn't keep from staring into his moss green eyes. They held her captive as the man held her captive in this small space.

"I see," Connor said as his head bent in slow increments to brush his lips across hers. It was just a caress, just a touch.

Grace had watched as he'd moved closer but did nothing to stop him. His lips were dry, soft. She'd never felt anything as sweet.

Connor lifted his head and stepped back. Taking a deep breath he leaned against the only wall not covered in shelves and crossed his arms. "All right, Grace. You can leave now."

Grace stared up at him. As before, his black wavy hair fell over his forehead—it would be so easy to reach up and brush the heavy strands back. Her heart pounded and her face felt flushed, yet she stood rooted in place.

"Grace? Did you hear me?"

"Uh, yes." She turned to leave then stopped. "Why did you do that?" she asked over her shoulder.

"Kiss you?"

"Yes."

"I surely don't know, but it won't happen again," Connor answered and hoped it wasn't a lie.

"Good. I didn't like it," Grace responded then dashed out the door.

Connor's soft chuckle followed her into the kitchen.

******

Connor told Fred and Roy what Grace had said before he left for his hotel. But his night was fitful. He'd woken several times and lay awake for hours. Between the encounter with Grace, their brief sweet kiss, and the story she told, he couldn't get his mind to rest.

He was a suspicious man by nature. His gut told him there was more to what Grace had told him but he needed to gain her trust before she'd open up to him further.

Why would someone ride so far out and not meet with the person they'd gone to see? Why not ride back to town with Thomas rather than alone, especially with a storm unfolding? And what was her connection to Ruth, a woman with a long legacy in Salt Lake and no other connection to Grace other than the fact that she frequented the small restaurant?

He'd been out all the following day, watching the jeweler, Calvin Wallace, and making plans for the arrival of Proctor and his comrades. Frustration ate at him. Not about the murderers who would be stalking him. No, his frustration was knowing that several people in this town knew the man in the drawing but refused to provide a name. He felt like throwing something across the room.

Instead, he threw his hat on the bed, unstrapped his gun belt, and dropped into a chair. His room was large and elegant. Something Louis Dunnigan would request, with all the features you'd expect from the best hotel in Salt Lake. As far as he knew, Fred and Roy had similar rooms. Dunnigan always went first class, even for his help.

Connor thought back on what they'd learned so far. Roy had more success than either Fred or Connor. Neither Parley Smith nor Calvin Wallace had gone anywhere the past two days. Almost as if they knew they were being watched.

He'd start again tomorrow. But there was something about Grace's trip to visit a friend on the same day that Ezra rode the same direction that bothered Connor. He didn't believe in coincidences. They needed to discover where Ezra went and pay that person a call.

A soft knock on the door pulled him from his thoughts. He opened it to see a tray loaded with the supper he'd order. His eyes traveled up and held on the beautiful woman holding the tray.

"Your supper, Mr. MacLaren."

Connor indicated she should bring the tray into his room and set it on the table near the window. He watched her move. Her long black hair was braided, then twisted to form a knot at the back of her head. Her eyes were golden, the color of honey. Although her dress was modest, in the style of a high-end hotel employee, it still clung to her curves.

She set the tray down and turned toward him. "Anything else, Mr. MacLaren?"

He looked at her a moment before shaking his head. She left, closing the door quietly behind her. Connor sat on the bed, staring at the food a few feet away. He walked to the window and looked out. The restaurant was only a few blocks away, but Grace was probably already gone. He wish he knew what it was about her that intrigued him.

She was pretty but not stunningly beautiful like some of the women he'd known. She was proud but not haughty, and he liked the way he could make her blush at the most innocent comments. He'd never met a woman whose mere presence sent heat coursing through his body. Connor was a controlled man by nature, not accustomed to the lack of restraint that gripped him whenever she was around.

He needed to shake her out of his thoughts. Get whatever information he could from her, find Meggie, and leave town. He'd decided years ago there was no place in his life for anything more than a short-term affair. Connor had simply never been drawn in that direction. Unlike his cousins who relished their lives as married men, he didn't need or want that kind of intimacy. Physical intimacy, yes. Emotional intimacy, never.

Connor ate the food. It was excellent but didn't satisfy his cravings. He pushed it away and walked to the wall hook that held his gun belt. Withdrawing one of his two pistols, he sat on the bed and examined it. He stepped to the wardrobe and grabbed a black leather case. Within minutes Connor had the contents emptied and was busy cleaning his weapons. Finally, near midnight, he finished his work, and stashed the kit.

Connor fell back onto the bed and slipped into another fitful night.

******

New York City

"You're sure this is the place?" Earl Swain looked up the street, then down before his eyes settled on the gated structure across the street. It had taken them hours to shake the men who followed them.

"This is the address Vance gave us for McCann's home. Fancy, huh?" Vance had walked around the corner where the house was located. It wasn't opulent by New York standards but compared to the homes the three killers had seen it was a mansion.

"What's your plan," Bert Newell asked Len.

"For tonight, to watch and see who comes and goes, just like we did yesterday at his office. We need to decide which will be the easiest way to get to him, and his body guard. What are your thoughts, Earl?"

"It's secure but I can get to it." The home was three stories, narrow, with a stone wall and iron gates. It was typical of the upper class townhomes popular in this area of the city.

"Easier than the office?" Len persisted.

"Depends on the number of people coming and going, and their schedule. Do we know if McCann has guards around his family?"

"We'll find out tonight."

Vance had done a good job setting them up. The three men made their way upstairs to an empty apartment in the building across the street. They settled in and began their vigil, hoping to learn what they needed by midnight. It was mid-morning. Alex McCann had left for his office a few hours earlier, just after the men had arrived. His body guard had been with him.

An hour later Earl nudged Len. "Look." He pointed across the street where a woman and two children, a boy and girl, left the house and stepped into a waiting carriage.

"Did you see anyone else? Any body guards?" Bert had moved behind his comrades.

"No, just their driver, wife, and children." Len stood and stretched. "We need to find out how many are inside. Let's set up a delivery."

They'd used this ploy many times in the past when their work had been comprised of being ordinary thieves and not the killers they'd become.

"Bert, you set it up and Earl will make the delivery. You and I will be watching while he enters. Make it a big package that requires he walk into the home and set the object down. We don't want him handing it off to someone else." Len thought a moment. "See if it can be delivered later today."

"Sure, boss." He grabbed his hat and left.

"From what I've seen so far, if there are few people inside, this will be the better location to hit McCann. Might get his family in the cross-fire though." Earl had no interest in hurting women or children, but knew Len didn't feel the same. He was ruthless. As long as there was money at the end, he didn't care who he had to kill.

"For now, prepare to take them from here. Provide me the details and I'll get what you need. No witnesses, Earl." Len eyes narrowed on his partner. "I don't want the same mess we went through before."

Earl knew what Len referred to, and agreed that it couldn't be repeated. He'd over-calculated the amount of dynamite needed to blow through a rock wall that connected with an abandoned room on the other side. Except it hadn't been abandoned or empty. Two women had died. They'd never been charged with the murders even though several other women had seen them. The witnesses were too rattled by the explosion and death of their friends. Although they hadn't gone to jail, the images had haunted Earl ever since.

"What about the children, Len? I don't hold with hurting them."

Len watched Earl. He knew his skills and limitations. That's why Bert had been with them from the start. Bert took care of the details that Earl couldn't. "Don't worry, Earl. I'll make sure you don't have to worry about the children."

Chapter Nine

Salt Lake City

It had been a long train ride and Jericho was tired. He knew where Connor and the others were staying, and was glad that McCann had seen to his accommodations as well. He looked up at the two story structure then walked inside. It was early, he hadn't expected to see Connor but there he was, sitting in the hotel restaurant, drinking a cup of coffee.

Jericho walked up to the table and threw his saddlebags down on an empty chair.

Connor looked at the tall, imposing figure. "Have a seat, Mr. Jericho." Connor signaled the server for another cup of coffee and menu. "What took you so long?"

MacLaren's features stayed neutral but Jericho could see the humor in his eyes. "It was a long, tedious trip, laddie. All the way out here just to protect your sorry arse, which we both know doesn't need to be protected." Jericho thanked the server when she set down his hot brew. "Have you seen them?"

"No. What are your thoughts?"

"I think they'll go after McCann first, then come here."

"Is Alex safe?"

"He's got Hatcher with him. Lee will guard Alex with is life, as we would. But those three are slime. There's just no telling what they'll do now that they're free to seek revenge." Jericho sipped at his coffee and ordered breakfast when the server returned. "Alex is sending the family out of town as well as keeping just a few people at the office. He's preparing as best he can."

"There's no doubt someone is behind them, providing money and other resources. We know someone had to come up with the false statements that got their guilty verdict overturned. Any idea who?" Connor asked.

"Alex thinks it's a man of wealth that he was hired to investigate several years back, Roscoe Vance. He found evidence of embezzlement, fraud, but it didn't stick. Alex suspects Vance bought off some witnesses and a judge. The allegations cost him his marriage and ruined several partnerships, but he still retained his money. Word is he blames Alex and you for all of it."

"The man is slime, like Proctor and his group. It got real messy."

"Yeah, it did." Jericho tucked into his breakfast, cleaning his plate within a few minutes then pushing the dish away. "What now?"

"We wait until they arrive, then take care of them, one way or another. Of course, that's assuming Alex hasn't been able to get them on something at his end. Fred and Roy are here, so we have enough eyes, but I'm going to keep focusing on finding Meggie. She's my first priority."

"Understood, and that's as it should be." Jericho pushed up from his chair and grabbed the saddlebags. "My horse is at the livery a few blocks down. I'm going to claim my room, freshen up, then make a visit to the saloons. That's where Proctor will go as soon as he arrives in town. I'll meet up with you later."

Connor watched his old friend leave, grateful for his presence.

******

Grace gathered her small reticule and bonnet before rushing down the stairs to the street. Ruth had invited her to go shopping, something Grace hadn't done in a long time. Ruth needed to stop at the mercantile, a dress shop, and drug store. Ruth was waiting in a wagon when Grace reached the street.

"Good morning, Grace," Ruth called as she steadied the horses. "Hop on up."

Grace climbed up next to Ruth, wrapping her shawl more tightly around her, and tying her bonnet down. "I'm so glad you included me."

"Well, it's good to have company. I like being in town but, sometimes, it's lonely without all the family." They moved down the street at a slow pace, unaware of being watched.

Connor hung back, not wanting the women to see him. He was on foot, deciding he'd have a better chance of staying hidden without his horse. There was more to Grace's ride than just looking for a friend, Connor was certain of it. Perhaps she was meeting another man, possibly Ezra Thomas. Jasper had said Grace didn't take to men, but after their brief kiss, Connor knew her boss was wrong. She'd enjoyed it as much as he had. There was a lot more to that girl than she wanted anyone to see.

Ruth stopped at the drug store. Grace stayed in the wagon, content to be away from her small room and work at the restaurant. She couldn't recall the last time she'd spent time with another woman, alone, in town. Within a few minutes Ruth had returned, directing the horses toward a small dress shop.

This time Grace did go inside, curious as to what she'd find. All the dresses she'd owned her entire life had been made either by her mother or herself. Her father, or Jeremiah, had selected fabric, usually cheap cotton or scratchy wool, not allowing the women to have a voice in the decision. Now she was standing in a real dress shop, staring at dresses of all colors and fabrics.

"Come on in, Grace, you don't have to stand in the doorway," Ruth called to her.

Grace entered a step at a time, absorbing everything and running her fingers over some of the dresses. She'd made it through half the shop when Ruth walked up next to her.

"Find anything you like?"

"Oh, I like so much I'd never be able to choose." As Grace spoke she looked around the store once more. "Maybe we'll be able to come back again."

"We can return next week if you'd like and stay longer. Perhaps you can try on some dresses.

The green one in the window would be stunning on you," Ruth said as they reached the wagon and climbed up.

Connor had stayed a couple of doors down knowing there was no chance he could walk into the dress shop unobserved. He hoped their next stop would give him a chance to listen to their conversation, possibly learn more about Grace's ride to the country.

He watched as Ruth pulled up in front of Ezra Thomas' general store. Another coincidence? Connor stepped into the tailor shop next door until the women had entered the mercantile, then walked to a window and peered inside. Ruth was talking to Thomas, while Grace held back, standing in another aisle, picking up an item then setting it back down while keeping an eye on Thomas. It appeared she was watching the exchange but not letting Ezra get a look at her.

Connor slipped into the store with a large group who'd entered just as Grace walked up to Ruth. It was obvious Grace was trying hard not to make eye contact with the merchant. He casually moved closer, taking off his hat, and positioning himself to listen.

"Grace, come over here and meet Ezra Thomas. He owns the store."

Grace placed a can on a shelf and pulled her bonnet down lower before moving toward the counter. She kept her head down until just before she stopped beside Ruth.

"Ezra, this is my friend, Grace."

"Well, it's a pleasure Grace." Thomas plastered a broad smile on his face but it seemed forced. She hoped he didn't recognize her. She'd only been in the small shop once with Jeremiah but didn't want to take any chances.

"Hello, Mr. Thomas. It's nice to meet you." She kept her head low, her eyes not making contact with his.

"Have we met before, Grace? You seem familiar."

"I don't believe so, but I meet a lot of people at the restaurant where I work."

"Which restaurant is that?"

"Oh, a small place. You've probably never heard of it." Grace hoped he didn't ask the name.

"Oh, I've heard about most of the restaurants. How long have you been there?" Thomas asked.

"A few months now."

"I'll have to stop by. What did you say the name was?" Ezra had been moving, trying to get a better look at Grace's face, but she'd outmaneuvered him each time.

Connor looked at the fear on Grace's face and stepped forward. "Hello, Grace." He stood between her and Ezra then turned to the merchant. "It's good to see you again, Mr. Thomas."

"Uh, yes. It's good see you again, Mr. MacLaren. Can I help you with something?"

"Not today. I spotted Grace and wanted to say hello." He zeroed in on Grace. "If you ladies have no plans, I'd be honored to escort you to dinner."

"Oh, I don't think..." Grace started.

"That's a marvelous idea, young man. My name's Ruth Dix." She held out her hand.

Connor gripped it gently. "I'm Connor MacLaren, and it's my pleasure, ma'am."

"Well, we best get moving along. Good to see you, Ezra," Ruth said and took Grace's elbow.

"You too, Ruth. And nice meeting you, Grace." Ezra stared at the pair until they were out the door, then called to someone in the back room. He spoke to the man who emerged, then sent him scurrying outside.

******

Meggie had risen early. It was a beautiful day—warm and clear with a slight breeze. She planned to dash to the creek, pull flowers, and teach the girls about drying plants.

She hurried to the stream, picking flowers as fast as her hands would move, and throwing them in her apron. When she could no longer carry any more, she ran back to the house, set the flowers in water, and placed them in a cupboard, out of sight.

She heard the voices before she saw them round the corner.

"Good morning," Meggie said as the girls took their places at the table.

"Good morning, Meggie," they replied, a big smile playing across each face.

Meggie handed them their breakfast and sat down for morning prayer.

"What's the surprise?" the oldest, Janie, blurted, stuffing eggs in her mouth.

"I'll show you as soon as breakfast is done and the dishes are washed."

"What's all the noise?" Jeremiah entered the room rubbing his eyes and pulling up one suspender. Meggie usually heard him enter, but not today.

"Meggie has a surprise for us, Papa!" The youngest, Essie, left her chair, jumping up and down in front of her father.

Jeremiah's eyes shot to Meggie. "What surprise?" His tone was hard.

"Oh, nothing really. I just thought the girls could use a lesson in something different today." Meggie realized she'd been slowly backing away from her husband, not wanting to be too close. She hated it when he touched her.

"Let's see it," Jeremiah insisted.

"I thought I'd show them once breakfast was over."

"It's over. Now show me your surprise."

Meggie walked to the cupboard and grasped the jar loaded with wildflowers. She glanced at Jeremiah and noticed that his eyes had grown wide when she set her surprise on the counter.

"Flowers? You're wasting their time and yours on flowers?" He stalked to the counter, snatched the glass jar and walked out the back door.

"Papa, wait, please. Can we see them?" Janie ran after him. He spun, grabbing her arm and turning her back inside the house. The other two girls stood motionless next to Meggie.

Jeremiah yanked the flowers from the water. Throwing them to the ground, he emptied the jar, and slammed back into the house. "No more foolishness, Meggie. These girls are to learn their letters and how to run this house. Not waste time on such frivolous things as flowers." He stopped within inches of her. "Am I clear, Mrs. Moser?"

Meggie squeezed her hands together and stared at her feet. "Yes. You're quite clear."

"Good." Jeremiah walked past his daughters on his way outside, not registering the fear he'd caused in the young girls. The smallest stood with tears streaming down her face while the two oldest stared after him, not understanding his anger over the flowers Meggie had gathered for them.

"What's going on?" Ada asked as she entered the kitchen. From the looks on everyone's face she guessed that Jeremiah had already soured the day.

Meggie glanced up but shook her head. "I'll explain later." She grabbed the girl's empty plates and began to the scape the remnants into a bucket. "Would you start Jeremiah's breakfast?"

"Of course," Ada replied as she walked up to Meggie, placing a hand on the younger woman's arm. "Whatever happened, it's just his way." She looked nervously over her shoulder then turned back to Meggie. "Someday, I pray this will all be behind us."

The women jumped as the door slammed open and Jeremiah entered. "I'm taking Nina to town for supplies, then we're going to the gathering. You two watch the girls. I expect all the lessons and chores to be done by the time I return."

To Meggie's relief, he ate in silence, ushered Nina to the wagon, and left.

"Would you like me to watch the girls and give them their lessons? Getting away for a walk will make you feel better."

"Thank you, Ada. That would be wonderful." Meggie hugged her friend, retrieved a sweater, and dashed outside before she had a change of heart. She hated leaving Ada to watch the girls by herself, but the opportunity for some time alone was too tempting. Meggie wanted to walk to the other side of the stream, look for wild berries, and enjoy her brief freedom.

Chapter Ten

New York City

"I'm telling you, Len, we can't get McCann at his home. He has three to four people there at all times." Earl had made the delivery that morning, then met Len and Bert back at the apartment Vance had set up. Earl had made it inside the McCann home and was left alone in the entry hall long enough to get a good count on the help. Killing McCann at his own home would be dangerous.

"All right, we'll get him at his office." Len looked out the window. He agreed with Earl, the home across the street wasn't the best place.

"Or when he travels between the two. That way we focus on him and his body guard. They have security at his office, but he rides home alone."

"Bert, we need to get ready. We'll set it up for tonight."

Several hours later the three men had positioned themselves a few blocks from McCann's office. They knew he left late each night, taking a route that wound through high traffic areas. The last few blocks were through quiet residential neighborhoods. There was one section of torn up road with only two homes. Even with the rough terrain, McCann still took this street. That's where they waited.

Earl had buried dynamite in a small mound of dirt centered in the road. He'd laid the fuse so that it would remain unseen until it was too late. Len and Bert positioned themselves on either side of the road, ready to pick off the occupants in the carriage, assuming the dynamite didn't complete the job. It would be over in a couple of minutes.

The three didn't wait long. Bert spotted the carriage a block away. He signaled the others, then knelt down with his rifle positioned to pick off anyone who survived the blast. He watched as Earl bent down to light the fuse. Bert could see the sparks as the small flame moved along the length of the fuse. If the carriage kept its current pace the dynamite would detonate just as the driver was on top of it.

A few moments later, the unsuspecting driver heard a loud explosion at the same time as his body was launched into the air. He landed with a sickening thud. The horse bucked and collapsed to the ground, pulling the carriage on to its side. The three men watched, waiting for survivors to climb from the destruction. They saw no one.

Len started toward the carriage but the distant sounds of alarm bells stopped him. They didn't wait to see the bodies loaded into the ambulance. Len motioned for Bert and Earl to run. He was right behind them.

The following day the New York Sun reported that two men were killed in an explosion that destroyed a carriage owned by prominent businessman Alex McCann. The driver was identified as J.A. Bean. The passenger was assumed to be Alex McCann, but positive identification had not been made public. McCann's family was reported to be out of town at the time of the explosion.

Satisfied, Len cut the story out of the paper, pocketed it, and along with Earl and Bert, left New York for Salt Lake City.

****

Salt Lake City

"Ladies." Connor pulled out chairs for both Ruth and Grace.

"Thank you, Mr. MacLaren, this is a real treat," Ruth said as she lowered herself into a chair.

Grace mumbled a weak thank you and took her seat next to Ruth. Her companion glanced over at her, wondering at the change in the young woman since seeing Connor in the mercantile.

Connor watched Grace squirm in her seat, fascinated at the change in her. At the restaurant she was confident, spoke to everyone, and offered an easy smile. Around him she was aloof, distant—except for their brief moment in the storage room. Perhaps that was it. The woman was uncomfortable about their encounter, maybe embarrassed. Hell, it was just a kiss, and barely that. But, as he continued to stare, he noticed a rose tone begin to form on her throat and move upwards onto her chin, then cheeks.

She lifted her head, no longer able to handle his continued scrutiny. "What is it? Why are you staring?" Her voice was strained, impatient, and she immediately chastised herself for the outburst.

"I must apologize, Grace. You are so lovely today that I can't take my eyes off you." Connor's eyes sparkled at her reaction.

"Now that's just plain nonsense. A man like you must be around truly beautiful woman all the time. Don't think you can charm me, Mr. MacLaren."

Connor sat back in his chair, acting as if she'd wounded him, and working to contain the laughter he felt. "Why Grace, whatever have I done to deserve such words?"

"You know perfectly well what. I don't intend to discuss it further. Ever." She opened the menu and pretended to read, having lost her appetite the moment she'd seen Connor in the store. She'd wondered several times if the kiss had affected him as it did her.

She'd lain awake most of the night reliving the moment, the touch of his lips to hers, remembering his unique scent. Leather, sunshine, and something else. She didn't understand it, but she'd wanted more than the one brief kiss. Now, sitting in this restaurant, all she wanted to do was wipe the image from her memory.

Ruth sat watching her two companions, turning from one to another, and trying to understand their conversation. There was history between them, but she had no idea what.

Connor softened as he watched Grace struggle to control her emotions—feelings he now realized were directed at and about him.

He held up his hands, palms out. "Whatever I did, I apologize. Now, do you think we can enjoy our dinner?"

Grace's face flamed red—she'd made a complete fool of herself. She smoothed her skirt and worked to control her shaking hands. What had she been thinking talking like that to their host? Why couldn't she have waited until she saw him in the restaurant? There was no reason to have lost her temper over something that meant nothing to her. Absolutely nothing.

Her eyes met Connor's. "Yes, I think that is a very good idea. I, well, I shouldn't have..."

"Don't worry about it. We won't speak of it again." Connor pulled the menu in front of his face to hide the obvious lie. He had every intention of speaking of it again, and much more.

******

Grace lay in bed, unable to sleep, and the clock kept ticking. She'd gotten home from work early at nine o'clock. It was now two in the morning, and her next shift started in four hours. She rolled to her side, pulling the covers more tightly around her and stared out the dust covered window at the full moon. Grace liked the light. She slept better with more of it, but not tonight.

Grace kept feeling Connor's lips on hers. She'd hated Jeremiah's foul breath and wet kisses. Thinking about him made her gag. Yet Grace had liked the way Connor's soft, dry lips moved over hers. It had been so unexpected. When he pulled away she'd wanted to draw him back down to make sure the tingling sensation she'd felt was real. But all she'd done was stare at him. Grace hadn't found her voice until he'd dismissed her, had spoken the lie without thought. She'd enjoyed the kiss, very much. The more time Grace spent around Connor, the more she discovered how much she liked the man.

******

It had been a wonderful day. Meggie had wandered a good distance from the farm, toward a road she knew ran west from Salt Lake. It was the road she planned to take the first chance she got.

Dark clouds were moving in, engulfing the mountain range north of the farm, and obscuring the sun. Meggie knew she had to start back. It was after twelve o'clock, maybe two. Jeremiah never stayed in town long and she didn't know how long the meeting would last—it could be early evening or late. She figured she had another three hours but that was all.

Lightening flashed several miles away. She counted until the sound of thunder reached her seven seconds later. A short time later another flash. Thunder cracked the sky ten seconds afterwards. The storm was moving away from her.

She sat beneath a large tree, pulled her knees up, and wrapped her arms around both legs, listening to the thunder and watching the lightning. Her mind went back to the night of

Eugene's accident. The night everything changed once more for her.

Charleston, South Carolina, several years before

Ben had ridden to Dodge Delaney's home late the next morning when Eugene hadn't returned. That's when he discovered his employer had never made it to his destination. Dodge organized a search and ten men rode out to canvass the road between the two estates.

Dodge was the one to find him. Eugene's broken body was cold and already stiffening in death. Dodge had ignored the sight, wrapping his arms around his friend, rocking him back and forth as tears rolled down his face. He didn't attempt to hide them. Eugene was the best man he'd ever known, his closest friend, more like a brother, and now he was gone.

There must have been two hundred people at the service. Eugene Jackson was well liked, respected, and a true son of Charleston. Most went back to the Jackson estate for refreshments, discussing their memories of him—some with sadness, others smiling as they thought of the charming rogue who'd done well with the little he'd been left after his parents died.

Meggie had hidden in Eugene's office, sitting in the large leather chair, and staring outside. The concern over her own situation was minimal compared to the sadness she felt over losing a man who'd treated her well, honorably. Meggie had no idea how long she'd been alone when the sound of the door opening and closing interrupted her thoughts. The footfalls were soft as they approached the desk and stopped. She looked up to see Dodge Delaney towering over her.

"Hello, Meggie. I wondered where you were hiding." His soft words drifted over her. She knew Dodge was in tremendous pain over the loss of his closest friend.

"I'm sorry. I wasn't hiding. Not exactly. It's just that I know so few of his friends, and Ben and Nettie didn't need my help. I think they wanted some time alone." Her gaze moved from Dodge to the view outside. People milled around, spoke in quiet voices, discussing the man they'd lost.

Dodge cleared his throat. "We need to talk, Meggie. Make plans for you."

She knew it would come to this, but hoped it wouldn't be today. "All right."

The sadness in her voice pierced Dodge's heart. He knew the girl had held great affection for Eugene, even if it was that of an older brother. He needed to tread gently.

Dodge rested a hip against the desk and shifted his drink from one hand to the other in an attempt to get his own feelings under control. He already felt the loss and had no idea what he'd do without Eugene. Now he had to make a decision about Meggie.

He took a deep, calming breath. "Did you know that Eugene had asked me to take you into my home if anything happened to him?"

Meggie's wide eyes flew from the view outside to Dodge. "He never said anything to me."

"I'm not surprised. Neither one of us ever thought it would come to pass. We were both young with so many plans. We never believed anything would happen to either one of us." Dodge's eyes had moved to a small photograph taken a couple of years before. It sat on Eugene's desk. Two young men with broad smiles and the world in front of them. "It's something I never thought much about, but I want you to know I intend to honor Eugene's request."

Honor Eugene's request. The words played through Meggie's mind. Dodge didn't say he wanted her in his house, or would be honored to have her. No, he was just complying with a friend's request.

"Please, Mr. Delaney. You are under no obligation to take me into your household. Mr. Jackson once mentioned that you had more help than you needed. I'm certain you have no space for another." Meggie pushed out of the chair to stand in front of Dodge. He towered over her five-foot five-inch height.

Dodge stared down into the girl's deep, moss green eyes. They were still red and moist, remnants of her own grief over Eugene's death. "Meggie, let me rephrase it as a request." He set down his empty glass. "I would be honored if you would agree to live in my house until such time as you decide to follow your own dreams."

The lump in Meggie's throat had grown to the size of a large stone. She was determined to stop the tears that threatened. "Will I be allowed to work in your home? I don't want to take charity or have people gossip."

"If that's what you want, then yes, I will find suitable work for you. And of course, with the number of people in my home, there will always be someone around. No one will gossip." Dodge was surprised at the relief he felt at her agreeing to Eugene's request.

"All right. I'd be very happy to work in your house, Mr. Delaney." The smile she gave him was tentative, but it was a start. For the first time Dodge looked at her coming to his home as a step in lessening the intense emptiness that now haunted him.

"Then it's settled. We'll move you over as soon as you can gather your possessions."

Meggie startled him with a beautiful smile. "Well, that will only take a few minutes. I don't have much."

"Good. Then you can ride back with me this afternoon." Dodge made a slight bow and left to rejoin the others.

He'd settled her into a small room near the kitchen. It was similar to her room at Eugene's and her duties were almost identical, but one of the maid's was instructed to teach her to sew. Meggie already had a good knowledge of stitching. Her mother had taught her before she and her brothers had come to the new country. Dodge ran an efficient home. She learned that he was quite wealthy, having grown the businesses his father had left to him, and expanded into other industries. He was twenty-two.

Present day

A huge explosion rocked Meggie from her memories of the past. The storm must have changed directions as it was now directly over her. She bolted from under the tree and took off in a run for the house. By the time she entered the kitchen her hair and clothing were drenched.

"Meggie, where in the world have you been? We've been worried." Ada walked toward her with a towel.

"Are they back?"

"Jeremiah and Nina? No, not yet, but I'm sure they'll be here soon. I was hoping you'd make it back before he arrived."

A moment later the women heard a horse pulling a wagon.

Neither spoke. Meggie ran up the stairs, closed the door to her room, and stripped out of her wet clothes. She braided her hair and crawled under the covers, refusing to let her day be ruined by Jeremiah. Her last thoughts were of Dodge smiling as she worked on a new tablecloth. How she'd loved his smile.

Chapter Eleven

Connor didn't know what had come over him. He was in Salt Lake to find his sister, take her home, not moon over some woman who'd made it clear she wanted nothing to do with him. The trouble was, he didn't believe her. In all his years, Connor had never felt so conflicted about a woman. Something warned him that she wasn't who she seemed.

Connor needed to ignore his feelings toward her. What he wanted was something else entirely. It was early, and he knew she would have already started work at the restaurant. Besides, he was hungry and Jasper made a great breakfast.

Grace heard the door open. "Take a seat anywhere," she called over her shoulder, not taking her eyes from the couple in front of her. "So that's an order of flapjacks and one order of ham and eggs, right?"

"That's right, dear. Also, more coffee when you have time." The older couple slipped back into their private conversation.

Grace gave Jasper the order, grabbed the coffee, and topped off four cups before looking toward the newest customer who sat alone near the door. Her breath caught at the same time as she felt a trembling sensation in her stomach. She didn't like her body's reactions to Connor MacLaren, but she couldn't very well ignore him.

"Good morning, Mr. MacLaren. The usual today?"

"Hello, Grace. Yes, that would be fine. Thanks." Connor studied her, trying to understand what it was about this woman that had him acting in ways that weren't normal—at least not for him.

He'd lived his life on the edge, making no commitments, creating no entanglements. Pierce had always told him he'd change if the right woman came along. Connor thought that was pure nonsense. At least he had until he'd met Grace. Hell, he just didn't have time for this right now. He should get up and leave. Find another place that served ham, eggs, and flapjacks the way Jasper did. There were probably a couple other restaurants close-by to choose from.

He didn't budge.

"Here you go. Let me know if you need anything else." She started to turn away but stopped when Connor grasped her arm. Grace looked at the hand that held her, wanting to pull away, and at the same time curious as to what he wanted. "What is it?"

"Have supper with me."

She eyed him, wanting to say yes, knowing she shouldn't. "I can't."

"Why not? Are you afraid of me?"

"No, of course not. I work late every night."

"Not every night."

"I, uh..."

“Grace, another order is ready,” Jasper called from the kitchen.

“I have to go.”

“Your next night off.” Connor didn’t know where the words were coming from. “It’s just supper, Grace.”

She stared at him a long moment before answering. “All right.”

He began to tuck into his breakfast when the front door burst open and Jericho walked over to stand by the table.

“We have to talk, Connor. Now.” Jericho pulled off his hat and threw it on one chair while he took a seat on another.

Connor set down his fork, focusing on his friend. “What is it?”

“One of McCann’s carriages was blown up after it left the office earlier this week.”

Connor waived to Grace for coffee then sat back in the seat, dread filling him. “Tell me everything you know.”

Grace brought a cup filled with strong, black coffee and set it before Jericho. Connor nodded his thanks then returned his full attention to Jericho.

“Neither Alex or Lee were in the carriage. He’d asked one of his employees to stop by his house for something. It happened just a few blocks from his home. The employee and driver were killed.”

Connor scrubbed a hand over his face. “Have they arrested anyone?”

“No, but they suspect Proctor. One of the men, Earl Swain, knows explosives, and all three men have disappeared. Hatcher is certain they believe

Alex was in the carriage, and is dead." He rotated the cup in his hand. "That means you're next on the list. They'll come by train, Connor, and be looking for you. We can't ignore their threat any longer."

"No, we can't" Connor grabbed his hat and threw money on the table. "Let's go."

******

Connor had spent another frustrating day passing around the sketch, talking to anyone who'd take a good look at the image. He decided to try one more block of stores then head to the saloon to meet Jericho, Fred and Roy. With luck one of them would've learned something more following Parley Smith and Ezra Thomas. Calvin Wallace, the jeweler, had left for Denver the day before which left Connor time to locate anyone else who might recognize the man he sought. So far it had been wasted time.

A bell sounded over the door as Connor strode through the entry.

"Good afternoon. Can I help you?"

"I hope so." Connor pulled the well-worn drawing from a pocket. "Does this man look familiar to you?"

"Well now, let me see." The shop owner reached for his spectacles and stared at the image. "You know, I just might recognize this fella." He adjusted his glasses and looked again. "Yes, I believe this looks like one of the Mormons who owns a farm outside of town. He comes in here every once in a while when he can't get what he wants from one of his own. Let me see, what is his name? Martin? No, that's not right. Moser? Yes, that's it. His last name is Moser. Don't think I ever heard his first name."

"Do you know where Mr. Moser's farm is located?" Connor couldn't believe he'd found someone who not only recognized the man but knew a name. The same name that was mentioned at the meeting.

"Sorry, son, I don't. He comes in, pays cash, and leaves. I'm lucky to remember his name. But hold on a minute." A few moments later he returned with an older woman. "This here's Margaret, my wife. Go ahead, tell the man what you know."

Margaret eyed the stranger. Black pants, vest, hat, and boots. She wasn't too sure about him. He didn't have the look of any of the men she knew.

"Margaret, tell the man what you told me. He doesn't have all day." Her husband nudged her just enough to get her started.

"Well, one of his wives mentioned living northwest of town. Way out from the way she talked. She'd wanted to say more but her husband, Mr. Moser, grabbed her arm and pulled her outside. Right rude of him if you ask me."

"Did you notice how many wives he had with him? What they looked like?"

"He doesn't come in here often and he only brings in one at a time. There's the older one. She has real dark hair. Kind of plump and short.

Another one has brown hair. Come to think of it, she's pretty short too, and a little round."

"How tall do you think?" Connor asked. He remembered Meggie's hair as reddish-brown, but maybe it had changed after all these years.

"Oh, maybe five-feet-three."

Not Meggie.

"There was one other that came in once. Pretty gal. Taller than the others. She had deep red hair, kind of wavy from what I could tell. 'Course they all wear bonnets you know." Margaret studied the man again. He seemed hard, but lots of men grew hard in this country. "Why are you asking?"

Connor hadn't gotten this far before. He'd never mentioned Meggie—never needed to. "I'm looking for my sister. Someone saw her with the man in this drawing. But she's not short or plump or has red hair. I'm going to head out to see Moser. Maybe she's a friend of one his wives."

"Good luck, son, 'cause you'll need it. With the new law, those in plural marriages stay out of sight and don't talk much with those not of their faith. Most aren't violent at all, but there are some who'll protect what's theirs no matter what." The merchant walked around the counter and stuck out his hand. "Hope you find your sister. I'm Edwin Miles. Come back in sometime, let me know what you discover."

"Thank you, Mr. Miles, Mrs. Miles. I'm Connor MacLaren, and I do appreciate the information." Connor folded the drawing and placed it once more in his shirt pocket.

He wanted to ride out that moment to find the farm, not wait to tell Fred and Roy what he'd learned. It was growing dark and he only had the slimmest knowledge of the location. Northwest. No, he'd share what the couple had told him with the other men and decide what to do from there.

******

"We'll be in Salt Lake by late tomorrow," the conductor told the passengers as they pulled out of Denver.

Len stared out the train window, anxious to get to the town where MacLaren had been spotted. One of the two men who'd cost him five years of his life. McCann was dead and MacLaren would be soon.

Late the following evening Proctor, Swain, and Newell unloaded their horses, tied on the saddlebags, and found the closest saloon.

"Three whiskey's, bartender," Len called out. "You wouldn't happen to know a man named Connor MacLaren, would you?" he asked as the drinks were set in front them.

"MacLaren? No, don't recall that name, but we get a lot of men in and out of here. Anything else?"

"No." Len didn't bother to look at the amber liquid, just tossed it back, and asked for another.

"What now?" Bert rested his arms on the table and looked around the crowded saloon.

"Get supper, sleep, and start tomorrow. How hard can it be with three of us looking?" At least, Len hoped it wouldn't take long.

"It's a big place, Len," Earl replied. "Might want to start at the Marshal's office. Vance said MacLaren was in town looking for his sister. My guess is he'd check with the law first thing."

"Good idea. Well, I'm ready to get some food and find the hotel Vance set up for us." Len walked through the swinging doors and slammed into another man. "Hey, watch it."

"My apologies, mister," the man said, then took a good look at the gent before him. He'd seen that face before but couldn't place it. Fred Helms was good with faces, especially those of men he'd arrested. Two other men walked up to stand by the stranger, and the face now made sense. Len Proctor, the man released from prison. Fred had to get to MacLaren. "Excuse me." He tipped his hat and kept moving.

"That guy look familiar to you, Len?" Bert asked.

Len followed the man's path down the walkway. "Somewhat, but can't say from where." He continued to watch until the man was out of sight. "Come on, I'm starving."

The three stopped at a small restaurant and ordered steaks from a pretty woman with flaming red hair, but not before each had taken a long, slow look.

"Three steaks, Jasper." Grace pulled down plates and looked back out to the dining area at the three men. Besides the fact that their stares had unnerved her, something about them seemed off. She'd never seen any of them before, Grace was certain of that. Being too close made her skin crawl, the same as when she'd been around Jeremiah.

"Order's ready," Jasper called.

Grace placed the meals in front of the men. "Anything else?"

"Yeah," Len said. "You ever hear of a man named Connor MacLaren?"

The use of Connor's name surprised her but she covered it well. "I've met a lot of men, mister, but I don't recall a MacLaren. Why? Is he a friend of yours?"

"You might say that. I haven't seen him in a long time and heard he was in Salt Lake." Len sat back in his chair to stare at Grace, wishing he had more time to get to know her. "Well, if you hear the name, we're staying at the Palace Hotel down the road."

"Sure, mister. What's your name?

"Len Proctor."

She walked back toward the kitchen, unease crawling up her spine. Grace wasn't sure why she'd covered for Connor, she hardly knew him, but something about those three just wasn't right.

Before meeting Len Proctor, Grace had decided to decline Connor's invitation to supper. Every time she was around him she felt things, emotions that frightened her. She'd made up her mind it was best to stay as far away from the cowboy as possible. Now, her thoughts had changed. Proctor and his companions were looking for Connor and every instinct she had told Grace they weren't his friends, no matter what they professed. She'd meet with him—if only to warn him.

Chapter Twelve

"Come on, keep up," Meggie laughed but kept running. Her pace was just fast enough to keep ahead of the three girls who giggled as they gained on her. She circled the house, then the barn, planning to wear them out before bedtime. After three turns Meggie stopped in front of the kitchen door. "All right, that's enough for now. I smell supper cooking."

She opened the back door to allow the girls to dash in ahead of her. "Walk," Meggie reminded them. "They're full of energy tonight," she told Ada and Nina before settling in a slat back chair. "I tried wearing them out, but I'm not sure it worked. Maybe they'll be tired after they eat."

"If not, Nina and I will read to them until they tire. They are a handful." Ada was a patient woman. Meggie had always thought she would've been happiest with a passel of children and a loving husband. Instead, she'd only been able to bring her one daughter into the world. Two others hadn't made it to the sixth month of her pregnancy.

Jeremiah worked longer than normal that evening, walking in tired and disgruntled. He hadn't been able to repair a piece of equipment that was needed, and would be making a trip into town if he couldn't fix it within a few days.

Jeremiah told Ada he'd take her and the oldest girls with him.

Meggie sat at the table silently praying that Jeremiah wouldn't be able to fix the broken tool. All she'd thought about the last weeks was escape. Her chance may now be upon her.

"I'll be in the office a while." Jeremiah stood and left the small dining room.

"Guess I'd better check on the girls," Nina said and excused herself. "Don't worry about them tonight, Meggie, I'll take care of getting them to bed."

"That would be wonderful." Meggie sat a few minutes more and then helped Ada with the dishes. It had been another long day. The girls had risen early, which meant the same for Meggie. She finished drying the last plate and wrapped the dishtowel around a small hook on the side of a cabinet.

"Why don't you take a walk," Ada said. "Things are fine here and I know how much you enjoy being outside, alone with your thoughts."

Meggie didn't wait. She grabbed a coat and quilt, and then hastened outside. Although it wasn't a full moon, the night was bright. She headed toward her favorite spot, walking first toward the small stream and following its path to the big tree. She'd come here as often as she could since Grace had left, but never, ever brought the girls with her. This was her private spot, away from all the obstacles standing in the way of her dreams.

Meggie ran to the tree, turned, and leaned her back against the rough bark. She threw the quilt down and slid to the ground. The blanket was large enough to pull around her, keeping the chill away from her legs. She drew her coat tight and leaned her head back. The stars were bright with little cloud cover. Meggie thought about Nina's two girls and Jeremiah's refusal to let them attend a regular school.

The two oldest had spent the entire morning working on their letters and simple addition, then helped Ada and Nina with dinner. The youngest had sat in a corner with a picture book she'd been given at one of the church meetings. The book was full of single-line drawings of animals. It was old, dog-eared and her most favored possession. In Meggie's mind the two oldest needed to be in a regular school with other children, not stuck in a farm house being schooled by someone who'd only made it through a few grades.

Even though Connor and Pierce had done what they could to continue her education, the need for all three to work had usually taken precedence. Survival came first. The fact that she was well-read and could write was a testament to how much her brothers pushed Meggie and her strong desire to learn—as well as the generosity of Dodge Delaney.

Charleston, South Carolina, several years before

The better your education, the better your prospects, Meggie. The words popped into her mind unbidden. Dodge had spoken them not long after she'd arrived at his home. It was beautiful, more imposing than Eugene Jackson's house, but the people who worked for Dodge welcomed her.

Dodge knew of Meggie's desire to improve herself, find skills so she could earn a living and move out on her own. It was a concept almost unheard of in this very southern community, yet she was determined to be independent, able to support herself. As many women learned, it was a goal few achieved.

One day, an older man appeared carrying tablets and books. Dodge ushered him into his study and closed the door. Not long afterward he threw the doors open and asked Meggie to join them. Mr. Holly sat at a table near the window. Dodge escorted her over, introduced the tutor, and closed the door behind himself as he left. That was the start of daily lessons in every subject Mr. Holly found relevant, which were many. It was the best gift she'd ever received.

The longer Meggie stayed the more she learned about the man who'd taken her into his home. Although he appeared carefree to most, he worked hard, worried about the people who worked for him, and found every subject of interest. He was constantly working on one business deal or another—many he'd previously shared with his friend Eugene.

She had watched Dodge leave several times a week for appointments in the city. His butler was discreet but had, at one point, confided that their employer had a special lady friend in town. At the time, Meggie thought nothing of it, conscious that many men in his circle had women they visited—

paramour was the word that came to mind. As the months progressed, the visits decreased until Dodge left for town only on rare occasions.

Instead, he stayed and worked on his numerous business ventures, read to Meggie, or taught her parlor games.

He encouraged her to ride and provided a beautiful gelding for her use. Dodge still expected her to complete her chores, and never let Meggie leave with him without checking her progress with Mr. Holly.

At first, Meggie had been hesitant to be alone with Dodge. She'd always been intimidated in his presence. Eugene had been the buffer, made her feel secure. After a few months in Dodge's home her thoughts about him had changed.

She was no longer intimidated—quite the opposite. Meggie now found herself increasingly attracted to the dashing Mr. Delaney.

He was five years her senior, wealthy, and a sought-after escort in the Charleston social spheres. She'd watched as beautiful, single young women would visit with their families, throwing themselves at him and fawning over the handsome bachelor. She wondered if these were the same type of women he would keep as a paramour. Probably not, she decided, but her knowledge in that area was small.

His time with Meggie was just a diversion. She was his employee, his ward, a young woman who would, in time, leave his household and be out of his life. He was gracious, attentive and, to the surprise of many, treated her as a treasured guest rather than as a female who worked for him. Dodge never once crossed the line.

Their time riding, walking along the river, and sharing picnics on his estate increased to the point Meggie had to concede that her intense feelings for Dodge were far beyond what was safe. She knew he'd never feel the same for her. After all, his life consisted of stunning women from wealth with impeccable manners.

He may not be with someone now but it was just a matter of time. A man as attractive, wealthy, and driven as Dodge wouldn't be without a woman for long.

Meggie was determined to hide her feelings, although it became more difficult as their time together continued. She'd come to realize that once Dodge selected his next paramour—or worse, a wife—she'd never again be able to watch him ride out, knowing he would be with another woman that evening. Her heart would break. Her only recourse was to leave.

Meggie planned to let Dodge know her decision soon and ask his help in finding a new employer.

Present day

She abruptly stopped her memories at hearing shouts from the direction of the house. It was Jeremiah's fierce, deep voice, and he was looking for her. It was late, past the normal time he'd be in bed. Meggie shuddered. There was only one reason why he'd care if she were away from the house. She took a deep breath and pushed up from the blanket. *Might as well get this over with*, she thought, and began the trek back into her present life.

******

"Hello, Grace." Connor stood at the entrance to her small room above the restaurant. He appeared the same as always—black pants, vest, coat, and boots along with a white shirt. Tonight he'd added a thin black tie. He held his hat between both hands, rotating it, worrying the brim as if he were nervous. Grace was certain that wasn't the case. He was one of the most confident men she'd ever met. She didn't know much about him, but Connor was one man who didn't back down from a challenge, and Grace believed he saw her as one.

"Hello, Connor." Grace hadn't been quite herself all day. Her heart pounded each time she'd thought of the night to come. This was the first time she'd been invited to supper by a man. Jeremiah never took any of his wives to a restaurant—they'd hardly ever left the farm. Her unease had grown each time she thought of spending an entire evening with Connor.

"You look beautiful." He knew she was attractive, but as Connor let his eyes wander over her hair, face, and the lovely, simple dress she wore, he realized she was a stunning woman. "Are you ready?"

"Yes, let me get my coat." Grace leaned to the side to grab her coat from a hook. Connor stepped into the room, took it from her hands, and helped her into it.

She glanced over her shoulder at him. He felt a quick, hard punch to his gut at the radiance of her smile. He'd found himself thinking of her almost constantly. It was an irritant and confusing. His mind was supposed to be full of ways to find Meggie, and although he walked the streets of Salt Lake every day, following those who'd recognized the drawing, he still couldn't shake Grace's image from his mind.

"What did you do today?" He'd gone ahead of her down the steep stair case and wondered how she made it up and down each day in the snow and ice that covered Salt Lake during many winter days.

"Ruth Dix invited me for dinner. She lives not far and it gave me a chance to get away for a while." Grace didn't confide in Connor that she'd told Ruth about some of her past, as well as her plans to help her friend Meggie. What Grace hadn't confided in Ruth was that she and Meggie were married to the same man. To her surprise, Ruth had been adamant about helping her, offering Grace whatever aid was needed.

"You've known her long?"

"Not really. She's been coming to Jasper's for many years. We struck up a friendship, and it's grown." Grace had never met a woman like Ruth, nor a man like Connor. She peered up at the hard, attractive looking cowboy. His hat was pulled low, his arm through hers as he guided her to the buggy he'd rented. "Is this yours?"

"It is for tonight." Connor helped her onto the padded two person seat. It was covered and drawn by a large, beautiful horse.

"Is she yours?" Grace pointed to the deep, blood-red, bay.

"Yes. He," Connor paused, "is my horse. Crusader's been my partner for several years."

"He's magnificent." Grace settled into the carriage as Connor stepped up from the other side. "Are you a cowboy?"

The question caught him off guard. He'd been a Texas Ranger, done private investigator work, and was now a Range Detective. At least, he had been. Now he was simply a man looking for his sister.

"No, not really."

"Then, what do you do?" She watched his profile, looking for signs he might seek to either embellish or lie about his work.

Connor heard her question just as he brought the carriage to a halt in front of the entrance to a well-lit hotel. It was the nicest place in Salt Lake. He wanted Grace to remember this supper long after he'd left.

"We're here." Connor jumped down and moved around the carriage, well aware he hadn't answered her question. Grace extended her hand but he ignored it and wrapped his large hands around her waist, setting her down on the boardwalk. He let his hands linger a moment before dropping them to his sides.

"I've seen this hotel, but never been inside."

"It's the Templeton. From what I hear, it's the best in the city." Connor placed a hand at the small of her back and guided Grace inside. Even though the night wasn't yet too chilly, warmth hit them the moment they entered the lobby. Connor helped her out of her coat and handed it to the maître d', who showed them to an intimate table in a corner.

Grace stared at the setting. A white tablecloth was adorned with candles, silverware, and a small vase of flowers. She'd never seen anything so stunning.

Connor moved to her chair and pulled it out, seating her opposite him. Her eyes wandered over the room and the other guests. The women wore elegant dresses and the men were in suits. Her simple dress didn't compare to those of the others in the room. Connor fit in well while she felt dwarfed, out of place.

"Wine, Grace?" Connor asked after their server had returned to their table.

"Um, yes, I think so."

"You think so? Is there something else you'd like?"

"No, wine is fine. I've just never had it before."

Connor watched Grace over the candlelight which enhanced her eyes, as well as her obvious unease at being in a place such as this. He hadn't thought about her background, if she had ever been inside an upscale hotel or restaurant. *Perhaps this was the wrong choice,* he wondered, then quickly discarded the thought. No, this was the exact place for her to be, with him, on a night out like she'd never had.

"Well, then tonight is another first for you. First supper with me, first time in the Templeton, and first time drinking wine. I hope you enjoy all three." He held up his glass to her. "To many firsts, Grace."

She lifted her glass and held it up the way Connor did. When Connor took a sip then placed his glass back on the table, she followed. The chilled liquid ran down her throat. It wasn't what she'd expected. She liked it.

"Are you ready to order, sir." Their server stood next to Grace, waiting for her response. She picked up the menu, trying to scan it so that the man would not grow impatient.

"Why don't we give the lady a few minutes," Connor said.

"Certainly, sir."

Grace peeked from behind the menu and smiled, grateful for Connor's intervention. "What would you suggest?"

"I haven't eaten here either, but you can't go wrong with a steak. There's duck and chicken, also."

"A steak sounds perfect."

Connor motioned the waiter over. "Two steaks, medium," he ordered, then turned his attention to his guest.

"Where are you from, Grace? Here in Salt Lake?" He picked up his wine glass and took a swallow, waiting for her to respond.

"No, not Salt Lake. I was born in St. Louis, but my family came out here several years ago." Grace sipped at her wine and felt herself relax.

"So your parents are in Salt Lake? That must be nice, being able to see them."

"No, they moved on, to California. I stayed behind and found a job at Jasper's." Her eyes shifted as she spoke, not meeting Connor's. Grace was hiding something. He'd find out what, eventually.

"Are you from this area?" Grace asked.

"No, originally from Scotland. My parents sent my sister, brother, and I here when I was seventeen. The prospects in America were here, at least that's what my parents thought."

"Were they right?"

"Yes, and no. My parents died a few years after we arrived in New York. I found work at the docks, Pierce worked for a man who made small tools, and my sister took a job as a maid. Pierce and I took turns schooling her because we couldn't afford to not have her work."

"So you worked at the docks then came here?"

"Not exactly. I've done a lot of things. I was an investigator for a private company, took a turn as a Texas Ranger, worked for Pinkerton's for a while. My last job was as a Range Detective. I quit that a month ago to come here."

"What are you doing in Salt Lake?" she asked, this time meeting his eyes.

"Looking for someone."

"Who?"

"My sister. She was kidnapped from the docks when she was sixteen. I've been looking for her ever since. Taking different jobs, following every lead, but nothing. Finally, last month, my last employer agreed to help me. His two private detectives, Fred and Roy, believe they spotted her here in Salt Lake, so, here I am." He wanted to steer the questions back to Grace, away from him. "How long have you been with Jasper?"

"Several months now."

"Here you are, sir." The waiter placed two plates in front of them, steam still rising from the cooked meat. "Will there be anything else?"

"No, this will be fine," Connor replied.

Grace stared at her plate, making no attempt to slice into the steak.

"Is there something wrong, Grace?"

Her eyes shot to his. "No, it's just that I've never been served on plates this nice. I'm just trying to memorize it. You know, for later."

Connor watched as she sliced into the steak and put a small piece into her mouth.

She closed her eyes and chewed, savoring the taste. This was nothing like the thinner meats Jasper served. His food was good, but this was the best meal she'd ever had.

They ate in silence for most of the meal. Finally, Connor placed the last bite of steak in his mouth then pushed his plate away. He took another sip of his wine and watched Grace. The dim light from the candle danced across her face as she finished her meal. She was very expressive—if she liked something, you knew. He hadn't noticed the freckles sprinkled across her nose and cheeks until tonight. Her red hair was up, but enough strands had fallen to enhance the color of her eyes. Connor guessed them to be violet, but he noticed they darkened to a very deep blue when she was agitated, as she was the morning he'd run into her outside the restaurant.

"I can't eat another bite." Grace placed her silverware on the plate and pushed it back. "I'm sure I'll burst if I do."

"Then we'll just wait a while."

"Whatever for?"

"Dessert, of course. We can't leave a restaurant like this without having dessert."

Her groan could be heard across the room, and various diners turned their heads to stare.

"Sorry," she murmured then placed a hand over her mouth.

He watched as a slight tinge of red crept up her neck and colored her cheeks. *God, she is a beautiful woman,* Connor thought. He found himself wondering what it would be like to spend more time with her, see where this deep attraction led. It was something that had never been possible before. His life was one journey after another, his focus on finding Meggie, not on finding a woman he could love or make a permanent part of his life. Once he found his sister all that would change. He'd be free to find someone like Grace.

Connor noticed her eyes widen as they moved to the restaurant entrance. Her eyes turned from surprised to frightened as she continued to stare.

"Grace, what is it?"

"Oh, Connor, I forgot to tell you something important and now it may be too late." Her voice was strained, shaking.

"What is it?"

"There." She nodded toward the direction of the doorway.

Connor turned to see a man he knew all too well, and had been expecting, just not tonight at the Templeton. Len Proctor had a hand on the butt of his gun. His partners, Bert and Earl, stood alongside, watching.

"How do you know them, Grace?" His eyes turned to slits and his voice hardened.

"They came into the restaurant today. Asked if I knew you, said they were friends of yours."

"What did you tell them?"

"Nothing. I said I'd never heard of you. Something about them wasn't right."

He glanced over his shoulder once more to confirm the three men were still watching, then turned back to Grace. "Listen carefully. Those three are more dangerous than you can imagine. I sent them to prison for murder, but they were released on some bogus information. They're here for me, not you." He threw his napkin on the table and stood. "Stay here, do you understand? If things turn bad, go out the back door and find the sheriff. Can you do that?"

Grace didn't answer. She stood, ignored Connor's surprised expression, and walked straight toward the maître d' who stood between her and the three men.

"Dammit, Grace, get back here," Connor hissed but she continued walking.

"Excuse me," she said to the maître d'. "Do you see those three men standing against the wall?"

"Of course, madam. I've been wondering why they are here."

She turned her back to the three intruders and spoke in a soft voice. "They have vowed to kill the gentleman I am with tonight. I'm thinking that would be a bad thing for this restaurant, correct?"

"Absolutely, but what can I do?"

"We'll wait at our table while you send someone to the sheriff. Tell him what is happening and ask for assistance. Will you do this for us?"

"What if they insist on entering the dining room?"

"From the little I know of them, I doubt that's what they'd do. The sheriff will know how to handle men such as these."

"Yes, madam. I will send someone right away."

Grace turned toward the three men and scowled. They stared back, enjoying her discomfort, murmuring to each other, and laughing. She hoped the sheriff could find some charge to lock them up.

She marched back to the table and took her seat. Connor stood with his hands on his hips, a grim expression filling his face.

"What the hell were you thinking, walking up there like that?" He growled the question, then sat down.

"I asked the maître d' to send for the sheriff. Those men are a nuisance and should be run out of the restaurant, don't you think?"

Connor's expression had turned from anger to disbelief to amusement as Grace explained her actions. She was either brave or stupid, he wasn't sure which at this point. However, bringing in the sheriff might prove to be a brilliant move, at least until he could get Grace out of there.

Chapter Thirteen

It wasn't long before a commotion in the lobby had all eyes focused on the three men plus the sheriff and two deputies. Fred Helms and Roy Crowley had informed the sheriff of the murderers release and the expectation that they'd end up in Salt Lake looking for trouble.

"Stop your complaining and come along with me, Proctor. We can straighten everything out at the jail." The sheriff had a gun drawn and was waving it toward the main entry. "You two also, everyone goes with us."

The two deputies stood behind Bert and Earl, nudging them with the barrels of their pistols.

"We haven't done anything, Sheriff. Just minding our business and watching all those good people eat their dinner," Len protested but followed the sheriff outside. At least he knew MacLaren was in town.

"Did you ever think those good people don't want to be watched, especially by three ex-cons? Now get moving that way." He pointed down the street to the jail. It was a large building made of stone with lights shining out of several windows.

The sheriff moved behind Proctor but kept a gun trained on the man. They'd get the three in a cell, at least for one night, then go back to speak with MacLaren. That man was causing more problems by the hour.

Connor had already paid the waiter, and the moment the sheriff removed the three from the lobby, he escorted Grace outside and lifted her into the carriage. He wasted no time getting her home. She was certain the men didn't know her living quarters were above Jasper's, but Connor wasn't as convinced.

"Get some things together. You're going to stay with Ruth Dix tonight," Connor ordered and walked her inside.

"No, I'm not. It's late and she doesn't know I'm coming. I'll be perfectly safe here." She'd crossed her arms over her chest and stood in front of Connor, blocking his path into her small room.

"This isn't up for debate or a vote. I know those men. As soon as they're released they'll come back here. You're the easiest link to me and they'll have no problem with forcing you to talk."

"But I don't know where you live. There's nothing I can tell them."

"They don't know that. After seeing us tonight they'll assume you know a lot more about me than you do. Now, get some clothes. I'm taking you to Ruth's."

She rotated away from him in frustration. "I don't like to be ordered around. You have no right..." but her words stopped when Connor grabbed both shoulders and turned her toward him. She stared into his eyes which had turned a deep, penetrating green.

"This is not a discussion, Grace. I need you to do this, for yourself, and for me."

She stood motionless, her eyes fixed on his. Connor's movements were so slow, a fraction at a time, that Grace didn't register how his lips hovered over hers until the moment he closed the distance. He brushed his lips across hers—once, twice—before claiming her in earnest.

Grace stiffened, ready for him to turn into the only type of man she knew, Jeremiah. But, when he continued to gently glide his lips over hers, coaxing her to accept instead of demanding she comply, Grace relaxed. Her arms moved from her sides to his arms, then crept up to rest on his shoulders as he deepened the kiss. Just as she was beginning to enjoy his touch and the feel of him, Connor pulled back. He rested his forehead against hers and took a steadying breath.

"Get your things together. We need to leave now, before the sheriff releases those men." His voice was calm, reassuring. He took a couple of steps back. "Do you have a bag?"

She cleared her throat, trying to focus on the present and not their kiss. "Yes, under the bed."

Connor knelt and pulled the small bag out. "Add what you'll need. I'll keep watch outside." He opened the door and walked out.

She opened the bag and stuffed a few things into it, not really focusing on what went inside. Her thoughts were still fixated on their kiss. It was so different, so tender, not at all repugnant like the ones Jeremiah forced on her. She began to believe perhaps her husband's way wasn't at all like those of other men.

Grace took a quick turn around the room, then closed the bag, and opened her door. Connor stood just outside, watching the street below.

"Ready?"

Grace shook her head.

"Let's go." He escorted her down the stairs and once again lifted her into the carriage. "Where does Ruth live?"

"Just three blocks away, that direction." She pointed away from the main street.

Ten minutes later, Connor helped Grace down and grabbed her bag. He placed a hand on the small of her back and walked to the front door, knocking until Ruth peered out.

"Good Lord, come in, both of you." Ruth held the door open then closed and locked it as soon as Connor passed through. "Sit down while I get you both some tea."

"None for me, Ruth. I just want to be sure it's all right if Grace stays here a couple of nights. There's been some trouble and I don't think it's wise for her to stay at her place."

Ruth moved her gaze from Connor to Grace but kept her thoughts to herself. "Of course, it's all right. You can stay here as long as you like."

"I really don't want to put you out, Ruth, it's just that Connor insisted my place might not be safe."

"Don't worry so much, Grace. Having you here is no imposition at all. In fact, it would be nice to have a little company." Ruth turned her attention back to Connor. "You sure I can't get you something? Whiskey, maybe?"

"No ma'am. I'll be going now that I know Grace is safe with you." He moved in front of Grace. "Don't go to work tomorrow. I'll let Jasper know you're ill and staying with a friend. Don't go anywhere for a few days unless I'm with you." When she started to object, he grabbed both her hands. "Grace, you have to do this my way. We need to keep both you and Ruth safe. Those men are ruthless killers. There's no need to be a target."

She truly hated to be bossed around and didn't want to let Jasper down, but what Connor said made sense. Grace didn't want to do anything that could place her friend in jeopardy. "All right, but don't think you can tell me what to do all the time, Connor MacLaren. I'll have none of it. You understand?"

He smiled down at her. "Yes, ma'am, I understand." He tipped his hat to Ruth and left, driving the carriage down several blocks and away from the Dix home. He hoped he was doing the right thing. What he felt like doing was staying with Grace, not letting her out of his sight. But she'd be safe with Ruth, he had to trust that.

******

"All right, Proctor, you and your friends are free to go. Just remember that my men and I will be keeping watch on you. Anything even the least bit suspicious happens, and you'll find yourself back behind these bars." The sheriff followed the three out front and watched as one of the deputies returned their personal belongings.

None of the three said a word as they took their possessions, and walked out into the bright morning sun. Len settled his hat on his head while looking up and down the street. “Let’s grab breakfast then we’ll go after MacLaren, and the woman who lied to us.”

They stopped at the first restaurant they saw, ate, and then found their horses for the ride to Jasper’s. At least they knew where the woman, Grace, worked. She’d tell them how to find MacLaren, then Proctor planned to deal with both of them.

“Where’s your help this morning?”

“Grace? Well, she’s ill and won’t be in for a few days.” Jasper stared to turn away when Proctor grabbed his arm.

“Where’s she staying?” The menace in Proctor’s voice wasn’t lost on Jasper.

“I don’t know. It could be several people but I don’t know where any of them live. Now, I need to get back to my paying customers.” Jasper yanked his arm away, dismissing the men, and returning to his work.

“Let’s go,” Proctor said.

“But, Len...”

“Not now, Earl. We’ll get the information, but not in front of a restaurant full of people,” Proctor said in a hushed voice. “Come on.”

******

It had been two days since Connor received the information about Moser from Edwin and Margaret Miles. The wife had said the family lived northwest of town, but nothing more specific. Connor was on his way to meet Jericho, Fred, and Roy after swinging by the restaurant to let Jasper know that Grace was ill and wouldn't be at work for a few days. He'd known Jasper was suspicious, but to his credit, Grace's boss had accepted the news and not asked questions.

"Fred and I checked with the sheriff. He's heard of a family named Moser living northwest of town, about eight or ten miles out. Thinks they're off of Old Pioneer Road, but wasn't sure." Roy pulled out a piece of paper to read his notes. "He said our best bet would be to ask at the livery on the north end of town. That's where most of those families get their repairs done."

Fred pulled out his pocket watch and checked the time. "Guess we best get moving," he said and slid the timepiece back into his shirt. "Heard you had some visitors last night, Connor."

"Yeah. Proctor and his friends are in town." Connor noticed Jericho's gaze had swung to his. He hadn't had a chance to tell his friend of the encounter. "Figure we'll find Meggie and get out of the area before there's trouble. The last thing I want is a gunfight with those three."

"You know they'll just keep following you. Mr. Jericho, Roy, and I are here which makes the odds even. Better to take care of that scum now than be looking over your shoulder every day."

Connor thought over the offer. He didn't want his life to revolve around three murderers with vengeance on their minds. "I may just take you up on that, Fred." He looked at Jericho. "I'd like you to stay in town. Pass by the Dix place a few times and make sure everything is quiet."

"No problem." Jericho would do whatever Connor needed. "Find me when you get back in town," he said before leaving to check the Dix home.

Connor watched him ride off, grateful for the unquestioned loyalty Jericho had always offered.

"Yep, we can find your girl, then flush those three out in the open. May make them do something that will put them back in jail for good this time." Fred reined his horse around toward the livery.

"Yes, I know a farmer named Moser. Lives off Old Pioneer Road if I remember right, maybe ten miles out. You got business with him?" the blacksmith asked.

"Some."

"You're not the law, are you?" The smithy had pulled off his gloves and set them aside. He was a large man, tall and wide, with thick hands.

"No, we're not with the sheriff's office if that's what you mean?"

"I know they've been trying to locate men with multiple marriages. I'm not too fond of arresting those men. Wouldn't want to see that happen to Jeremiah."

Jeremiah. Now they had his full name.

"Thanks for the information," Roy called over his shoulder as they turned north.

Old Pioneer Road turned out to be the way most travelers moved from northern Utah to Idaho or California. It was wider than most country roads with more traffic. They passed a few farmers heading toward Salt Lake and a few riders who passed them on their way out of the city.

They'd ridden about an hour, the sky darkening more with each mile, when they heard a loud crack of thunder followed by a flash of lightning. It didn't stop them but, when the storm hit a couple of miles later, it slowed their pace and made it difficult to see sign posts.

The storm increased until they had to find shelter. Fred noticed a cabin a hundred yards from the road. At first glance it appeared to be abandoned, but as they got closer they noticed a light coming from the inside. Connor and Fred stayed put while Roy pounded on the door. When there was no answer he turned the knob. The door opened to reveal a small, two-room home with a fire in a pot-bellied stove with a large kettle on top.

"Someone lives here but they're not inside. What do you want to do?" Roy yelled.

"Let's get out of this weather. Whoever lives here is bound to return soon," Connor said and slid off Crusader.

They led their horses into the small stable and dashed back to the cabin, their boots soaked and caked with mud. They took off their oil-skins and hung them on hooks near the door. Roy stoked the fire and checked the kettle, but swung around when the cabin door burst open. The barrel of a shotgun was followed by a small, stooped figure bundled in layers of clothing.

"What are you doing in here?" the old man said pointing the weapon at Connor.

"Just getting out of the rain, nothing more."

"Well ain't you ever heard of being invited?"

"We knocked but no one answered. We'll get going now that we've had a chance to dry off," Connor said and moved to grab his coat.

"Stay right there, young man. That's a miserable storm and getting worse. If you ain't from here, you'll just get lost." The man's voice was rough, raspy, but not as harsh as when he'd first entered the cabin. He still hadn't lowered the gun. "What do you want out here?"

"We're looking for Jeremiah Moser's farm. You know him?" Fred asked, rubbing his hands together for warmth.

"Yep. What you want him for?"

"One of the women on the farm may be a relative of someone we know. Just want to check it out, see if it's true." This time Fred stood and moved to the stove, trying to find the warmth he sought.

"You're not deputies are you? I don't hold with what some of the Mormons do, but I don't hold with arresting the men either." He glared at the three.

"No, sir. Just trying to find the woman, that's all." Connor sat back down and watched the old man. He rested his hand on the butt of his pistol even though he saw little danger from the cabin owner.

"Well, Jeremiah is a different sort, that's for sure." The old man twisted around and placed the shotgun against the wall before shaking out of his heavy coat. "Don't like visitors, and likes lawmen even less. You best be prepared."

The old man sauntered toward the stove, picked up the kettle, and poured hot water into an old, dented coffee pot. He set the pot back on the stove to let it boil while he pulled four tin cups from their hooks, then turned toward the others.

"I'm Homer Erickson. Why don't you tell me who you are?"

All three introduced themselves.

"I knew a MacLaren years ago. Lived in the Arizona territory somewhere. Stuart I think his name was."

"My uncle, Stuart MacLaren," Connor said.

Homer shook his head. "Don't remember much about him, just that he was building himself a cattle ranch."

"My cousins and brother work it now. I'm hoping to join them when this trip is over."

When the coffee was ready he filled each cup and handed them out, finally taking a seat in an old rocking chair.

"Why would you want to see Moser anyway? He don't seem like the type to get social calls. Might be easier to just wander up that way and look around. Maybe you'll see the woman you're after." Homer sat back in the chair and rocked.

Connor looked at the others. “We’ve been thinking the same thing, Mr. Erickson. We don’t want to disturb the man if the woman we’re trying to find isn’t there.”

“He ain’t there now anyway. Took off earlier today for one of those meetings he’s always going to. He stopped here to fix a wheel that was acting up. Had a couple of the women with him. Doesn’t usually come back for a day or two but then he stays put for a while. Might have better luck in a few days. Anyway, his road washes out in heavy rains. Don’t expect you can get back there until late tomorrow or the next day with this weather.”

“What road do we take?”

“You’re at it. Just behind the barn is his road. You’ll see it when the storm moves out.”

Homer stood and set his cup down on a wooden table. “I’m for sleep. You’re welcome to bed down on the floor or the stable, but it appears mighty crowded already.” Another crack of thunder shook the cabin. “’Course, you can always head back to Salt Lake tonight, but I wouldn’t advise it.”

Chapter Fourteen

"We'll meet at dawn tomorrow and ride back," Connor told Fred and Roy as they rode through Salt Lake. "With luck we'll catch everyone at the farm."

They'd decided to stay over in Homer's cabin, leaving for town as soon as the storm had passed the next day. As Homer had predicted, Moser's road was washed out. They found the road to Salt Lake almost impassable in some stretches, leaving one deserted wagon stuck in mud a foot deep.

The three traveled to the other side of town, stopping to grab their mid-day meal at Jasper's. When Connor walked in, the first person he spotted was Grace, delivering plates of food to a hungry family. He didn't even slow his stride, but stormed toward her, grabbing an arm and pulling her back to the kitchen. Connor spun her toward him, his anger evident in the set of his face and narrowed eyes.

"What the hell are you doing here? You're supposed to be at Ruth's, not putting yourself right where Proctor and his men know where to find you."

Grace tried to yank her arm free, but Connor's grip was too strong. "Let go of me," she snapped. "You have no right to come in here and tell me what I should or shouldn't be doing."

If anything, his grip tightened a little, his anger not subsiding at all. "I have every right to do what I can to keep you safe, alive. Those men are here for me, but make no mistake, they'll do whatever it takes to learn my whereabouts. That includes hurting you, and possibly Ruth." His rage had lessened, his voice settling into a low growl.

Indignation seeped from Grace's face as Connor spoke. She knew he'd be angry if he found her at the restaurant, but she needed the money to help free Meggie, and Jasper needed the assistance. She raised her chin and glared up at him. "I need to make my own decisions, not rely on you or any man to protect me. Now, let go of me." She pulled free and pushed past him.

He made no move to stop her. She was right, it wasn't his decision to make, even though he wished it otherwise. Grace was a stubborn woman, which was a good trait and a bad one. That obstinate streak could get her killed as well as others. Connor wasn't her guardian angel, just a man who didn't want her hurt or killed on account of him.

Connor strode through the kitchen and out the front entrance.

"He's right, you know." Jasper was drying the dishes Grace washed after the dinner crowd left. "I knew something was going on but, if what he says is true, you should leave and not come back until he's taken care of the men who hunt him."

Grace's head swung around. "How'd you know about that?"

"I haven't lived this long and not learned a few things, Gracie. I knew something wasn't right the moment Connor told me you were sick and staying with friends. The only friends you have are Ruth and me, so that narrowed it down a bit." He stacked the dishes and started on the pans. "Anyway, Ruth stopped by yesterday to let me know you wouldn't be in today either. She told me what had happened, about the men who are after MacLaren."

"Why didn't you say something when I walked in this morning?"

"For the same reason as you. It was your decision. It may have been mule-headed, and selfish, but it was still yours to make." He folded the towel and draped it over a hook. "Now, however, it's not. I'm still the boss and, if you want to stay working for me, you'll head back to Ruth's and not come back until those men are taken care of. You hear me?"

Grace stared at Jasper, at first not believing she'd heard him right. When his expression didn't change or soften, she knew he meant every word. She untied her apron, wadded it into a ball, and threw it on the counter. She slid into her coat and slammed through the back door, crashing into the hard, impenetrable form of Connor MacLaren.

******

Jeremiah had changed his mind, taking Nina and Ada with him to the gathering, leaving the girls with Meggie. The chance she'd been waiting for had disappeared in an instant. It had rained without a break since they'd left. The girls were in bed, asleep. It was late—the first time in hours that she'd had any time to herself.

Meggie selected a book from Jeremiah's shelf, brushing the container of money with her fingers in the process. She set the book down and removed the canister from the shelf, opened it, and counted the money once more. The amount hadn't changed.

She knew the adults would be back in the morning. Her mind screamed that she should leave, take the money, and make a dash for it. The oldest girl knew how to make breakfast, take care of the other two. She'd done it before when Jeremiah had taken Nina and Meggie to town, leaving Ada with the girls.

Within hours Ada had lost her breakfast, was burning with fever, and become delirious. The oldest, Janie, had taken over and done a wonderful job with Mary and Essie. That was almost a year ago. Meggie knew Janie could, and would, do it again. She made her decision in an instant.

She dashed to the kitchen, canister in hand—grabbed bread, leftover meat, and some cookies—and stuffed them into an old fabric pouch. Meggie emptied the money into the pouch as well. She set the food on the table then ran up the stairs to her room. Clothes, her brush, a blanket, gloves, and a bonnet were stuffed into an old carpet bag. She reached for her coat that hung on a peg by the door and was back in the kitchen within minutes.

Meggie grabbed the bag of food, took an old rain slicker and water skin then slipped out the back door, pulling the raincoat on as she ran. She knew the way to town, had been there many times with Jeremiah. It was close to two in the morning—dark, still raining, and the winds were gusting—but her mind was made up. She'd stay in the trees that bordered their dirt drive to Old Pioneer Road and follow it to Salt Lake. After that, well, she didn't know. It didn't matter, as long as she stayed hidden from Jeremiah when he came to find her, and he would try.

The rain pounded harder, faster. She kept going, determined to never turn back, never return to a life she hadn't chosen.

Darkness turned to early morning. The rain had let up but the air was cold, damp, and the ground was muddy, sticky, and slippery. She'd fallen more than once. So far, her bags had been spared but her body was beginning to tire. Before long, she'd need to find a place to hide, rest, and start again.

Meggie was a mile down Old Pioneer Road, heading south toward Salt Lake, when three riders approached from the north, heading straight toward her. She'd been in the middle of the road, trying to stay away from the muddy slopes that fell away on either side. She dashed to one side, attempting to hide behind a large bush on the edge of the road. Just as she slowed to reach for a branch, her feet gave way and propelled her several yards down the slope. She screamed as her body rolled into a stand of dense, prickly, shrubs then stopped.

She squirmed as far within the menacing bushes as possible before hearing riders pull up and stop their horses at the point where she'd slipped.

"Did you hear something?" Connor asked Roy and Fred who'd reined up beside him.

"Like what?" Fred asked.

"I thought I heard a scream. Sounded like a woman." Connor looked around once more but saw nothing. He sat a few more minutes, listening. "Guess it was nothing. Let's go."

Meggie lay still, hearing the voices but not making out what the men had said. She stayed in her hiding place several more minutes, until she was certain the riders had left, then clawed her way up the slope. Her body ached, her feet hurt, and she felt dizzy from the fall. No matter. She had to keep going on her mission to put as much distance between herself and Jeremiah as possible.

The sun began to peak through the clouds, warm rays falling on her face as she kept going south. Her legs were heavy. She hated to, but needed to stop. There was an old, abandoned shack not far up the road. She'd seen it several times on their way to town. It would be perfect.

It took longer than Meggie remembered, but an hour later she spotted the cabin. By the time she reached the dilapidated structure her legs were giving out and she'd developed a cough, deep and hard, that burned in her chest. The door barely stood on two rusted hinges. She pushed hard and it fell to the ground, leaving an opening about two feet wide. Meggie looked around, and then dashed inside.

She dropped her bags as another cough started in her chest, except this one went on for several moments. Her eyes began to tear and her lungs ached. She dropped to an old pallet and pulled her knees to her chest. At last, the coughing subsided but it left her aching and exhausted.

Meggie reached into one bag to pull out her blanket, then the other bag to grab some bread and meat. She stuffed some of both in her mouth, chewed, and then opened the water bag to wash it all down. Coughs racked her body once more, causing intense pain to burn in her chest. She lay back on the filthy pallet, tucked the blanket around her, and rolled into a ball. Within minutes she drifted into a fitful sleep and dreamed of Dodge.

Charleston, South Carolina, years before

"Meggie, wait up," Dodge called as he followed her deeper into the trees. They'd been riding for quite a while, looking for the perfect place to stop and eat. She pulled ahead of him, laughing as she glanced back over her shoulder.

Every time she smiled and laughed like that the hook set a little deeper. Dodge wasn't sure how much longer he could ignore his growing feelings for her. Meggie had become more and more important to him, almost as if she were an elixir he required each day. He found himself looking for her around the large house while she completed her chores. Mr. Holly would frown at him when he'd find an excuse to enter his study during her lessons, and Dodge was certain his longtime butler had suspicions but had yet to utter a word. He didn't know what he was going to do but whatever it was, the decision needed to be made soon.

He spotted her several yards ahead. She'd stopped her gelding beside a tall oak and waited, her eyes sparkling with mischief. Dodge reined beside her, slid from his horse, and strode directly to her. In one swift move he'd lifted her off the sidesaddle, slowly letting her slide down his body to stand in front of him. He moved his hands from her waist up her arms to her shoulders, clasping them with his strong hands.

"Whatever am I going to do with you, Meggie?" His voice was unsteady, rough, foreign sounding, even to his own ears. His eyes locked with hers.

Meggie wanted to look away, tried to look away, but found she could not. Her smile faltered then faded as he lowered his head and brushed his lips lightly over hers, once, then again, before settling on them for a slow kiss.

She held still, not knowing what to do, her arms rigid at her side. His lips felt pleasantly soft and wonderful. Meggie knew she should push away, tell him to stop, but the words wouldn't come.

Dodge let go of her shoulders to wrap his arms around her, pulling her close. "Put your arms around my neck," he whispered in her ear before claiming her lips once more.

She moved her hands up his arms to his shoulders then around his neck, moving into him, wanting to get closer.

His hands traveled up and down her back while his lips shifted over hers one way then another before capturing her lower lip between his teeth. He heard her sigh and felt her melt into him, straining to get closer.

He pulled back, resting his forehead against hers, breathing heavily. His hands moved back to her shoulders, steadying her, and creating a slight distance between them.

Dodge stared at Meggie, not sure what to say. He'd known it would come to this if he didn't stay away from her. His pull toward her was too strong, more than anything he'd ever felt for a woman.

"We need to go back, Meggie. Now." He tried to make his words soft but they came out more forceful, rougher than intended. Meggie stepped back, one pace, then two before turning to grab the reins of her horse. Dodge walked over to help her up before mounting his own horse.

He had avoided her for three days afterward, taking his meals in his room or office, and never appearing for their rides or walks. On the fourth day the butler told Meggie he'd ridden into town to see an old friend. She knew immediately what that meant—he'd returned to his former paramour.

For Meggie, it was the most wonderful experience she'd ever known. She'd wanted him to continue and never stop—now she believed he'd been disappointed at her inexperience. It humiliated her to think he'd found her so lacking that he'd avoided her, seeking out another woman.

She finished her work then went to her room, changing into night clothes, crawling beneath the covers, and trying to decide her future. She couldn't stay with Dodge any longer. The time had come to leave.

Hours later a noise awakened her. The room was dark except for a slip of light that came from her door as it slowly opened. She could see someone entering her room. Dodge. She stayed still, pretending to sleep as he moved to the side of her bed and stared down at her.

She felt him sit on the edge of the bed. Dodge brushed his fingers over her forehead, moving an errant strand of hair off her face. He stroked her cheek, then placed a soft kiss on her temple, caressing her check with his lips before placing another kiss on the corner of her mouth. Meggie turned her face, allowing him to capture her lips completely.

Dodge moved closer, placing his arms on either side of her head and lowering his lips fully to hers. His tongue traced the outside of her lips. "Open for me, Meggie," he whispered. Her lips parted and he took control, tasting her, and deepening the kiss until he'd moved his arms around her, lifting her to him.

He steadied her with one arm as his hand came up, stroking through the sheer fabric of her night dress. She moaned and pushed into his palm, feeling the warmth spread.

He lifted his eyes to hers. “Meggie, if you don’t want this you need to tell me to stop.”

Her glassy eyes searched his, knowing what he meant but not completely understanding what to expect. All she knew was that she loved him, wanted him, and had no desire to push him away. “I love you, Dodge. Please, don’t stop.”

Her declaration washed over him. He’d known how she felt, could sense it in the way she looked and responded to him. He wasn’t certain how things would work out for them, but tonight, they belonged to each other—the rest would come in time.

North of Salt Lake, present day

Meggie stirred, waking from her dream, and pulling the blanket tightly around her. She felt chilled and coughed several more times, causing her lungs to burn. Her glassy eyes looked around the small, dingy shack. She could hear the slight pounding of rain, see the water dripping through the porous roof but made no effort to move. The pallet was dry, she was warm. All she wanted to do was drift back to sleep and her dreams of Dodge.

Chapter Fifteen

Grace burst through the back door of the restaurant kitchen just as Connor had made the decision to go back in and drag her out. She wasn't safe from Proctor and the others. He had to convince her of that.

She slammed into him. Connor placed his hands on her shoulders to steady her, and keep her from stumbling back.

"Let go of me!" Her face was red, her violet blue eyes had turned a deep blue and appeared to be sending sparks his way.

He dropped his hands. Grace lost her footing, falling backwards, and landing on the hard wooden step with a thud. Instead of jumping up and responding, she surprised Connor by taking a deep breath, and lowering her head into her hands. Connor watched her struggle with something then sat beside her, taking a hand from her face and encasing it in his two larger ones.

"Where were you going?" he asked when she finally lifter her eyes to meet his.

Her voice had lost much of its defiance but her features told him she'd lost none of her determination to do things her own way. "I don't know. Jasper told me to leave. Said you were right and I needed to hide until those men had been arrested, or..."

He moved his arm around her shoulders and drew her to him, holding her close, not letting go of the hand he held in his lap.

"He's right, you know. Those men are vicious killers and don't care if their victims are men or women. You are their way to finding me—that's all you mean to them, Grace, nothing more." He tightened his hold on her and placed a kiss on her fiery red hair. "I'll take you to Ruth's. Either my friend Mr. Jericho or I will stay with you until we're sure the threat has passed. We'll make sure you are safe."

Her eyes searched his. "Why would you do that? Why would you place yourself and your friend in danger because of me, someone you know so little about? You could just leave."

He glanced away, looking up and down the dirt alley behind the restaurant, searching for hidden dangers before returning his gaze to hers.

"You are an innocent in the history I have with those men. I can't just walk away and leave you unprotected."

"Oh," she whispered and realized in that moment that is wasn't the answer she wanted or hoped to hear. She shifted away and prepared to stand, but he held her still.

"You're right that I don't know much about you, but I want to change that. I came to Salt Lake to find my sister, except I find my thoughts are consumed with you." He took a breath and stood, reaching out a hand to help her up. "It's frustrating, and damn inconvenient, but that's the way it is."

The disgust on Connor's face caused her to smile as she took his hand. She knew how he felt since she felt the same about him. He was as distraction, a nuisance, interfering in her plans to get Meggie and leave. At the same time, she wanted to stay, get to know him, find out if the experiences with Jeremiah were coloring her judgment about men, especially this man.

They didn't speak on the way to Ruth's. He helped her off Crusader, looking around once more before escorting her into the house. Jericho stood by a window looking out.

"About time you got here." Jericho glanced at the woman. "I stopped in to introduce myself to Mrs. Dix and Grace, and learned Grace had gone to Jasper's." He gave the young woman a pointed look. "Ruth got a message from one of her sons that she was needed at the ranch. She left a few minutes ago. I was just about ready to ride to the restaurant when I saw you two. Ruth said you can stay as long as you want. She said you're welcome to use her other horse and buggy."

Grace looked up at the large man. He was tall and broad, perhaps in his fifties with a thin scar that ran from his left ear to left edge of his mouth.

"Grace, this is Mr. Jericho. He'll be watching out for you when I'm not here."

"Ma'am," Jericho touched the front rim of his black bowler, a style he favored to the more common western hats of the region.

"Pleased to meet you, Mr. Jericho." She laid her coat on the nearest chair and walked into the kitchen. "I'll make us some coffee," she called over her shoulder as she reached for the old pot and tin of grounds.

Jericho walked up to Connor. "What are your plans?"

"I need to speak with Fred and Roy to arrange plans to return to the Moser farm. I'll be back this evening. I'm counting on you to watch out for Grace while I'm gone." Connor stood at the window, peering out, but saw no movement or indication they'd been followed from the restaurant.

"I won't let anyone near her. Find Meggie and don't worry about us. We'll be fine." Jericho turned when Grace walked into the room with cups of coffee. "Thank you, ma'am."

"Please, call me Grace. I have a feeling we'll be fine friends by the time this is over." She smiled at Jericho as she handed a cup to Conner. Grace watched him wrap his hands around it and thought of what he'd said about wanting to get to know her better. He was looking for his sister, she was trying to free a friend. Perhaps they could work together to do both for the young women who were important to them.

"I need to leave for a while, Grace. Mr. Jericho will stay here. Do as he says." He pinned her with a look meant to indicate how serious her compliance was. "I'll be back in a few hours." He finished his coffee and handed her the empty cup.

******

Charleston, South Carolina, several years before

Dodge had ordered Meggie's belongings be moved upstairs into a bedroom next to his. He knew the implications of his actions, knew she'd be looked upon in a different, and unflattering way, by many.

They'd spoken for hours the night he'd gone to her. He'd spent the previous days at his men's club in Charleston, deciding what to do. His feelings for Meggie were strong, but were they strong enough to break with tradition, create scandal, and marry a woman of such low rank. Dodge had intended to marry as a convenience, for the sake of having an heir, not for love. Meggie had changed all that. Dodge was unsure how this would play out, but he had no intention of being too far away from her ever again.

Several weeks passed. Few visitors came to the Delaney mansion and Dodge received only a rare invitation to a social event in Charleston. Word had gotten out that his relationship with Meggie had changed. He was being ostracized in a complete, if civilized way.

He'd arranged for a seamstress to prepare a selection of dresses for the few parties that included them. They walked, rode horses, and fell more in love each day. Dodge knew he had to make a decision. It wasn't fair to Meggie to keep her as a mistress in his own home when his feelings for her were so strong, so total. He'd gone to town and selected an engagement band. He'd had it inscribed, *Always, D.* They would have a quiet supper at home and he'd propose.

"May I escort you downstairs?" Dodge asked and looped Meggie's arm through his as they made their way down the wide staircase. "You look beautiful tonight." He had leaned over to whisper in her ear and place a kiss on her neck. Her bright smile and sparkling green eyes sent a fierce longing through him. He'd rather be pulling Meggie into his room to make slow, passionate love. Tonight, however, was important. Her answer would determine the future for both of them.

He'd planned a special meal with candlelight and her favorite foods.

"Are we celebrating something?" Meggie asked as she looked at the tempting spread in front of her.

"Perhaps." Dodge watched as she placed a forkful of meat into her mouth. He smiled at her perplexed expression and focused on his supper.

They took their dessert in a small parlor. Dodge knew this was Meggie's favorite room with its comfortable chairs and fireplace. She loved to curl up with a book in the evenings and read while he worked on business proposals.

Dodge placed his plate aside and walked to Meggie's chair, looked down, and then knelt before her. He took her hands in his and placed a kiss on each palm before holding them to his heart.

"I love you, Meggie, and want to marry you. Will you do me the honor of becoming my wife?"

Dodge could tell he'd shocked her by the stunned expression on her face. Tears welled in her eyes at the same time a broad smile brightened her face. She pulled her hands from his grasp to swipe the tears which threatened.

"I love you so much, Dodge. Yes, I will marry you." She threw her arms around his neck but stopped at a sudden noise from the other room.

Their heads rose when they heard pounding at the front door. They could hear Dodge's butler answer the door, and what sounded like a cordial conversation turn to shouts in a matter of seconds. Dodge began to rise when he heard a shot ring out, and then the closed doors of the parlor burst open to reveal several armed men, all hidden behind masks.

"Stay where you are," the tallest of the men hissed while pointing his pistol at Dodge's chest.

"What do you want?" Dodge growled back. His guns were in the office. He'd seen no need to have them near him this night.

"Your safe, where is it?"

"In my office. I'll show you, but you will promise not to hurt the lady." Dodge glared at the intruder and wondered as to the safety of the rest of his staff.

The gunman nodded and indicated with his pistol for Dodge to proceed him out of the parlor. Dodge walked to the picture which hid a wall safe, pushed it aside, and worked the combination. He reached in and pulled out a box, which he dropped on the desk behind him.

"There. Take all of it and get out." Dodge glanced behind the man holding a gun on him and saw Meggie being held against an average height man with thick arms, a gun pointed at her head. "We won't follow. Just take the money and leave."

"Oh, I know you won't follow, as we're taking the lady with us," the gunman replied and started to step back.

"No!" Dodge yelled and began to follow the robber.

One shot rang out. Dodge felt a sharp pain before looking down to see a red bloom of color appear on his shirt. His gaze swung to Meggie, seeing her panicked eyes, hearing her scream, but unable to stop himself from falling forward onto his desk, then slipping to the floor.

North of Salt Lake, present day

Meggie tossed and turned, burning up below the blanket cocooned around her. Hard coughs racked her body. She tried to sit up and reach out for the water skin, but her fingers fumbled with the pouch and she found herself unable to close her hand around it. She fell back to the pallet, coughing until her lungs burned and there was no strength left to fight the savage hacking.

She wrapped the blanket tight and thought of Dodge and the last time she'd seen him, covered in blood, and falling to the floor of his study. The robbers had taken her with them that night and sold her to a man with a promise that he'd get her out of the state. Edgar Skanks had taken her west, toward Kansas and Colorado. Most nights he kept her tied to his peddler's wagon. Days were spent driving the horses that pulled his rig. Meggie didn't care. Dodge was dead. She had nothing left to care about and little will to live. As long as Skanks provided food, she ate. If he hadn't, she knew her will to survive would have dried up like the hope she'd lost when Dodge was killed.

Earlier that morning the rain had been dripping through the openings in the roof. Now it was dark. *Had she missed a whole day*, she wondered before drifting back into a restless sleep.

******

Salt Lake, present day

It was dark when he rode into Ruth Dix's property. Fred and Roy wanted to ride out the following morning to stake out the farm, watch for Meggie. He'd agreed to meet them at Jasper's then ride north.

"Mr. Jericho," he nodded to his friend who stood at the entrance to the kitchen, gun drawn even though Connor was certain the man knew who was walking through the door. "How were things here?" He threw his hat on a chair but kept his gun belt on.

"Quiet." Jericho holstered his gun. "She went to her room an hour ago."

"Why don't you bed down, too? I'll keep watch tonight."

"Wake me if you hear anything. Coffee's still hot," Jericho said and walked down the hall to an empty guest room.

Connor entered the kitchen, poured some coffee, and walked to the front room. He sat next to a window, his back to a wall. His thoughts drifted to Meggie, wondering if they'd find her tomorrow, and if so, would she even remember him. He'd never considered that his sister might like her life, not want to leave with him. It had been eight long years, half a lifetime for someone who'd disappeared when she was sixteen.

He looked up at the sound of a door being opened and footsteps walking down the hall. Grace appeared a moment later. She stood at the entrance to the front room, staring at him as if deciding whether or not to enter.

"Hello, Grace." Connor shifted on the small divan and took in the sight of her. She wore the same dress she'd been in all day with a blanket wrapped around her shoulders. Her hair was disheveled and her feet were bare. She was beautiful.

"How long have you been here?" Grace asked as she walked toward him.

"Not long." He reached out a hand to her. She grasped it and let him pull her to him until their knees touched. "You've been sleeping."

"I didn't think I could sleep. The back room is cold and a little damp from the rains." She shivered and pulled the quilt tighter.

Connor tugged her hand until she sat down next to him on the divan. He wrapped an arm around her shoulders, pulling her close, and rested his chin on the top of her head. He could feel her relax, meld to him. She rested a hand on his stomach. He moved his hand up and stroked her hair then cupped the back of her head and tilted her face to his. He looked into her sleep filled eyes. She didn't glance away but held his gaze. Grace didn't resist when he dipped his head to hers and took her lips in a long, passionate kiss.

She moved into him, turning to wrap her arms around his neck and pull him to her. He angled his mouth over hers, outlined her lips with his tongue, coaxing her to open. When she did, he thrust in, enjoying the taste and feel of her as he explored in leisurely strokes. Her heavy sigh encouraged him, as did the heat that engulfed his body, pulsing through him.

Connor lifted her, positioning her on his lap, and deepened the kiss. He unbuttoned her dress and pushed the material aside. She tensed when his lips moved over her through the sheer chemise, the new sensation causing heat to form and spread through her already sensitized body. She gripped his head in both hands, holding him to her.

"Connor," she said in a low, husky voice, and arched toward him.

He lifted his head to stare into her glassy, deep violet eyes, knowing he needed to end this before passion overtook them. He had to concentrate on the danger Proctor presented, not on the desirable woman in his arms. "You are so beautiful, Grace. I want you, but not here, and not tonight." He placed another kiss on her already swollen lips, and reluctantly pulled her dress together.

Grace knew he was right to stop. She'd never felt anything like the sensations that exploded through her at his touch. She continued to watch him until he shifted her on his lap, tucked her head on his shoulder and rested his chin, once again, on the top of her head. She snaked an arm up around his neck, sighed, and closed her eyes.

He held her for a long time, watching her sleep. Her breaths came in short, labored bursts, and he wondered for the hundredth time who she was. If she'd lived in Salt Lake as long as she'd said surely there would be other friends besides Ruth Dix. Ruth and Jasper were the only two people she spoke of as friends, which made no sense for a woman who'd been here for years.

Her natural passion surprised him. He didn't know if she was experienced or an innocent. His guess was somewhere in between. For the first time it occurred to him that she may have been married and he wondered if she would have told him or kept it hidden. There was much about this woman he didn't know and for the first time in his life he wanted to.

Connor pulled back the curtain to peer out. It was dark and he saw no movement indicating that Proctor had located them. Connor needed to concentrate on taking care of the men who pursued him, and finding Meggie. After that he could focus on Grace and his growing attraction to the red-haired vixen who had proven to be a considerable temptation.

Chapter Sixteen

Meggie's head pounded as her feverish body was racked once again by a burst of painful coughing. The coughs had grown worse through the night, leaving her with little energy and even less ability to continue her journey. She knew it must be a few more miles to Salt Lake, much too long a journey on foot in her present condition. Her stomach growled but she felt none of the usual hunger pangs that were common upon waking.

Meggie shifted on the hard pallet, causing her head to spin from the effort. Chills gripped her as she slid back under the blanket and tried to curb her dizziness before attempting to stand. Her eyes ached and her mouth was dry. She tried to reach for her water skin but it was too far of a stretch and she fell back to the pallet, covering her mouth as another surge of coughs consumed her. Meggie rolled into a ball and wished for sleep. She drifted off hoping she'd wake to a clear head and healed body.

"I know I saw someone go in here, George." Meggie's sleep clouded brain could just make out a woman's voice. The light coming through the roof openings told her it must be late afternoon.

"That was a couple of days ago, Agnes. They're probably gone by now."

"I just saw one person. That's all."

Meggie could hear the creaking of boards then a gasp. "George, look."

"Is it a man or woman, Agnes?"

Meggie felt the cold air assault her body as the blanket was pulled back.

"It's a young woman. Come on over here." The woman placed on hand on Meggie's forehead. "Good Lord, the girl's burning up. We've got to get her out of here."

Meggie tried to open her eyes. It wasn't surprising that she didn't recognize either of the voices. Jeremiah isolated them from most people, preferring to keep their solitary life at the farm. Her eyes felt heavy and her head still pounded from the raging headache she'd woken to earlier.

"I..." Meggie tried to talk but couldn't get the words out.

"Now don't you worry, girl. Agnes and me will get you to our place real soon."

The next thing Meggie remembered was being placed in a warm, comfortable bed. She'd drifted off during the journey with no recollection of how they'd gotten here.

"I'll get cool water and a cloth while you grab extra blankets," she heard Agnes say to George.

Each time she'd drift off she would wake to someone wiping her with a cold cloth, giving her sips of water, or honey with lemon to help her cough. She knew she'd lost at least another day and night while they tended to her. Dreams assaulted Meggie when she slept. Images of Dodge would combine with those of Grace, Eugene, Skanks, and Jeremiah. She saw herself running, trying to get away, but being restrained by a man with a mask. She screamed, sat up, and lashed out at the man, kicking and slapping at his covered face.

"It's okay now, you're going to be all right," a voice soothed. "You're safe with us."

Meggie could feel herself relax and fall back onto the bed. She opened her eyes to see an elderly woman leaning over a basin of water to wring out a cloth then place it on Meggie's forehead.

"Who...uh...who are you?" she managed to ask through her parched throat and mouth.

"So, you're awake." The woman put a hand behind Meggie's head and lifted. "Let's see if we can get some water down you, all right?"

With the woman's help Meggie was able to get a few sips of water down her throat. It felt wonderful.

"Thank you."

""We're just glad we found you when we did. You were in pretty bad shape in that old shack. No one's lived there for years."

Meggie didn't respond but stayed still, watching the woman move around the small bedroom. She heard a door open, then close.

"George," the woman called. "She's awake and I think her fever's broke."

"Well, that's real good."

Meggie looked up to see an elderly man, lean and stooped, stand over her. He placed a hand on her forehead. "Yep, seems like it has broken." His eyes moved from his wife back to Meggie. "You have a name, girl?"

"Meghan," she coughed out. It was her given name, though no one had ever called her that. Not even her parents.

"Meghan, huh? You got a last name?"

"Delaney." *A small lie*, she thought.

"Well, Meghan Delaney, I'm George Hines and this is my wife, Gladys. You from around here?" He sat down on a ladder back chair a couple of feet away.

"No, not really." She had no intention of mentioning Jeremiah Moser.

"So, how'd you come to hole up in that shack alone?"

"Now, George, don't badger the poor girl."

"I'm not badgering her, Agnes, I'm just trying to find who her kinfolk are." He turned his attention back to Meggie. "You got kin here?"

She hesitated a moment. "No, I don't have any family. Here or anywhere." Meggie pulled the heavy quilt up under her chin as exhaustion overtook her.

"That's enough for now. Meghan needs her rest." Agnes grabbed the washbasin and cloth. "We'll figure things out when she gets her strength back." She closed the door behind her and George.

"Agnes, you know that Mormon farmer, Jeremiah Moser, came by a couple of days ago looking for one of his wives. He called her Meggie and she fits the description. She's got to be the same person."

"Yes, she most likely is." Agnes continued into the kitchen wondering why the girl had lied to them and what had made her run.

"We can't just keep her with us when he's looking for her."

She turned from the sink and laced her hands in front of her. "That girl is sick. She ran from the man and she's lying about not having a family. Something is wrong, and I'm not sending her back until I know what's going on."

"But she's his wife," George began.

"That's what he says," Agnes interrupted. "But I'll bet Meghan will say different. You know I don't hold with the Mormon way of having more than one wife and I won't interfere if she wants to be with that man. But if she doesn't want to go back, or she isn't his wife, then I don't see how we can send her away until we know why she ran. She's a grown woman, not a child."

George understood his wife's thinking. Neither of them approved of the multiple marriages practiced by some Mormons. However, they'd never interfered with the beliefs that several of their neighbors shared. Living so far from the city was challenging and it was wise to maintain strong relationships with those around you. He had no intention of letting the arrival of this young woman damage the friendships Agnes and he had developed over many years.

"We'll give her a couple of days to rest up. After that, I want some answers from her. Truthful answers, not the lies she told us today." George jammed his old hat down on his bald head and trudged out the door.

******

"Don't let her out of your sight," Connor cautioned Jericho. "I'll be back as soon as I can, but it could be late."

"I'll watch her, as if she were my own," Jericho said and turned to walk back into the house. "You be safe," he called as the front door closed behind him.

Connor had met Fred and Roy then rode to the Moser farm. It had been a quick journey with clear skies. They'd stopped at Homer Erickson's, thanking the man, and dropping off coffee and supplies to replenish what they'd used.

"He's at the farm, all right. At least, he was a couple of days ago. Came by here looking for one of the women who lives with him. Moser called her his fourth wife. Guess she took off while he and the other ones were at some kind of meeting. He was as mad as I've ever seen him." Homer shook his head and chuckled. "Don't believe he found her because I saw him ride out again yesterday and he came back without her. It sure don't bode well for that gal if he does find her and it's my guess that he will. There just aren't many places a young woman can hide around here, not with all the other people of their faith who live out this way."

Connor, Fred, and Roy exchanged looks.

"We best get going, Homer. Thanks again for your hospitality." Connor swung up on Crusader and nudged his horse forward.

"You let me know what happens," Homer called after them as they made the turn up the long dirt road to the farm.

It was mid-morning when they slid from their horses and hid them behind a thick stand of trees. They were about two hundred yards from the farm house. A buggy, and a wagon were parked alongside the barn, and two horses were in a corral. Three children, all girls, played as one woman watched them. Connor pulled out his field glasses. It wasn't Meggie.

They moved forward, staying behind trees, and bushes until they had gotten as close as possible without being seen.

"I'm going to get as close to the back of the house as possible, see if I can see anyone else," Connor whispered.

"What if Moser comes out and leaves?" Fred asked.

"Follow him. I'll catch up with you." Connor moved away, toward the barn, staying low, and hoping no one spotted him.

He made it to a small corral behind the barn where the two horses grazed. Neither looked up at his approach. He'd made the decision to move again when he heard a man's voice.

"Ada, bring the girls in with Nina. I'm leaving and I want everyone inside."

"Yes, Jeremiah," the woman called Ada responded. She gathered the three children and scooted them in through the back door.

A few minutes later Moser walked out, hitched horses to the wagon, and climbed onto the seat.

"Jeremiah," another woman called. "You want us to wait supper?"

"No. I don't know when I'll return." He slapped the reins on the horses to begin the slow trek off the property.

Connor watched him move past where Fred and Roy waited, then made his way back to them and their horses.

"Shouldn't be hard to keep him in sight. He doesn't appear to be in much of a hurry." Roy said as the three mounted.

Roy had been right. Moser moved at a slow pace turning away from Salt Lake on Old Pioneer Road, heading north. They followed him for almost thirty minutes before Connor reined his horse to a stop. Fred and Roy pulled up next to him.

"You two continue to follow him. I'm going back. See if I can get anyone at the farm to speak with me."

This time Connor rode straight to the house and knocked on the door. It took a while before a woman opened the door a couple of inches and peeked out.

"Mr. Moser isn't home now. You'll have to come back," the woman said and began to close the door before Connor stopped it with his boot.

"I'm not here to see Mr. Moser." His foot didn't budge.

"We aren't buying anything if that's what you want."

"Nope. I'm looking for a young woman named Meggie. She's..." Connor started but at the mention of Meggie's name the woman pushed hard on the door almost dislodging his boot. He held his hand up to stop her efforts.

"Who is it, Nina?" another woman called from inside the house.

"I can handle it, Ada. He's leaving," Nina replied as she again tried to shove the door closed.

"Ada," Connor called into the house. "I'm speaking to Nina about a woman I'm looking for. Her name's Meggie and she's my sister."

"We don't know any Meggie," Nina began but Ada's voice stopped her.

Connor looked through the open door to see the other woman make her way across the foyer.

"Of course we know Meggie. Why would you tell this man that we don't?" Ada stopped to look at Connor ignoring Nina's angry expression. "You say you know Meggie?"

"Yes, ma'am. I'm her brother, Connor MacLaren."

Ada looked him up and down before letting her eyes return to his. "What's your brother's name?"

"Pierce."

Her face stayed expressionless. "Where were you from?"

"Scotland, originally, but we lived in Red Hook before Meggie disappeared." This last had the woman's face break into a smile.

"Well, I'll be. This is Meggie's brother, Nina." She glanced at Nina, waiting for her to move away. "She mentioned a different last name, though, not MacLaren." Ada nudged Nina aside and pulled the door open.

Connor wanted to scream with satisfaction that he'd finally found her—at least where she lived. His heart pounded as he worked to keep his composure. The last thing he wanted was to scare the women.

"Jeremiah won't like this when he comes home," Nina hissed but stepped out of the way so Connor could enter.

"May I get you anything, Mr. MacLaren?" Ada asked as she showed him into the front room.

"Water would be fine, ma'am."

Ada left, leaving him alone with Nina who didn't sit but stood against a wall, glaring at him. The three young girls returned with Ada, one handing Connor a glass of water.

"Thank you," Connor smiled at the girl who blushed and stepped behind Ada. He took a swallow of water, watching the five females stare at him. None of the girls looked anything like Meggie, or Pierce, or him. "What's your name?" He asked the tallest girl who stood apart, near the foyer.

She looked up at Nina, her mother, who nodded. "Janie."

"And how old are you, Janie?"

"Nine. My sister Mary is seven," she pointed to the next oldest, "and Essie is four."

"Well, you're all real pretty." He finished the water and handed the empty glass to Ada. "Thank you. That was just right."

"Why do you want Meggie?" Nina asked, trying to pull her two girls behind her.

"He knows Meggie, Mama?" Mary asked Nina.

"Shush, Mary, and let the man talk."

"She went missing years ago and I've been looking for her ever since. Found out that someone had spotted her in Salt Lake and learned she might be living out here on the farm." Connor watched Ada. She seemed to know Meggie better.

"Meggie ran away," the littlest girl blurted before being hushed by her mother, Ada.

"Ran away?" Connor asked.

Ada took a seat near Connor and laced her hands together in her lap. "We believe she left about three days ago, during the rain storm. The girls were in bed and the rest of us were at a church meeting. We didn't get home until morning and that's when the girls told us they couldn't find Meggie."

Connor absorbed the words, taking a deep breath to calm the disappointment that engulfed him. "Could she have been taken?"

"I don't believe so, Mr. MacLaren. Some of her clothes were gone as well as some food. Plus, well," she looked at Nina before proceeding, "some money Mr. Moser kept for emergencies is missing."

"Has Mr. Moser been looking for her?"

"Oh, yes. Every day he takes the wagon out and looks for her. He's gone all the way to the edge of Salt Lake over the last two days and today he's going north. We just hope she's safe," Ada said. She was glad no one could read her thoughts. If they could, they'd realize that she'd prayed over and over the last three days that Meggie was safe and far away from Jeremiah Moser.

"Well, I thank you ladies for the information. Best I get going and help Mr. Moser look for her.

I'm sure she's safe, somewhere." Connor placed his hat back on his head and started for the door.

"Mr. MacLaren, wait just a minute," Ada said and hurried out of the room and up the stairs. Moments later she was back downstairs, holding something out to him. "Here, you take this with you. It was Meggie's. She kept it all these years. Told me it was what she wore the night she was kidnapped. I was surprised it was still in her room."

Connor stared at the ragged shawl Meggie loved to wear. It had been their mother's. He held out a shaky hand and gently took the woven garment from Ada.

"Thank you, ma'am." His voice was strained and almost broke from the emotion he felt at seeing the shawl. He looked at Ada, nodded once more, and then walked out the front door, closing it softly behind him.

Chapter Seventeen

Jericho walked around the Dix property once more, checking for anything that might indicate Len Proctor, Earl Swain, or Bert Newell had found Grace. He'd done this several times today and each time found nothing to indicate anyone had been on the property.

It wasn't a large lot. There was a short drive for the wagon, a small stable for the horses, and a corral behind the house. A wagon couldn't get through the back area but a horse and rider could. There were several trees but not much shrubbery that would hide a man. The sun had set, leaving the sky dark on a night that featured a sliver of a moon. He knew Grace was in the kitchen making supper while they waited for Connor's return.

Jericho had just opened the door when a bullet whizzed past, breaking a window, and sending shards of glass in all directions. He pulled his gun, turned toward the front yard, and crouched low as a second bullet nicked him in the shoulder, sending him falling backward into the house. He kicked the door closed and rolled in front of a sofa, resting his back against it and checking his injured shoulder.

"Grace!"

At the sound of gunfire she'd dropped behind the cabinets. She pulled a handgun Connor had given her from her dress pocket and held it in front of her.

"I'm in the kitchen," she yelled back.

"Get to the back room and lock the door. Don't come out until I tell you."

"But..."

"Just do it, Grace."

He watched as she dashed into the hall and disappeared into the last bedroom.

"Come on out and we won't hurt the woman," a man called from outside. "We're after MacLaren. You tell us where he is and we won't harm anyone."

Jericho knew the lie for what it was and ignored the threat. He rolled so that his body was positioned under a window. Jericho looked out. He could see one man about thirty feet away moving from the trees toward the house. Jericho aimed and fired. The man dropped his gun, grabbed at his chest, and fell.

"Damn it, Earl. I told you to stay put," the leader called.

Jericho figured Len Proctor was the one yelling orders. Earl Swain was down. Bert Newell was still out there with Proctor. Grace was safe in the bedroom. Jericho prayed she'd stay there.

Jericho shifted his weight, and rolled, needing to move to the other side of the room where he could get a better view, but the front door bursting open stopped him. Len Proctor pointed his pistol at Jericho and fired. The bullet pierced his wrist, causing him to release his gun.

"Where's MacLaren?" Procter sneered stepping closer, aiming at Jericho. "Tell me, or the first bullet will be to a knee. The second to your other knee, then your arm until you'll beg to tell me where he is."

"I don't know who MacLaren is. Why don't you enlighten me?" Jericho spat out while trying to locate his gun.

Proctor pulled the trigger, the shot splitting the wooden floor a few inches from Jericho's chest. "Not good enough. Try again," Proctor hissed.

Connor heard the shots from a couple of blocks away and pushed Crusader into a run. He pulled his gun as he approached the Dix property and saw one man down, another crouched behind the wagon. As Connor got closer he could see it was Bert Newell—they'd found Grace. He charged full speed into the yard and aimed just as Bert started to stand. One shot from Connor's gun and the killer fell backward.

Connor jumped from Crusader and ran toward the front steps, dropping behind the rails when he heard a shot from inside.

"Tell me where MacLaren is or you'll wish you had," he heard Proctor yell.

Connor took a tentative step toward the porch, then another before he could see through the open door and into the room where Proctor stood, his arm stretched in front of him, a gun in his hand.

"I'm telling you, I don't know any MacLaren," Jericho threw back.

"Proctor." Connor's cold, commanding voice pierced the night. He stood eight feet away, his Colt aimed at Len's heart. "Drop it, now."

Len swung his gun toward Connor but never uttered a sound before a bullet blew through his chest, a second through his skull.

Connor dashed through the door, spotted Jericho's bleeding shoulder and wrist, and started toward him.

"Grace is in the back bedroom. Go check on her," Jericho ground out as he pushed himself up and walked over to check on Proctor.

Connor hurried down the hall, shoved open the bedroom door, and came face-to-face with the gun he'd given Grace. "Whoa, honey," he said in a low, calm voice as he slowly holstered his Colt and walked toward her. "It's over. All three are dead."

Grace's eyes were wide, her two-handed grip shaky, but she didn't lower the gun.

"Grace. It's me, Connor. Put the gun down, sweetheart. It's all right." He continued to walk forward, arms at his sides, palms out.

"Connor?" she whispered, her voice as shaky as the gun she held.

He watched as she lowered the gun a few inches, then reached out a hand, and took it from her loosened grip. "It's over, Grace. They're all dead." He wrapped his arms around her, holding tight, then stroking her hair. He pulled back to look at her. "You all right now?"

She looked up him. "Yes, I'm fine. I've never been around anything like that." She took a step back.

"You did real good. I've no doubt that if one of those men had made it past Jericho they would have been looking square into the barrel of your gun, just like I did." He reached out and grabbed her hand. "Come on. Let's check on Mr. Jericho."

Grace walked with him into the front room to see Jericho using his one good arm to drag a body outside and down the porch steps. She looked around at the mess, not dropping her hand from Connor's. She'd never been near a gunfight, seen blood like this, or a dead body. It made her stomach roll but she was determined to keep herself together. The last thing she wanted was for Connor to see her as weak.

"I guess I'd better get started cleaning this up before Ruth gets back." She turned toward the kitchen but Connor pulled her hand, drawing her to him, and lowered his head to capture her lips. Her hands moved up his arms and around his neck. She held tight, savoring the taste and feel of him.

"Uh, I could use your help out here." Jericho's voice broke the moment.

Grace's arms dropped and she jumped back a step before walking to the kitchen.

Connor watched her walk away before turning to Jericho. "Your timing is, as always, perfect."

"Come on," Jericho chuckled. "Let's get these bodies loaded and to the sheriff. Then you can tell me what you found out about Meggie."

******

"You've been in town less than a month, MacLaren, and already the number of dead men exceeds what is seen over six times that long." The sheriff had accepted their accounts of the deaths at Ruth Dix's home. He was aware of Proctor, Swain, and Newell and their quest for vengeance against MacLaren. Fred and Roy had told him of the attempt on Alex McCann's life, and although there had been no confirmed proof they were the men who'd blown up the carriage, everything pointed toward them. "Do you think there's any chance you can get done with the rest of your business and leave before anyone else turns up dead?"

"I have no regrets on any of the deaths, Sheriff. You know as well as I, each one was a justified kill." Connor was at peace with each shooting. He never second guessed himself when it came to dispatching a man who held a gun to another. "The odds are pretty good that I'll find my sister within a few days and be out of your hair."

"Not that we don't welcome newcomers, but in your case, the sooner you leave the better for all."

Jericho and Connor walked outside onto a quiet, dark street. It was close to midnight.

"Drink?" Jericho asked.

"Yeah."

The two walked to the closest saloon, taking a table in the corner, and ordered a couple of whiskeys.

"You going to tell me about you and Grace?" Jericho sipped his drink and stared at his friend. He'd watched the two together and guessed something was going on. Until now, he hadn't said anything. Connor was in his teens when Jericho had first met him. In all that time he'd never known him to be serious over any woman. He had his share, his pick as most would say, but all were short term without meaning. This one had all the signs of being more.

"Nothing to tell." Connor held his glass up to the dim light and rolled the amber liquid around in the short glass before tossing it back. He let the warmth trickle down his throat, then signaled the bartender for another.

"That's not the way I see it."

Connor debated about sharing his feelings. Truth was, he didn't know for certain how he felt. Grace stirred emotions that he'd never felt before for any woman. She got under his skin in a way that made him anxious and wary. He felt a protectiveness toward her that he'd felt for no one else except his sister, Meggie, and their brother, Pierce.

"I like her," Connor said before downing his second whiskey.

"You bedded her yet?"

"Hell, no."

"You plan to?"

"That's none of your damned business." Connor slammed his glass on the table and stood.

"Got to take that for a yes, laddie," Jericho replied and stood to walk outside. "I'm heading to the hotel, unless you need me back at the Dix place."

"No, you go ahead. I'll pick up Grace and take her home. Not sure she'll want to stay at Ruth's place after what happened."

Connor was right. Grace wanted nothing more than to return to her small room. She planned to return the next day to make sure nothing had been missed when cleaning up, but other than that, Grace wouldn't go back until the next time Ruth was in town.

Connor followed her up the narrow steps to her place, carrying her small bag, and set it down on the floor inside.

"You going to be okay here tonight?"

She slipped off her coat and hung it on a nearby hook. Grace wanted to be alone but didn't want him to leave. Her heart told her to walk up to him, lace her arms around his neck, and ask him to stay. She shouldn't. She was still married and it would be wrong, even if her marriage was a mockery. She planned to obtain a divorce, which was simple to do in Utah. The laws were lenient and divorce common with people coming from other states to take advantage of the quick dissolution procedures. She simply hadn't had time to do it with work and planning how she was going to free Meggie.

Grace walked to a window and stared at the dark sky, deciding what to do. She needed to tell him about Moser but the words wouldn't form. Say something tonight, or let him leave—she was conflicted. She continued to look out when she sensed him walk up behind her, felt his strong arms wrap around her waist, and draw her flush against his chest.

He pulled loose strands of hair away from her neck, bending to place kisses up to the tender spot behind her ear. "Ask me to stay," he whispered before tugging a sensitive earlobe with his lips. She sagged against him, letting her head fall back against his chest and giving him access to the soft column of her neck.

Connor moved a hand around to splay over her stomach as the second held her tight against him. He continued kissing her soft skin as he unbuttoned the front of her dress and pushed it from her shoulders. He let it fall to her waist leaving her in only a thin chemise.

Grace's body trembled at his touch. She could feel her body warm, heat coursing through her limbs. She inhaled his unique scent as his lips moved down her neck to her shoulders.

She moaned and he turned her to face him, kissing her, and outlining her lips with his tongue until she opened for him. Her hands sifted through his dark, silky hair, pulling him down, holding him in place.

Grace was on fire. She'd never felt sensations like this before, waves of heat moving up and down her body, and settling between her legs. She squirmed against him, pulling Connor tighter, trying to get closer, the friction of his clothes through her sheer chemise sending shudders through her body. She wound her hands in his hair, angling her mouth one way then another over his, matching each thrust of his tongue with hers.

He untied her chemise, pushing it and her dress to the floor, leaving her wearing only her thin drawers. He gazed down at her. "You are so damn beautiful, Grace." His voice was husky as he stared at her creamy skin and soft curves.

Connor picked her up and walked to the bed, settling her on his lap. He buried his face in her graceful neck, nipping, and kissing his way down. She bucked against him, arching up, and holding his head in place.

One of his hands rested on her thigh, kneading, and moving upward toward the ties at her waist.

"Grace," he whispered. "Tell me to stop, or that you want me to stay. I need to hear it from you." He lifted his gaze to hers, waiting for an answer.

"Stay, Connor. Make love to me." Grace pulled him back down to her knowing her decision was both wrong and right.

Chapter Eighteen

The night passed and Connor stayed, something he'd never done with any woman. They made love twice more before the sun cast its light through the slits in Grace's curtains. He held her close, not wanting to let go or leave, but knowing he had to search for his sister. It couldn't wait another day.

Connor turned Grace to face him, watching her slowly wake and cast her sleep filled gaze up at him. "I need to go," he leaned down to kiss her. She snaked a hand behind his head and held him, then let her grip slip away.

"Your sister?" she asked, her voice husky from sleep and their night of love.

"Yes. We found where she lived and know she ran away as the storm hit a few days ago. No one has seen her since. I must find her before her husband does."

"She's married?" Grace sat up in bed. He'd never mentioned that his sister might be married.

"Looks that way. We talked to the man's other wives and they confirmed Meggie lived there."

"Meggie?" Grace jumped out of bed at the mention of her friend's name. "Meggie is your sister?"

"You know her?" Connor was stunned.

"Did you speak with a woman named Ada, and one named Nina?"

"Yes, both were at the Moser farm." He gripped Grace's shoulders and pulled her to within six inches of him. "Tell me what you know of my sister."

She stared up at him. Grace couldn't wrap her mind around the fact that the woman Connor had been searching for was her close friend. "Meggie is a good friend—a very good one." Her voice had grown soft as she thought of Meggie, running away, alone.

She pulled away from him and grabbed her clothes. "We have to leave. Now. We must find her before Moser does." Her voice was urgent.

Connor watched her, his body shaking at the knowledge that the woman he'd fallen for, made love to all night, knew his sister. Meggie was the reason he'd come to Salt Lake. Grace had been a distraction, up until last night. Now she might hold the key to finding his sister. He pulled on his clothes, buttoned his shirt, and grabbed his gun belt.

"Do you have any idea where she'd go?" Connor asked as Grace slipped into her coat.

"Not for sure, but I believe she'd head for Salt Lake, not north. She'd have to find money and a way to get out of this area before her husband finds her. If it was during the storm, she may have taken shelter with a neighbor on the way to town. We'll just have to search."

Within an hour they'd found Jericho, Roy, and Fred and began their search. Grace rode one of Ruth's horses. She wasn't as proficient as Connor but they kept a moderate pace, letting her gain confidence until she sat easily in the saddle.

Connor kept watch on Grace as they rode. There was so much he wanted to know about her. He was convinced she hadn't told him the complete truth about herself and her life in Salt Lake—too much didn't add up. This was all new to him, these feelings and his desire to be around her, reach out and touch her. He didn't know the rules, what was expected in a normal relationship. But he did know that he needed her to be honest, as he intended to be with her.

About a mile north of Salt Lake, they began to see farm houses on either side of Old Pioneer Road. Roy and Fred took the farms to one side while Connor, Grace, and Jericho talked to the owners on the other. An hour passed, then two, without anyone acknowledging they'd seen Meggie. Several mentioned speaking with Jeremiah Moser several days before, but the man hadn't been back since.

It was coming up on midday. The riders were about a mile from the turnoff to the Moser farm and Homer Erickson's shack. Connor pulled up.

"I want to speak with Homer again, find out if he's seen anything."

"You know Mr. Erickson?" Grace asked.

"Met him on our search. Nice enough guy. Not sure how much he cares for his neighbor, Moser, but he was decent enough to us. You know him?"

"No, I know he's lives alone, but never got to meet him."

As they spoke Jericho noticed a farm house several yards off the road, hidden somewhat from the road. A man stopped a wagon to the front of the house then went inside. A few minutes later he came out carrying something wrapped in a blanket and laid it in the back of the wagon before climbing onto the seat. He was followed outside by a woman who climbed into the wagon next him. From this distance the man and woman appeared to be older, maybe in their sixties or seventies.

"Look there, Connor," Jericho said and pointed toward the house. "The man just carried something out in a blanket and laid it in the back of the wagon. I think we should speak with them."

The man slapped the horses and the wagon moved at a slow pace to the main road, then stopped when the couple saw the group of riders approach.

"Morning," Connor said and tipped his hat.

"Morning," the old man replied. "Can I help you folks?"

"Maybe so. We're looking for a young woman who got lost during the storm the other night. She's about twenty-four with dark, reddish-brown hair, and green eyes. You happen to see her?"

The man glanced at the woman beside him, then back at Connor. "What you want her for?"

"She's my sister and was kidnapped eight years ago. We heard she lived at the Moser farm but took off during the storm."

"She got a name?" the old man asked.

"Meggie. Meggie MacLaren."

"She calls herself Meggie Delaney," Grace interjected and saw the look of surprise on Connor's face.

"Agnes?" the man looked to the woman.

"I suppose it'd be all right, George."

"We got a young woman in the back of this wagon. Found her over yonder in that shack," he pointed across the road to the falling down cabin. "She was sick, got better then took a turn yesterday. High fever, delirious. We're on our way to find the doctor."

By this time Connor, Grace, and Jericho had all dismounted and stood by the wagon, peering into the back but not touching the blanket.

"May I," Connor asked, his voice shaky, too afraid to hope the woman under the blanket was Meggie.

The man nodded. "Go ahead and look."

Connor reached in, touching the edge of the blanket, and slowly pulled it back. His breath caught. Even sick, Connor recognized Meggie curled into a ball, clutching a coat that had been wrapped around her. "My God, Meggie." He looked up at Jericho. "It's Meggie! We finally found her!" He jumped into the wagon and lifted his sister, cradling her in his arms, rocking her, everyone else all but forgotten.

The others watched as Connor held his sister, speaking in soft whispers to her, telling her everything would be fine, that he'd take care of her.

"Uh, son, we best get going to town. She's in a bad way," the man interjected.

Connor took a hard look at Meggie this time, touching her face, and noticing the fever. Her teeth were chattering and her body shivered even with the burning fever.

"I'll bring Crusader," Jericho offered. "You stay in the wagon with Meggie."

Connor just looked up and nodded.

******

Connor refused to leave the room even with the threats the doctor and nurses threw at him. He stayed, back against the wall, arms crossed, and watched as they worked on his sister. It had been eight long years, there was no chance he'd let her out of his sight for even a minute until he knew she'd be all right.

The doctor walked up to him after tending to Meggie. "Let's talk outside a minute."

Connor glanced at Meggie, obviously not wanting to leave.

"She's in good hands."

They walked down the hall a bit, then stopped.

"Your sister has pneumonia. As you heard, Mr. and Mrs. Hines told us she had a hacking cough and fever when they found her. She hasn't been able to keep food down, her fever has spiked back up, and she's having chills. They said she's been delirious much of the last few days. We're bringing down the fever but there's not much we can do about the infection. We may have caught it early enough and she's young and seems pretty healthy.

Even so, you need to know that the odds aren't good she'll pull through."

Connor stared at the doctor, not believing the man's words or accepting them. "What can I do?" His words were strained as he began to comprehend that Meggie might never recover. He may have found her only to lose her forever to the life-threatening disease.

"Pray, Mr. MacLaren, and don't stop."

Connor nodded and started back toward the room. The doctor reached out to stop him.

"It's best that you not be in the room. Stay with your friends. We'll let you know as soon as we know anything."

******

A full day passed without much change. Connor and Grace refused to leave the hospital. Jericho got a message off to Alex McCann, and Fred sent word to Louis Dunnigan, the man paying Roy and him to help find Meggie. Dunnigan offered to send his personal doctor from Denver. Alex replied asking Fred to let him know if there was anything at all that Connor needed to help Meggie. Truth was, there was nothing more anyone could do except wait.

The second day Meggie showed some improvement, giving everyone hope that she might still beat the disease. Jasper Bing came and went, bringing food and anything else Grace, Connor or the others needed. Ruth Dix arrived back in Salt Lake late that day, finding a note on her front door left by Jasper. She wasted no time getting to the hospital, demanding to speak with the doctor and nurses, refusing to accept that Meggie could not be saved. She'd never met the young woman, but she was Grace's friend and Connor's sister, that's all that mattered.

"Grace, you and Connor need to get away, if just for a while. Go outside, take a walk. Mr. Jericho and I will stay. Nothing will happen while you're gone," Ruth said later that evening.

"I don't know, Ruth. I hate to leave, even for a short time."

Connor heard the exchange. He sat a few chairs away, his arms on his knees, hands clasped, head bent. He wasn't a praying man, never had been, not since his parents had sent them to America from Scotland. Not since learning that you could achieve your dreams in this new land if you were willing to fight, claw, and sometimes kill. Not since Meggie had been taken eight years before. Not since he'd turned from the optimism of his youth to the deadly reality of the present.

But now, he prayed. Not for himself or the men he'd killed. All righteous, he'd stated after each one. No, he prayed for Meggie. He'd phrased his prayers every way he could think of—from asking for her recovery, to begging God to spare her. He was out of words. He figured if God hadn't heard him by now, he never would.

Connor stood and reached out a hand to Grace. "Come on. Let's get out of here for a while."

They walked into the cool night air with no destination in mind. Neither said a word for several minutes, each absorbed in their own thoughts. Grace was the first to break the silence.

"Where will you go once Meggie recovers?"

Connor glanced at her and stopped walking, still holding her hand tight to his side. It was a question he knew the answer to but hadn't thought about since they'd found her. He'd planned to take her back to Fire Mountain for a fresh start. After years without her family she deserved to be near them, surrounded by people who would accept and love her. Maybe if he voiced it the thought would become reality.

He started walking again, still not letting loose of his hold on Grace. "Fire Mountain, where our family lives."

"Is it nice there?"

He shook his head and snorted. "I don't know, never been there. But Pierce says it's one of the most beautiful places he's ever seen." Connor glanced over at Grace, wanting something, but not sure what it was. "Will you stay in Salt Lake?"

She was quiet a long time. Her dream had been to go back for Meggie and travel south to the Arizona territory. More than anything she wanted to follow that dream, except now Meggie had her family. Grace would be in the way.

"I...I don't know."

Connor came to a halt and turned Grace toward him. "Come with us." He was surprised he'd voiced his thoughts. He'd never asked a woman for more than a short, physical relationship—never wanted one—but one night with Grace wasn't enough. He didn't think a thousand nights would ever suffice.

"What are you saying, Connor?" She stared up at him, surprised by his invitation.

"I'm not sure what I'm saying except that I can't ride out and leave you behind. You and I, we're good together." He looked up to the clear sky trying to find the words that would best convey his feelings. "I've never asked this of any woman, Grace. I need you with me. I can't promise anything more than that."

She let his words roll around in her head. Her intent had been to travel to Arizona anyway as soon as she'd saved enough money. She had no interest in staying in Salt Lake. It would be safer to travel with Connor and Meggie than to go on her own, and perhaps his family could help her find a job once they arrived in Fire Mountain. She couldn't depend on Connor. He'd been clear about that. He wanted and needed her, but didn't love her. She'd realized over the last several days how much she cared for this man. *Did she love him?* Grace wasn't certain, but suspected that yes, she did. She made a quick decision.

"All right. I'll travel with you and Meggie to Fire Mountain. She's my friend and she'll need someone who knows her and understands the life she's had the last few years."

Connor's relief was immediate.

"There is a condition," Grace added.

"What is it?" Wariness crept into his voice.

"I will get a job, build my own life once we get there, and not be dependent on you in any way."

Connor stared at her, not liking the sound of this condition. He understood her need to be independent—he'd made no promises of any kind. At the same time, he wanted her to himself. Did her condition mean that she'd let other men court her?

"Grace, does that mean..." he started, but stopped at the sound of someone yelling his name.

"Connor! Come quick!" Jericho caught up with them, out of breath and bending over. "It's Meggie," he wheezed. "The doctor says she'll make it."

Connor grabbed Grace's hand and took off at a run, never stopping until he stood outside Meggie's room.

Chapter Nineteen

Even with the doctor's news, he hadn't allowed Connor or anyone else in Meggie's room that night. She'd woken off and on but was weak and disoriented. He asked that Connor wait until morning, and if she continued to improve, he'd be allowed to visit for short periods.

It was now ten in the morning, and Connor's patience was wearing thin, as was everyone else's. Just as Connor was preparing to insist they finally be allowed to see his sister, the doctor walked out of her room, gesturing to Connor and Grace.

"She's asking for someone named Dodge and for Grace. Do either of you know him?"

"I didn't know him, but Meggie has spoken of him often." She looked at Connor, knowing he knew nothing about this part of his sister's past. "He died several years ago."

"I see. Well, then, it should be fine if both of you go in at one time. It's unusual for non-family to be allowed in at this point, Grace, but since she's asking for you, we'll make an exception." He opened the door for the two to pass through. "Please understand, she is still tired and extremely weak. You can only have a few minutes."

The room was sterile, colder than Connor anticipated. Meggie was the lone patient. She was covered in thick blankets and a turban had been wrapped around her head to keep in the warmth. As they approached the bed Connor noticed her pale skin and labored breathing, as if she still had to battle for each breath. She looked to be no more than the sixteen years of age she was when she'd been abducted.

He leaned down, close to her ear. "Meggie, darlin', can you hear me?" He watched her eyes flutter, then stop. "Meggie, it's Connor. Can you hear me?" Her eyes fluttered once again before a small slit exposed her pale green eyes. She looked toward Connor, then the woman standing behind him—her eyes held.

"Grace?" Her voice was low and hoarse from lack of use.

"I'm here, Meggie," Grace stepped closer.

Meggie's glazed eyes never left Grace's. "I've missed you." She coughed, causing the nurse to walk over.

"I'm so sorry I left you, Meggie. I was coming back for you as soon as I had enough money."

Connor's gaze turned to Grace at these words. It was the first she'd spoken of trying to save money to help his sister leave Moser. He wished he'd mentioned Meggie's name to Grace sooner, perhaps they could've gotten to her before she tried to run.

Meggie's eyes closed and she took a shallow breath. "I knew you wouldn't leave me, Grace." She dropped back to sleep.

Connor watched her, disappointment washing over him at the realization that she hadn't recognized him. He was eight years older, had changed a great deal during the life he'd led trying to find her. Yet she looked the same. He would have known her anywhere.

They nurse walked up and touched Connor's arm. "She'll sleep for a while, maybe a couple of hours or even the rest of the day. Why don't you get breakfast, go outside. She'll be fine here."

Connor knew the nurse was right. He needed some air and food, and to learn who this Dodge person was that Meggie had asked for.

"Come on. We'll get the others and grab something to eat," Connor said to Grace and walked into the hall. Ruth, Mr. Jericho, Fred, and Roy stood at their approach.

"How is she, laddie?" Jericho asked, stretching to his full six-foot-six height.

"She spoke to Grace for a moment before she got tired and went back to sleep. She didn't recognize me."

Grace touched his arm to get his attention. "She will. It's been years and she has no idea you've been looking for her."

"Of course I've been looking for her. From the first day—I've never stopped searching." Anger and frustration laced his voice. He knew he was overreacting. Of course she wouldn't have known how hard he'd tried to find her, traveled through so many states he couldn't name them all, and chased too many dead ends to count. But she wouldn't know that because he'd never gotten close, until now.

Grace turned to the others. "The nurse said to come back in a couple of hours."

"Let's get out of here and grab some food. I'm famished," Jericho said before walking outside.

They ended up at Jasper's.

After he served them each an oversized portion of the special he sat down next to Grace. "Tell me how she's doing."

"The doctor says she'll pull through. Connor and I saw her for a few minutes, but she's weak, tired, and so pale it made my heart ache."

Connor watched Grace as she spoke to Jasper. She'd known Meggie much better than he'd realized. He'd thought they were mere friends, acquaintances, but now he understood they were much more than that. Grace held secrets to Meggie's past that Connor wanted to learn. He suspected there was also more to Grace's life in Salt Lake than she'd shared with him.

"Well, that's all good news," Jasper said and clapped Connor on the shoulder. "It won't be long and you'll have your sister back in the fold. And Grace, you'll be able to get back here to work, where you belong." He pushed from his seat and headed to the kitchen.

Connor looked over at Grace, knowing it would be a difficult conversation when she told Jasper of her plans to leave for Fire Mountain.

******

Meggie hadn't woken enough to have visitors again that day. Connor had taken Grace to her room, conflicted about whether to stay or return to his hotel. He was exhausted, in need of a bath and shave, plus he needed to figure out what to do with Meggie once the hospital let her leave. He didn't want to bring her to the hotel, Grace's place was too small, and he had no contacts for something larger. He'd speak with Ruth the next morning, see if there was a chance Meggie and he could stay at her place a few days until she could travel.

"Will you stay with me tonight?" Grace's voice cut through his thoughts.

He looked down at her and all his thoughts of needing time alone to think dissolved. "Yes, I'll stay."

They took turns cleaning up before Connor slid into bed next to her. He pulled her to him, wrapping strong arms around her waist, and held tight. He'd intended to simply hold her, feeling her warmth wrap around him, and push away the pain of the last few days watching his sister hover on the edge of death. He took a deep breath, inhaling Grace's clean scent. She snuggled back against him causing his body to respond even as his mind fought the idea.

He turned Grace to him, kissing her with all the pent up hunger of a man who'd denied himself the basic human feelings a man felt for a woman for too long.

Grace wrapped her arms around him, knowing her heart had already taken the dangerous step of falling in love with this man. She wanted him, returning his kiss with all the passion she felt, straining to get closer.

He deepened the kiss, his tongue tracing her full bottom lip and coaxing her to open for him.

His hands moved up and down her back, shifting lower, and pressing her to him. He dipped his head, kissing his way along the soft column of her neck, drawing a low moan from her, then moving lower. He continued until they were both feverish with need and could wait no longer.

They made love until the early hours before falling into an exhausted sleep.

******

The following morning, Connor woke early, pulled Grace closer, and thought of what he could say to keep her in his life. He knew he'd lost his heart to this woman and didn't want to lose her.

He finally climbed out of bed and scribbled a quick note. He kissed a sleeping Grace on the cheek, and arrived at the hospital early—wanting time with his sister before anyone else came to visit. The doctor was just leaving Meggie's room.

"She's doing much better today. If this continues, you may be able to take her home in two or three days. Good thing that girl was healthy or we would have lost her."

Connor opened the door to her room and peered inside. She was sitting up, talking with a nurse, and had what appeared to be a smile on her face. The nurse looked up as Connor entered.

"It appears you have a visitor. I'll leave the two of you alone for a bit." The nurse nodded at Connor as she walked out, closing the door behind her.

"Hello, Meggie," Connor said in a cautious tone as he walked toward the bed. He saw her face turn from confusion to curiosity.

"Do I know you?" Her eyes held his, then dropped to his shirt and back up to his hair and face. "You look so familiar."

"It's been a long time I'm afraid. Much too long." Connor now stood by the bed, looking down at the most wonderful sight he'd seen in a long time.

"Connor?" The words were soft, tentative.

"Yes, Meggie. It's me."

"Connor!" she squealed and tried to launch her still weak body from the bed and into his arms. He held her, holding her tight, still not quite believing they were in this room, together, and that she'd survived the deadly illness.

She pulled back to look at him. "I thought you'd forgotten me," she said as she swiped tears from her eyes.

"Never. I've been looking for you all this time."

"Good morning," Grace said as she entered the room to see Meggie and Connor holding hands. "So, I see you recognize your brother. Connor was afraid you wouldn't."

"I wasn't sure at first, but..." she smiled up at her brother and gripped his hand tighter. "How did you find me?"

"It's a long story, one I promise to tell you all of once the doctor lets you leave." Connor sat down on the edge of the bed. "He says you might be able to leave in a couple of days."

"I'd like to leave today, now."

"Doubt he'll allow that, but soon." He turned to Grace. "I thought I'd ask Ruth if Meggie and I could stay with her a few days until Meggie's able to travel."

"Travel?" Meggie asked, her voice wavering, betraying her exhaustion.

"I had hoped you would want to come with me to Fire Mountain, Arizona. Pierce and I were able to find our MacLaren cousins. They have a ranch there and would like us to settle with them. Pierce is there now." He knew this was a lot to take in all at once. "You don't have to decide today, there's time."

"I don't need time. It sounds wonderful," she covered her mouth to conceal a yawn. "Anywhere you go is where I want to be."

"I hoped that's what you'd say," Connor smiled at Meggie. "There's one other thing." He looked at Grace. "I've asked Grace to come along."

"Truly, you'd want to come with us, Grace?" It wasn't hard to miss the excitement in Meggie's voice, even though her head began to bob and she fought to keep her eyes open.

Grace glanced at Connor. Their eyes met and held, a gesture that wasn't lost on Meggie. There was something going on between her good friend and her brother. She'd have to ask Grace about this when they had time alone.

Grace broke contact with Connor and turned her attention back to her friend. "Yes, I'd like that very much."

"I would love to have you with us," Meggie said as another yawn escaped. Her eyes began to close, and this time stayed shut.

"Meggie, we'll leave you to rest, but I'll be back this afternoon." He leaned over and placed a kiss on his sister's forehead.

"All right, this afternoon," Meggie said as she drifted to sleep.

******

Fire Mountain, Arizona Territory

"Hello there, Pierce. You here to pick up the mail?" Tom had been the telegraph operator in Fire Mountain for years. He'd handled the stage lines that came through before the town got rail service to most places. Now he also handled mail for the growing town and surrounding ranches, including the MacLaren ranch.

"Sure am, Tom. Got anything for me?"

Tom reached behind him. He pulled a package, letters, and a telegram from the cubby-holed wall. "Here you go. Telegram just came in from Salt Lake an hour ago."

Pierce took the mail and walked outside, placing everything but the telegram in his saddlebags. He was still surprised how easily the MacLarens had accepted him and his brother, Connor. It was as if they'd always been a part of the family. None of them had ever met until a couple of months before when Drew MacLaren was involved in some trouble in Colorado.

He tore open the telegram and read the brief contents. *Connor had found Meggie!* He stepped back into the telegraph office. "He found her, Tom. Connor found our sister! He hopes to be in Fire Mountain within the month."

"That's wonderful news," Tom said, walking around the counter to slap Pierce on the back.

Pierce folded the message, stuffing it in his pocket. They'd been disappointed so many times in the past, but this time Connor had found her. His brother had never stopped searching, never given up, even when Pierce had been afraid the search would drive Connor mad. But his brother had been right to keep up his crusade. It had finally paid off.

He should ride back to the ranch, share the news with his cousins. Instead, he looked toward the saloon. He wanted a drink—to celebrate, before the restaurants and saloons became crowded with ranch hands and local townspeople.

Pierce pushed the door of the Desert Dove open and took a seat at a table in the corner. He'd been here a couple of times with his cousins—Niall, Jamie, Will, and Drew. It made sense that it was their favorite saloon. A few years earlier the oldest brother, Niall, had bought the place from the previous owner, Gloria Chalmette. She'd been a close friend of Niall's before he met and married Kate Garner. Now Gloria was married to Sam Browning, the town sheriff. Niall's ownership of the saloon hadn't been made public until last year.

Pierce signaled for a whiskey from the longtime bar keep, Ross, and then sat back to watch the people. It was a good town and a great place to raise a family. Trouble was, with all the single cowhands and other locals, most of the good women were spoken for.

"Here you go, mister." The soft voice flowed over him, breaking his thoughts.

"Thanks, uh..."

"Mollie. I just started yesterday." She didn't look like she could be more than eighteen or nineteen, with dark golden hair laced with strands of soft red. Mollie's soft, golden brown eyes looked him over. It wasn't provocative, more her way to really see and remember him.

"Nice to meet you, Mollie. I'm Pierce MacLaren." He saluted her with his glass and took a sip.

"Yes, I know. Ross told me you were one of the MacLarens. Well, I better get back to the bar. Good to meet you, Pierce. Just wave if there's anything else you'd like."

He watched her slow walk and swaying hips, almost choking on his drink. Hell yes, there was more he'd like—and it was wrapped up in the bundle that had just left his table. Pierce continued to follow her until his eyes caught Ross's knowing smirk. Smart-ass, but the man sure knew what he was doing when it came to hiring women.

Pierce started to stand when the door flew open and a group of businessmen came strolling into the saloon, headed for a large round table near his. One he'd met, Jerrod Minton, an attorney. He handled most of the business matters for the large ranches and more prosperous property owners. According to Niall, Minton had handled the legal affairs for the MacLarens for years. Honest, hardworking, and didn't tolerate any bull is the way Niall had described him. Jerrod saw Pierce and extended his hand.

"Hello, Pierce. How are you settling in?"

"Good, Jerrod. Learning things, helping the cousins as best I can. It's a new life, that's for sure."

Jerrod chuckled. "I'm sure it is. Niall invited Madeleine and I out for supper next week. Hope there's plenty of food because that boy of ours sure can eat for being only four." Jerrod had married Madeleine Rutherford, the town's school teacher, a few years ago. They had a four-year old boy and three-year old girl. Jamie MacLaren had courted her for a brief period before the woman he'd loved all his life had returned to Fire Mountain. Torie and Jamie were a perfect match. "If you have some time in the next few weeks, I'd like to learn more about what you've done for Connor. Investigation work and such."

"I'll make time."

"Better get back to my meeting." Jerrod tilted his head to the waiting table.

Pierce watched Jerrod take his seat, then let his eyes roam over the other occupants. He recognized the banker, but the others were strangers. One in particular caught his eye. He was about Pierce's height at over six feet, with thick blond hair. The clothes were what distinguished him—black trousers and coat that fell to within six inches of his knees. His white shirt had a stand-up collar with an emerald green silk ribbon tie that matched his brocade vest. It was unusual for Fire Mountain, but he'd seen the style often back East. The one difference was the western style black hat he'd placed on a hook behind his chair.

"Anything else, Pierce?" Mollie had come up beside him, eyeing the man the same way Pierce did. "I'm thinking back East with money," she said in a quiet voice.

Pierce grinned. "Probably so. Nothing more for me, Mollie. See you next time." He favored her with a wicked smile, waved to Ross, and started back to the MacLaren ranch.

Mollie walked back up to the bar, leaning against it as she watched Pierce mount his horse. She'd met quite a few men the last couple of years, but none that had made such an immediate impact on her. Pierce MacLaren. She'd sure like to get to know him better.

Chapter Twenty

Salt Lake City

Ruth had been delighted to offer her house to Meggie and Connor, and two days later Meggie found herself settled into a guest room at the Dix home. She'd never met Ruth before, but after only a few hours, felt as if she'd known the older woman her whole life.

Meggie had fought Connor about carrying her into the house, but she'd ultimately given in when it had become apparent there was no chance of winning that argument. Now she was fidgety, ready to move around, and get back to a normal life. *Normal*, she thought. *What was that?* She'd had so few choices over the years that the thought of being able to do whatever she wanted was a little daunting.

She and Connor had said their goodbyes and thanks to Fred Helms and Roy Crowley, who'd been called back to Denver now that Meggie was out of danger. Jericho had agreed to return with them to Fire Mountain, saying that—even at their older ages—he felt both Connor and Pierce needed *looking after*. Meggie remembered meeting Mr. Jericho a couple of times before being kidnapped and thanked God her brothers had kept him as their friend.

"Supper will be ready in a few minutes," Ruth called from the kitchen. Meggie heard the back door slam. "Hey, MacLaren, wipe those boots before you track mud into my kitchen."

"Yes, ma'am. Sorry about that," Connor replied. Meggie could hear the chagrin in his voice and almost laughed. "I'll let Meggie know about supper."

As he walked through the front room the entry door swung open.

"Good evening, Connor," Grace said.

Connor moved toward her, wrapping an arm around her waist to pull her toward him for a welcoming kiss. Her hands grasped his strong forearms, steadying herself, then relaxed into the kiss.

"All right, that's enough, you two," Ruth said as she stood in the kitchen doorway.

Connor and Grace pushed apart. "Uh, good evening, Ruth," Grace managed. "I hope it's okay that I came by tonight?"

"Of course it is. In fact, you can help me set the table while Connor gets Meggie."

Jericho showed up just as Grace was placing the last of the food on the table.

"I set a place for you, Mr. Jericho, just in case you decided to join us," Grace said and smiled at someone who'd become a good friend in a short time.

"I never pass up an invitation for home cooking." Jericho smiled and placed his gun belt on a nearby table as Connor and Meggie walked in from the hallway.

"Look at you, missy. No one would even know how sick you've been by looking at you tonight," Jericho said and meant every word of it.

"Thank you, Mr. Jericho. I feel wonderful and it's so good to get out of that hospital." Meggie took her seat as Connor held the chair. He did the same for Grace.

"Mrs. Dix, this sure is a good spread," Jericho said as he pulled out the chair for their hostess.

"It's a celebration, Mr. Jericho. Meggie being home and those three murderers out of our lives. Overall, it's been a real good week," Ruth replied. "Mr. Jericho, would you say the prayer?"

"It would be my honor," Jericho replied and bowed his head.

Connor looked at Jericho. He'd never known his friend to bless his food before eating. You just never knew everything about anybody.

"Dear Lord, thanks for bringing Meggie home, keeping us safe from those miserable varmints who tried to kill Connor, and introducing us to Ruth and Grace. You've been mighty generous, Lord, and we thank you. Oh, and bless this food. Amen."

"Amen," everyone said and tucked into their supper.

The table was quiet as the food was passed around. After a while, Connor looked toward his sister.

"They told us you ran away from your husband, Meggie. Is that true?" Connor asked in a gentle voice.

She looked at her brother then down to the table. "Yes, it's true."

"And the reason?"

"It's hard to explain." She looked at Grace then back at Connor. "It's complicated."

He looked around the table. "We have time. Tell us." Connor settled back in his chair.

Meggie told them of the kidnapping, being sold to Eugene Jackson, and then being taken in by his close friend, Dodge Delaney. She told them of the robbers who killed Dodge and took her hostage, leaving out the part where she and Dodge had fallen in love and he'd asked her to marry. Finally, Meggie talked about being sold to Edgar Skanks, working for the man until he'd sold her to her husband, a Mormon.

"A Mormon. So Ada and Nina are also his wives?" Connor was sickened at the tales coming from his sister. He'd failed her in so many ways, and had a lot to make up for.

"Yes, I'm wife number four." Her voice had grown small.

"And your husband is Jeremiah Moser." It was a statement, not a question.

"Yes, our husband," she gestured toward Grace then looked back at Connor, "is Jeremiah Moser."

Grace flinched at Meggie's words and looked down at her plate waiting for the consequences she was sure would come.

Connor couldn't believe what he'd just heard. He turned a stunned expression on Grace. "You're married? Married to Jeremiah Moser?" His voice was hard, incredulous.

"Well, I guess you could say that," Grace managed, her voice weak and unsteady.

"You guess? Are you married to the man or not?"

Grace and Meggie could see his anger rising at the realization that not only his sister, but Grace were married to the same man.

"Yes, but I can explain," Grace added, hoping he'd give them each a chance to share what life had been like in Jeremiah's home.

"Shit," he ground out, threw his napkin down, and pushed from the table. He paced away, turned his back to Grace, and ran both hands through his thick, wavy hair.

Ruth and Jericho sat quietly, absorbing the news for the first time, just like Connor.

He could hear the legs of a chair scrape against the wood floor. Grace walked up behind him, touching his back lightly with her hand. He spun toward her.

"Let us explain, Connor. Please."

He took a deep breath, stepping away from her, but sat back down, listening as they told of life with Moser.

Connor tried to push away the anger he felt toward Grace as he listened to them explain. She'd lied to him, if not outright, then by omitting the fact she was still a married woman. He had only two firm rules when it came to women—no innocents and no married women. Ever.

He suspected they each left out important details about life with Moser, but it was plain that it had not been a willing marriage for either.

They'd had a roof, food, but the marriage itself was something Connor couldn't imagine.

Did all this excuse Grace from lying to him, letting him believe she was free to be with him? What else could she be hiding from him?

When they'd both finished, Grace continued. "Divorce is easy here, Connor. I've read some and heard people at Jasper's talk about it. All I need to do is file and give the reasons. Most divorces are granted. I was waiting until I'd taken Meggie from him. I thought it best if we did it together."

Connor sat back and crossed his arms over his chest. "And if he tries to stop you?"

"He won't," Meggie said. "Ada, wife number two, heard several men talking at a meeting. With the ruling against plural marriages, many men are considering divorce so they're not arrested. It's the family situations that stop them from doing it right away." She stood and walked over to stand by Grace. "Ada said Jeremiah planned to divorce Grace and me. He felt he owed us nothing and there were no children. He hadn't made up his mind about Ada, but I know she wants to leave."

"Why would he do that if he'd already made the decision to hideaway and keep the marriages?" Jericho asked.

"I don't know for certain, but Ada thinks his half-brother, Parley Smith, encouraged him to rethink his marriages. Parley is going to divorce also rather than face arrest. He told Jeremiah the church would work out housing and other needs for the divorced women. I didn't quite believe what she'd heard was true, but now it makes sense. If I'd stayed he probably would have divorced me anyway, but I couldn't live there any longer. I wanted to get away, like Grace did." She grabbed her friend's hand and squeezed.

The room fell silent. Jericho watched Connor, knowing how his friend felt about deceit of any kind, and his strict avoidance of married women. His gaze switched to Grace and the misery he saw etched in her face. He hoped his friend could move beyond this. In Jericho's opinion, Grace was the second best thing to ever happen to Connor. The first was finding Meggie.

Connor pushed from the table and looked at Meggie, avoiding Grace's pleading stare. "Tomorrow, we do whatever is needed to file for divorce, Meggie. Then we leave for Fire Mountain."

"And Grace?" Meggie asked.

"She can do whatever she wants. It's up to her." Connor turned and walked outside, leaving them all to stare at his retreating back.

Meggie reached over and grabbed Grace's hand. "He didn't mean it, Grace. Anyone can see he cares a great deal about you. Right, Mr. Jericho?"

Jericho took a deep breath, looked at Meggie then Grace, before answering. "I've known that boy a good, long time. When he cares about someone, like you, Meggie, he'll move mountains to do what he can for them. He never stopped searching, which meant he never built a life of his own. His focus has been on finding you." He stopped to consider his next words. "Yes, I do believe he cares about you, Grace. It's the first time I've ever seen him open up to a woman, ask her to follow him. But, you've got to understand—Connor's beliefs are very black and white. No lying, no deceit, and no married women." Jericho stood and shoved his hands in his pockets. "Grace, you should've told him about Moser. My guess is he would've waited, understood, and helped you. Now? Well, now I just don't know. I'm sorry, Grace." He didn't follow Connor out front, but made his way out the kitchen door, preferring his own solitude.

Meggie squeezed her friend's hand tighter. "You can't give up, Grace. You must go with us tomorrow, file for divorce, and leave for Fire Mountain. I won't leave without you."

"You saw the look in his eyes. He hates me." Grace swallowed hard and lowered her face to hide the tears that threatened. "I should have told him."

"Yes, but you did what you thought was best at the time. We'll figure it out and move on. Give him some time. Let him work through it and figure out how much he cares about you. Please?"

Grace took a ragged breath. "I'll go tomorrow with you to file for divorce. After that, well, I don't know."

******

Connor walked the perimeter of Ruth's property, coming to terms with the fact that Grace hadn't been honest with him—and it was no small omission. He'd suspected she'd been married but thought her a widow. It never occurred to him that the woman he'd fallen for, hard, was still married.

He needed to get away from Grace, forget how he'd been duped, and move on.

Leaving for Fire Mountain without her was the best thing for both of them. She'd meet someone else, a man she could be honest with, and go on with her life. He and Meggie would join Pierce at the ranch, then he'd figure out what to do next, without Grace. The sharp pain in this chest should've been a warning that his line of thinking wasn't the answer, except he had no experience with a woman running a knife through his heart. He turned at the sound of a horse approaching.

"I'm going to the saloon for a drink. You care to tag along?" Jericho asked as he reined his horse to a stop in front of Connor.

"Not tonight."

"All right. I'll be back here in the morning to go with you to the file the papers. You plan to leave tomorrow or the next day?"

"Tomorrow. The sooner I get out of here, the better."

Jericho studied him a moment before speaking. "You make sure that's what you want, laddie. Women like Grace don't come into your life every day."

Connor gazed up at his friend, taking in the words, but knowing they held no meaning for him. "She stays here. It's over." Connor turned back to the house and sat down on the front step, not ready to face the women inside. He watched Jericho ride out, wishing circumstances were different.

A door slamming around the side of the house had him standing. He saw a lone figure walk down the drive toward the street, open the gate, and leave. Grace. She never lifted her eyes from the ground, never looked for him. She just kept walking until she was out of his sight. The stabbing pain returned to his chest, stronger this time, more intense. He knew he might never see Grace again, hold her or make love to her. Connor knew he had to live with it the way he had so many other things in his life.

He opened the front door, his hand gripping the handle much tighter than needed, and turned to look once more over his shoulder. Grace was gone. Out of his sight and now, out of his life.

Chapter Twenty-One

"Can I help you?" One lone clerk stood at a counter, scribbling on a piece of paper.

"This woman wants to file for divorce. Can you help her with that?" Connor asked and nudged Meggie forward with his hand on the small of her back. She'd begged him to stop at Grace's so that she could come with them. He'd refused. She kept looking over her shoulder, certain she'd see Grace walk through the door at any moment. She didn't.

The clerk reached for a form below the counter. "Fill this out and hand it back to me." He slid the paper across to Meggie.

Fifteen minutes later she turned the form in, Connor paid the man in cash, and, according to the clerk, they were done. The final papers would be mailed to them in Fire Mountain, in care of the MacLaren ranch. He walked her outside and down the steps.

"Let's go," Connor said to Meggie and the waiting Jericho, who'd stayed with the wagon. He guided the wagon back to Ruth's.

It didn't take long for them to pack. Jericho had purchased a horse and tack for Meggie that morning. He'd also purchased a second horse, for supplies he'd told Connor. The reality was, he hoped Connor would change his mind and let Grace ride along.

"Thanks again, Ruth. You've been more than generous to us," Meggie said as she hugged the older woman.

"I'm glad to have met all of you. You be sure to come visit if you're ever back in Salt Lake. I'll be real angry if I hear of you coming to town and not stopping to say hello," Ruth said and shielded her eyes from the mid-morning sun.

"We'll do that for certain, Ruth," Connor told her. "You ever get an itch, come south to Arizona and visit for a bit. I have a feeling you and our Aunt Alicia would become fast friends."

"Thank you, Connor. I may just do that." She stepped back and watched the three ride out the front gate, wishing there had been a different outcome for Connor and her friend Grace.

******

"I'm not going," Meggie stated as they left Ruth's and turned onto Main Street.

"What are you talking about? Of course you're going," Connor replied, not expecting his sister to put up a fight about leaving Salt Lake.

"I will not leave Grace behind. She's my friend, and even if you don't care about her anymore, I do." Meggie had brought her horse to a stop and refused to budge.

Connor reined his horse around and stopped next to his sister. "She's not coming to Fire Mountain. Don't argue with me on this. Grace stays here."

"Then so do I." She didn't know where Grace lived but she knew who could tell her. She'd stay with her friend until either Grace agreed to go with her to Fire Mountain or until Connor came to his senses and let her leave with them today.

"Ah, hell, Meggie. Can't you just let this be? Whatever Grace and I had, well, it's done."

"Only because you're too bullheaded to understand why she didn't tell you about Jeremiah."

"She didn't tell me she was still married. That's a big deal in my way of thinking."

"Do you love her?" Meggie glared at him. There was no way he'd win this argument. She knew Connor would never leave without her. They'd all stay or all leave, and that was it as far as Meggie was concerned.

"That's none of your business," Connor fumed, not comprehending there was no way he'd win this discussion.

"Well, I love her and I'm not leaving without her."

They sat astride their horses, each waiting for the other to give in. Neither budged even when Jericho rode up next to them.

"I can shift the supplies from the extra horse to our saddlebags so Grace can come with us," Jericho offered.

"You know damn well that's not the reason she's not coming," Connor stated and shifted his gaze to Jericho who nodded for the younger man to follow him. They rode a few yards away, coming to a halt.

"Listen to me, Connor. Meggie knows no one but you, Pierce, and me. Sure she'll make friends and the MacLarens will take to her easy." He glanced back at Meggie, sitting erect atop her horse. "Now Grace, those two are thick—know things about each other they may never share with anyone else. Not because they don't want to but because they may not trust anyone enough. They're more like sisters than friends. You just found Meggie, don't be losing her so quick to pride." Jericho held up his hand when Connor started to protest. "Take Grace with us. We'll get her settled in Fire Mountain, help her find work, then you don't have to ever see her again. At least Meggie will have her there and that is what's important right now."

Connor didn't like it, not any of it. He'd made his decision last night and hadn't planned to change it. Now this. What he hated most was that Jericho made sense, even if Connor didn't agree. He thought Meggie would be fine, with or without Grace, and Grace would certainly be all right in Salt Lake, where she'd grown up. He stopped on that thought. At least, she implied she'd grown up here. For all he knew that was a lie, too. He'd been honest with her, laid his past out for her to accept or reject. Why hadn't she done the same?

"Connor? What do you plan to do?" Jericho asked.

"Hell, I guess we'll take Grace with us." His disgusted tone hung in the air. Jericho knew it would take Connor a long time to forgive Grace.

Connor rode back to Meggie. "Let's get Grace and get out of Salt Lake."

"What if she still needs to file her papers?" Meggie asked. "You refused to pick her up this morning and she may not have had time."

"We'll take her to the clerk and get it done before we leave. Satisfied?" He was angry and frustrated. Connor wasn't used to being backed into a corner, forced to do something he felt was wrong, and all of this felt wrong. He didn't wait for Meggie to say anything more, just nudged Crusader toward Grace's place.

It was two blocks away. Connor walked up the steps and knocked. No answer. He tried again, still nothing. He tried to peer inside but the curtains were drawn. Maybe she'd gone back to work at Jasper's. They'd stop by the restaurant, but if she wasn't there, he was going to leave with Meggie and Jericho, even if he had to tie Meggie to her horse to get out of town.

Connor descended the stairs and looked up the street to see Grace walking toward them. Her head was bent, eyes on the ground, as she approached. It wasn't until she'd begun to cross the dirt street that she saw Connor. She came to a halt and started to turn around to head back toward where she'd been but stopped when Connor called to her.

"Grace! Hold up a minute." He didn't run to her, didn't walk fast, just ambled across the street to within a couple of feet of her. "Meggie wants you to come with us to Fire Mountain. Get your things." He started to turn away.

"And you, Connor? What do you want?"

"I'm letting Meggie make the decision on this. If you want to come, fine. If not, that's okay too, but you'll have to explain it to Meggie." This time he did leave Grace standing alone with her hands in her coat pockets. She watched as Connor said something to Meggie, who dismounted and made her way over to Grace.

"Come with us, Grace, please? Connor's agreed and I don't want to go without you. We'll start our new lives together."

More than anything, Grace wanted to go with Meggie to Arizona, start over, and forget the past. She'd find work and a place to stay, and forget Connor MacLaren. All she had to do was make it from Salt Lake to Fire Mountain, three to four days according to Jericho, without letting Connor see how much his rejection hurt.

"Did you file your divorce papers yet?" Meggie asked.

"Yes. I was coming home when I saw Connor. They'll send the papers to Jasper." There was no excitement in her voice at the step she'd taken to free herself from her hated marriage. She should've been elated, but all she felt was a tired emptiness.

"Good, Jasper can forward them to you in Fire Mountain. You can grab what can be packed in saddle bags and we'll leave. Connor's ready to get moving." Meggie grabbed Grace's hand and tugged her across the street. "I'll tell Connor and Jericho."

An hour later, they were a couple of miles outside of town, heading south at a steady pace. Connor in front, Meggie and Grace in the middle, with Jericho at the back. Meggie kept up a steady stream of conversation, attempting to focus Grace on her future and not on Connor. Unfortunately, Grace's eyes had been focused on Connor's back since they'd left Salt Lake—if she stared long enough, maybe he'd turn around and acknowledge her.

"Do you want to work in another restaurant?" Meggie asked after another couple of miles.

"Yes, that would be best. Maybe a laundry or general store."

"Connor says it's a good sized town and the territorial capital. There must be lots of work in a town like that."

"What will you do?" Grace asked.

"I hadn't thought about it much as I've only been a maid. Eugene and Dodge had their servants teach me how to sew, but I'm not a real seamstress. I might be able to take care of children, help out in someone's home." She took a deep breath then continued. "I'm just glad to be away from Jeremiah."

Meggie lapsed into silence, not knowing what else to say without repeating herself.

They stopped in a small town later that night. Connor left the three of them at a restaurant while he sought out the sheriff to confirm their route for the next day. He returned to the small boarding house where he'd taken rooms and ate his supper alone.

Connor took a few bites, then threw his fork on the plate. He hadn't been able to get Grace off his mind all day. He'd felt her eyes on him, staring, as if she intended to bore a hole straight through him. It was a damn uncomfortable feeling, and one he didn't intend to live with tomorrow. He'd change places with Jericho and ride behind the women.

******

Fire Mountain, Arizona

"Have you met the man Torie's parents sold their hotel to?" Pierce asked his cousin Jamie MacLaren as they worked fixing fences in one of the outlying pastures.

Torie was Jamie's wife. Her parents had owned the large hotel and mercantile for years until their recent decision to retire to spend more time with their grandchildren, Torie and Jamie's boys, Isaac and Caleb. "Last week. Torie, Niall, Kate, and I met him at a dinner Jerrod Minton hosted. Her folks were there." Jamie tore off a glove and wiped his hand over his damp forehead. "We'll have a party for them sometime soon to celebrate their retirement. They wanted to let things settle first. Why?"

"He from back East?"

"Yeah, I believe so. Wanted to expand his properties. Don't know what all he's into, but sounds like a couple other hotels. He also has some lumberyards. The way he tells it, he won them in some sort of poker bet. Drew wants to have him meet Dunnigan."

All the MacLarens knew and respected Louis Dunnigan. Three of them had worked for him—

Connor, Drew, and Pierce. Drew still handled all the legal affairs for Taylor-Dunnigan, a company half owned by Drew's father-in-law, Grant Taylor. Their business dealt in cattle and timberland, but the two men wanted to expand into the lumberyard trade.

"Makes sense," Pierce answered. "Wonder what brought him all the way out here to Fire Mountain?"

"Says he wants to open a lumberyard here. Heard it was a growing area, with rail service. He met Torie's parents right after he got to town. Guess things progressed from there." Jamie straightened from his position, bending to wrap wire and cut it. He stretched his arms above his head and twisted his body from side to side, eyeing his cousin. "Why all the questions?"

"No reason. Saw someone with Jerrod at the Desert Dove the other day. Looked to be from back east. You know, clothing and all. Just trying to get to know the people around here." Pierced mimicked his cousin and stretched his tight muscles. They were of similar size. Jamie was several years older, the second oldest of the four MacLaren brothers.

"Well, you'll meet him soon. Torie and Kate are already planning the party." Jamie warmed at the thought of his wife, Torie. A few years ago he would've never thought he'd be in this position—married, with two sons. He'd been a U.S. Marshal, and the woman he'd loved his whole life had been as far out of reach as the stars. Now they were together. You just never knew what surprises life held.

Chapter Twenty-Two

"You haven't said two words to Grace since we left Salt Lake. Don't you think that's a little childish?" Meggie had slowed her horse so that Connor would catch up. He'd been riding behind them all day. It was dusk. She knew he wanted to make it all the way to Fire Mountain that evening, but it looked as if they'd have to find a place in Flagstaff and finish their journey the following day.

Connor continued to stare straight ahead, directly at the back of the woman who was the object of Meggie's concern. He'd made it a point to distance himself from Grace. She needed to know—the secret she'd kept was a major issue for him and their relationship. Relationship. The word passed through his brain and stuck. He'd never been this attracted to a woman before, at least not in any romantic way.

He lived his life by simple rules. These rules had guided his journey to find Meggie, saved him from stepping over the line in sticky personal situations, and kept him alive in some tough circumstances. As far as Connor was concerned, they weren't open for interpretation or negotiation. You broke a rule and there was hell to pay, pure and simple.

Except, he'd never been in love before. Being this close to her for two days and not daring to speak with her, touch her, was about to drive him insane. He needed to get to Fire Mountain, help Grace find work, and a place to live—then make the final break with her.

He turned his head toward Meggie. "I understand your friendship with Grace, and I respect it. That's the only reason she's with us. You've pushed me enough on this, Meggie. You have to let go. I won't be with a woman I can't trust to be honest. It's that simple. I'll do what I can to get her set up in Fire Mountain, but after that, I'm through with her."

Meggie settled deeper into her saddle and thought about his words. He was right. This was a decision he had to make for himself, even though she felt it was wrong. She knew Grace was in love with Connor and suspected he felt the same toward her friend—at least, he had. Connor had always been stubborn. Once he made up his mind, no matter what else transpired, he seldom changed it. Meggie wished it were different.

"You're right. I know this is your decision, it's just hard to watch."

Connor didn't respond but focused his attention forward toward the town that had appeared in the distance.

It didn't take long to find rooms in the Weatherly Hotel and board their horses. Flagstaff was a growing town with rail service to California, cultural attractions, and booming commerce.

"Why don't you take the ladies to supper?" Connor asked Jericho as they stood outside the hotel. "I'll meet you in the morning after breakfast."

"If that's what you want," Jericho replied and walked up the steps. Connor hadn't taken one meal with Meggie and Grace since they'd left Salt Lake. It wasn't right but Jericho wasn't going to get in the middle of this one.

The ride to Fire Mountain took four hours the following morning. Connor wanted to take Grace into town and get her settled some place, except he didn't want to keep Pierce from Meggie any longer than necessary. He'd just have to put up with her presence for one more night. He could do that.

The MacLaren ranch wasn't hard to find. Everyone in the area knew the way and, just before noon, the four riders entered the large, impressive ranch. Three men were getting ready to mount their horses when one of them looked toward the road and saw the riders.

"By God, they're here," Pierce said to Jamie and jumped on his horse, racing to see his brother and sister. A couple of minutes later, he had Meggie off her horse and was swinging her around. "Ah, Meggie. You've no idea how good it is to see you," Pierce exclaimed and set his sister down. "You look wonderful—grownup and as beautiful as I remember." He reached up and shook hands with Connor and Jericho. "And who's this?"

When Connor didn't answer, Meggie walked over to where Grace still sat astride her horse. "This is my good friend, Grace Moser. She decided to come with us to Fire Mountain."

"Well, it's a pleasure, Grace Moser." Pierce smiled up at the beautiful woman, who blushed at his perusal. "It's a wonderful town. I'm sure you'll like it."

They looked up at the sound of more riders approaching.

Jamie and Will greeted Connor and Jericho. "This must be Meggie," Jamie said and looked at the woman who no one could mistake for anyone other than a MacLaren. "I'm your cousin, Jamie MacLaren, and this is one of my brothers, Will. We're glad you're here."

"Thank you," Meggie smiled at her cousins. "I'm very glad to be here. This is my friend Grace Moser. She's decided to settle in Fire Mountain."

Even though both Jamie and Will were happily married men, Connor still didn't like the way each looked at Grace with obvious approval. "It's a pleasure to meet you, Grace," Will said and tipped his hat. "Now, let's get you all to the house. Aunt Alicia can't wait to meet Meggie."

******

Supper was a grand event. Aunt Alicia and the other women had been cooking all day, getting ready for Meggie and Connor's arrival.

Alicia watched with interest the way Grace and Connor went out of their way to avoid each other, even taking seats at opposite ends of the table. Yet, Connor's eyes rarely left the lovely young woman all through the meal.

"Mr. Jericho tells me you plan to find work and a place to stay in town. What kind of work do you do, Grace?" Alicia asked as she passed around dessert.

"I worked at a small restaurant in Salt Lake, so that would be my first choice. I can also clean rooms or perhaps find work in a laundry." Grace said as she fidgeted with the napkin in her lap. It was easy to see that Meggie would be well cared for by a family who worked hard and wanted for little. She deserved it, Grace told herself, while at the same time realizing she didn't seem to fit. Her discomfort rose with each new discovery about the MacLaren family.

"We have a new proprietor at the hotel, plus he owns the mercantile," Alicia commented. "Bought it from Torie's parents. Perhaps Torie and Jamie could introduce you to him. I hear he's been real fair to all the workers."

"That's a wonderful idea, Aunt Alicia," Torie said and looked toward Grace. "I'll be happy to introduce you as soon as the new owner is back in town. I heard he had some business to attend to back east."

"I'm ready anytime. I need to find something and get settled as soon as I can." Grace looked around the table then down at her lap. She'd noticed Connor staring at her throughout the meal. Each time she looked up, his eyes were on her as if he were judging her and finding her wanting.

Connor had treated her the same on the entire journey. Grace knew he didn't want her with them, had agreed only to keep Meggie from staying in

Salt Lake. The truth was, she was fed up with his actions and wanted to be away from him as much as he wanted to be out of her life. She needed to get out of this house and away from him without delay.

******

Meggie and Grace helped clear the table, then excused themselves to walk outside. It was a beautiful, cloudless night and a sky full of clear, bright stars. They headed toward the barn. Amanda had told them that one of their mares had birthed a colt the day before and they wanted to take a look.

Meggie held a lantern as they entered the dark, cavernous space. "Over there," she pointed to a stall near the back.

It was large, built for the purpose of holding a mare and her newborn foal. The women peered through openings in the slats and watched, neither speaking.

"Do you still dream, Meggie?" Grace asked after a while.

"About Dodge?"

Grace nodded.

"Yes, quite often. I don't know why after all these years, but the dreams still come. Sometimes a couple a week."

"You loved him and still miss him. The dreams may never go away."

"I hope they don't. It's the one way he stays in my life—I don't want to let him go."

Grace reached over and grabbed her friend's hand. "He'll always be in your memories. Always."

Meggie looked at her friend. Even during the worst times with Jeremiah, Grace stayed positive, certain a better life lay ahead. It had been rare to see her without a smile. That had changed since Connor found out she had kept her marriage a secret.

"Are you planning to stay in Fire Mountain?" Meggie asked.

"I'd like to. Your family is wonderful and they're so committed to each other. I just need to put my feelings for your brother aside and forget he ever meant anything to me."

Grace continued to watch the mare and colt. They were so at peace while she felt as if her insides were being torn apart. She didn't understand how she'd developed such intense feelings for Connor after a few short weeks.

Grace glanced at Meggie. Her friend had been through so much in her short life and still she was the strongest person Grace knew. She thought back over the last few weeks and all that had happened, including dissolving her marriage to Jeremiah. She was a free woman, with a chance at a new start.

"I can't let Connor's inability to forgive me ruin what could be the best opportunity I may ever have. I'll stay for now, find a good job, and a place to live. Maybe, in time, I can become a part of this town." She smiled at Meggie. "Besides, you're here."

Meggie threw her arms around Grace. "We'll have a good life here, I'm sure of it."

******

"You want to tell me what's going on?" Pierce asked. He and Connor had ridden into town and taken a table at the Desert Dove.

"What are you talking about?"

"You and Grace. What's going on between you two? And don't tell me nothing."

Connor's gaze shifted toward a curvy brunette who strode toward their table.

"Hello, Pierce. Who do you have with you tonight?"

"Good evening, Mollie. This is my brother, Connor. He arrived from Salt Lake a couple of days ago."

"Welcome, Connor. What can I get you gentlemen?"

"Two whiskeys."

"Coming up." Mollie turned toward the bar.

Connor's eyes followed her, moving from her head to her toes.

"Don't even think about it," Pierce said. "She isn't one of the upstairs girls. According to Ross, the bartender, she serves drinks, nothing more." He sat back and enjoyed the same view as his brother. "She is something, though."

Connor's head swung to his brother. "So that's how it is."

"No. At least, not yet." Pierce watched Mollie walk to their table.

"Here you are. Two whiskeys. Anything else?"

"No, Mollie. That'll do it." Pierce held up his drink. "To having all three of us in one place again."

Connor returned the gesture, downed his whiskey, and held up his empty glass. "A couple more, Mollie, when you have a chance."

A minute later Mollie returned with two more glasses and a bottle. "Thought you might want this." She set everything on their table. "Let me know when you're done."

Pierce tore his eyes away from Mollie and sat back in his chair. "Now, tell me about Grace."

Connor poured another whiskey and held up the glass, studying the amber liquid. "She and Meggie were married to the same man, Jeremiah Moser."

"I've already heard that part, plus that they both filed for divorce. Now, tell me the rest."

Connor's jaw worked as his gaze took in the saloon owned by his oldest cousin, Niall. He'd heard it was the most successful bar in a town that boasted at least fifteen drinking establishments. Niall was thinking of buying out one of his competitors. If he did, he'd need someone to manage both places. He'd asked Connor to consider it. The time had come for Connor to focus on what he'd do next—stay in Fire Mountain or leave. The last person he wanted to talk about was Grace.

"All right. How's this for a guess. You fell for her, got involved. The first woman you've ever felt anything for, besides Meggie. My guess is she feels the same for you. Except something happened that went against your strict set of rules, and now you're both paying for it. Am I close?"

Connor sat up in his chair and rested his arms on the table. He rolled the glass between his hands. "She should've told me she was married."

Pierce studied his brother. Now it made sense. "She wasn't up front about her marriage and you bedded her, thinking she was free."

"Yeah."

"The problem is, you still care for her. Too much."

"Yeah."

Pierce knew his brother well and understood this was no small issue for Connor. Trust was something he valued above all else. When that was lost, it was almost impossible to reclaim.

"Jericho says she's a good woman."

"She is," Connor replied.

"Just not the woman you fell in love with?"

Connor's gaze shifted to his younger brother. "Hell, I don't know what or who she is. And I never said I was in love with her."

"That's good. You'll be able to walk away without a backward glance. Let her pick up her life, meet someone else, and forget about you. Sounds like a wise plan."

Pierce watched the effect his words had on Connor and saw what he expected—uncertainty and hesitation. Perhaps his brother hadn't made a firm decision about Grace after all.

"I've got to get out of here. You coming along?" Connor asked as he pushed up from the table.

"Not right now. Think I'll stay around and see what develops."

Connor nodded, knowing the development Pierce referred to was the pretty new bar maid, Mollie.

He pushed opened the doors and stepped outside. It was another clear, crisp night. He was about to walk down the steps to Crusader when a man stopped beside him.

"You must be Connor MacLaren."

Connor looked to see a tall, dark haired man with a badge offer his hand. "Sam Browning. I'm the sheriff."

"Nice to meet you, Sam. I've heard a lot of good things about you."

Sam didn't respond to the compliment. "Word has it you found your sister after a long search. Must've been hard. Congratulations."

"Eight years, but Meggie is finally where she belongs."

"My wife, Gloria, and I have been invited out to Anna and Hen Wright's retirement party. We'll look forward to meeting Meggie." Sam glanced up and down the street. "Well, better finish my rounds. Have a good evening, Connor."

Connor watched Sam move down the street. He knew Sam had a deputy named Cord McAllister who'd grown up with his cousins, plus a few other deputies. His cousin, Drew, mentioned that even though Fire Mountain had little crime, everyone felt it smart to have a strong sheriff and several deputies. The town was the territorial capital and they believed it sent a message to those who might not agree with the peaceful atmosphere. So far it seemed to be working.

Perhaps, if Niall did buy another saloon, he should consider his cousin's offer to manage it. He could always go back to being a Range Detective or an investigator for Alex McCann, but that would involve traveling and he didn't want to be away from Meggie now that they'd found her. Niall said he could always work the ranch, like Pierce. The cousins had already deeded off a section of land for Pierce and planned to do the same for Connor. At least there were options.

He needed to decide if he could stay in this town, with Grace, and not regret his decision to walk away.

Chapter Twenty-Three

Connor joined Drew and Tess on their ride to check on the horse stock. Drew, along with his brother Will and their wives, were in charge of the horse breeding program at the ranch which was growing at a rapid pace. Niall and Jamie ran the cattle operations.

Each of the brothers had their own place. Connor was staying with Drew, the first MacLaren cousin he'd met while working for Louis Dunnigan. When Connor arrived at the ranch Drew had been insistent he stay with them. Meggie and Grace were at the big house with Niall, Kate, and Aunt Alicia, while Jericho bunked down at Jamie's.

"What are your plans, Connor?" Drew asked as they rode toward the northern most pasture.

"Not sure yet. I've never been a rancher, so this is all new to me. Dunnigan offered me a position with Taylor & Dunnigan, but I'm not sure I want to go back to detective work."

"The way I hear it, Dunnigan would be willing to offer you just about anything to get you to stay with him and Grant." Drew turned his head toward Connor. "You've got a lot of skills that could be put to good use in their expanding operations. And I've got to tell you, the pay is good."

Drew was the attorney for the growing cattle, timber, and lumberyard business the two men were building. Even though the business was headquartered in Cold Creek, Colorado, Louis Dunnigan and Grant Taylor had allowed Drew to work from Fire Mountain, only traveling to Colorado when needed.

"I'll see what they offer. I've done a lifetime of traveling, searching for Meggie. Might be good to settle some place."

"You're welcome to stay here, carve out your own place on the ranch. We'd love to have you." Tess smiled over at him. He'd met Tess when she and Alicia had traveled to Denver, before she and Drew had married. He liked her, as well as all the MacLaren women.

"Been thinking about that. Guess I need a little time to let things settle in now that Meggie's here. She's turned into a strong woman, yet there are things that went on over the years still causing her pain. She's become good at hiding her feelings, covering things with a smile. I sense she struggles with accepting the events of the last eight years." Connor paused a moment, deciding how to best say what was on his mind. "I want to be here for her, not make any decisions until I know she'll be okay."

"Grace mentioned Meggie doesn't use the last name of her ex-husband in Salt Lake. Moser, is it?" Tess asked. At Connor's nod, she continued. "Grace didn't say what last name she uses, but it's not MacLaren. Grace is going to use her maiden name, Madison. It's understandable that neither of them want to acknowledge their marriage to Moser."

Connor's gut clenched at hearing Grace's name. With them living in different houses he hadn't seen her since the day they'd arrived. Meggie had told him she and Grace planned to go around Fire Mountain, look for work, and a place for Grace to live.

Drew stopped at the top of a small hill and pointed. "Those are the horse pastures, fenced off for different uses. We've put the mare and her new colt in the small one closest to us. Those three over in that area," he indicated another fenced area where other horses grazed, "are all due in the next few weeks. It won't be long before we'll need to get them to the barn. We're in the process of planning out a couple more birthing stalls. It all takes time."

Time, Connor thought. He needed more time to decide his future, see how Meggie did in Fire Mountain, and forget his feelings for Grace. It would all work out with enough time.

******

"Aunt Alicia and Torie may be right about waiting until the new owner of the hotel comes back into town. We've been to every restaurant except the hotel and no one seems to be hiring." Meggie was surprised at the size of the town. She'd expected a small, quiet, out of the way settlement. Instead, she'd learned that Fire Mountain was the territorial capital with new people moving in all the time and new businesses opening at a rapid pace.

"You'd think with all the building that someone would be hiring. Seems I'm either too early or too late. At least a couple of places asked me to come back in a couple of weeks." Grace wouldn't let herself get discouraged. A job would open up someplace and, in the meantime, Niall had fronted her the money to find a place of her own. That is, after Grace had turned down he and Kate's third offer to let her stay with them.

"Do you want to see the boarding houses Alicia mentioned? Two are right down the street." Meggie shielded her eyes from the sun and looked in the direction of the two homes with rooms for single women.

"Yes, I need to find out if they have any rooms available and what they cost." Grace had every intention of paying Niall back as soon as she could. She didn't want to be in anyone's debt.

An hour later, Grace counted out money for two weeks at a boarding house one block from the central business area, which meant a block from many of the saloons. The one upstairs room available was large, with new linens, and included a shared bath the landlady had added a few months before. There were three additional bedrooms downstairs plus a parlor, dining room, large kitchen, and another bath.

Maude, the owner, lived in a small place behind the boarding house. She and her husband had built both, first the small home when they were newlyweds, then the larger home when they'd raised their family. Her children were now all grown and her husband had passed three years before.

"Will you stay here tonight?" Meggie asked, disappointed that she and Grace hadn't had more time to talk over the last couple of days.

"I think that would be best. Connor needs to feel free to visit any of his cousins, and you, without believing he'll run into me. Besides, I want to be in town to meet the hotel owner as soon as he arrives."

Grace took her belongings off the horse Jericho had provided for her in Salt Lake. She didn't own much—everything fit into two small bags, plus a heavy coat tied to the back of the saddle.

"Please tell Mr. Jericho thanks for the use of the horse."

Meggie stood beside her friend, knowing the time had come to leave, yet her stubborn feet wouldn't respond. "When will I see you again?"

"Why don't you come into town this weekend? Maude said the boarders can have a visitor for supper on Saturdays."

"That sounds wonderful." Meggie hugged her friend. "You'll get a message to me if you find work, right?"

"Of course I will. See you Saturday." Grace watched her ride away, waving when Meggie turned and raised her hand.

******

"Meggie. Meggie, wake up, you're dreaming." Alicia sat on the edge of Meggie's bed trying to wake her from what appeared to be a bad dream.

It took a moment for Meggie to come out of whatever was troubling her. Eyes wide, she stared around the room, trying to remember the identity of the woman sitting beside her.

"Was I dreaming?"

"Sounded like more of a nightmare," Alicia said and poured Meggie a glass of water from the pitcher on the dresser.

Meggie accepted the glass, taking a couple of swallows, and trying to clear her head.

Dodge. Another dream about Dodge—except this time he was lying in a pool of blood and clutching his chest. He was saying something but she couldn't make it out.

She was screaming, trying to free herself from the grasp of two men who pulled her from the room where Dodge lay dying. She kicked at them and tried to dig in her heels, spitting at one who reared back and slapped her before wiping the dampness from his face.

Meggie had passed out, not waking until they'd ridden a long distance from the house. She had no idea of the carnage left behind. Her thoughts were focused on one man, Dodge, and whether he'd survived. Her brain told her it wasn't possible, not with the wide swatch of blood spreading across his chest. Her heart, however, wouldn't let go. It hadn't in all these years.

"Do you want to talk about it?" Alicia asked.

"No, not tonight, Aunt Alicia. Perhaps in the morning." Even as the words came out Meggie knew she wouldn't talk about the nightmare with her aunt. The only person Meggie had ever shared her dreams with was Grace. "Thank you for waking me. I'm sorry if I woke you."

"Don't be silly. I can't tell you how many bad dreams and nightmares I've interrupted over the years since the boys first came to live with Stuart and me." Alicia's eyes wandered over Meggie's face, knowing it had been a terrible nightmare. She wouldn't push Meggie. It was her decision to talk about the dream or keep it locked away.

"Well, if you're sure you're all right, I'll go back to bed."

"Goodnight, Aunt Alicia."

"Sleep well, Meggie."

******

"Grace, Meggie is downstairs to see you," Maude called from outside Grace's bedroom door.

It was early afternoon. Even though Grace had said to come for supper, Meggie couldn't wait any longer.

Grace raced downstairs. "Meggie, I'm so glad you came early. We can walk around town for a while. You won't believe all the different items for sale in the shops or the beautiful window displays." Even though they'd walked the town a few days before, neither had taken the time to look in the windows. She linked her arm with Meggie's and walked outside.

They strolled along the wooden walkway, peering into shops featuring beautiful dresses, jewelry laid out on black or green fabric, and stunning hats. They were looking into the window of once such shop, Meggie pointing to a particular item, when they heard a man clear his throat.

"Good afternoon, ladies. Allow me to introduce myself. I'm Chaz Yarbrough." He removed his hat and made a slight bow. Meggie recognized the southern inflection to his voice, the same as Dodge's. "I couldn't help but wonder what the two of you are looking at in the window."

"Nice to meet you, Mr. Yarbrough. I'm Miss Grace Madison and this is my friend, Miss Meggie MacLaren." Grace noticed Meggie wince out of the corner of her eye. Meggie had insisted on using Dodge's last name ever since his death, even when married to Jeremiah Moser. To Grace's way of thinking it was time she went back to MacLaren, especially now that she'd settled in a place where people thought of the family as almost the town founders.

"Pleased to make your acquaintance. Now, show me what it is that has you so fascinated." He peered over their shoulders.

"Do you see the cameo brooch, the one in the center with a dark rose colored background and figure of a woman in white?" Grace asked.

"Why, yes, that one is especially lovely. It's made of shell, you know. It is from an estate in the south. As I recall, it belonged to a woman who died very young."

"Really? Did you know her?" Grace asked, startled that the gentleman knew so much about the cameo.

"No, not personally. A friend of mine was acquainted with her family. I bought it from him and brought it to Fire Mountain."

"You own this shop?" Grace took a longer look at Chaz Yarbrough, wondering what an east coast gentleman was doing opening up a small shop in what many would consider a frontier town.

"Yes, I do, along with four others. Not all are jewelry or antiquity shops, however all do quite well." He turned to his left. "You see that drug store? It has a soda fountain. May I buy you two ladies a sarsaparilla or ice cream soda?"

"Ice cream soda? I've never heard of it, have you Meggie?"

Meggie hadn't been able to take her eyes away from Chaz Yarbrough. His clothes, his manner, and southern drawl pulled her in, allowing memories of Dodge to wash over her.

"Meggie?"

"Oh, I'm sorry, Grace. What did you say?"

"Ice cream sodas. Have you ever heard of them?" Grace repeated.

"No, never. Why?"

"Because Mr. Yarbrough has offered to treat us to one at his drug store." Grace flashed the most stunning smile that Chaz had seen in a long time. It was a smile he had a hard time pulling away from.

"I met a man in Philadelphia a couple of years ago, a Mr. Green, and he'd invented a drink he called the ice cream soda. People loved it, so I asked him if I could purchase the recipe and bring it west. It took some coaxing, but I am now able to offer it in my drug stores."

They walked slowly toward the store, looking into more windows as they passed by.

"You own more than one drug store?" Grace asked.

"My partner and I own three, or is it four? This is the latest one." He stopped to open the door and allow the women to pass in front of him. "Timothy, three chocolate sodas, please," Chaz called to the boy behind the counter.

"Yes, sir," Timothy called back and grabbed three glasses from a shelf behind him.

A few minutes later Meggie, Grace, and their host sat drinking the delicious beverages.

"This is wonderful, Mr. Yarbrough," Grace exclaimed and continued to sip on the frothy drink.

"And you, Miss MacLaren, do you like it?"

"Yes, very much. This is a real treat."

An hour later Chaz escorted them back to Grace's boarding house.

"Thank you so much, Mr. Yarbrough. That was the best afternoon we've had in a long time." Grace looked up into the handsome face with sparkling blue eyes. She noticed some of his mahogany colored hair had escaped his hat to fall on his forehead. It gave him a boyish, mischievous look. He swept the hat from his head in one fluid motion.

"I wonder if it would be all right to call on you, Miss Madison? Perhaps take you to dinner?"

Grace was so stunned her mouth fell open. Regaining her composure, she fumbled with her small reticule before answering. "Why yes, Mr. Yarbrough. That would be lovely."

"Good then. I will call for you on Tuesday evening, if that is acceptable?"

Grace nodded, a slight trace of color staining her cheeks.

"Ladies, it was a pleasure. Miss Madison, I will look forward to seeing you on Tuesday." He set his hat back on top of his head and strolled away, leaving two very surprised women behind.

Chapter Twenty-Four

Grace and Meggie dashed upstairs, hardly containing themselves from talking about Mr. Yarbrough before they entered the bedroom. They chatted about Chaz, his different businesses, southern drawl, and his invitation to take Grace to dinner.

"I hope it was all right to accept," Grace commented after they'd exhausted all they knew about Mr. Yarbrough.

"Why wouldn't it be all right?" Meggie asked, confused by the question. "You're a beautiful, single woman. Of course you should have said yes. That is, of course, unless you find him unattractive."

Both women burst into laughter at Meggie's comment. The man was exceedingly handsome, more so than most men either woman had ever met.

Meggie stayed the night, riding home just after breakfast to a house full of people. It was Sunday morning and everyone had just come home from church.

"Where have you been, Meggie?" Pierce said as he walked up to her. "Connor is in a state, so watch out."

"Oh, no. I'm so sorry." She looked into the room to see Connor glaring at her. "I rode into town yesterday to have supper with Grace. One thing led to another and I decided to spend the night rather than ride home alone in the dark."

She hated causing either of her brothers to worry. They'd been through enough over the last few years without her doing something else that caused more concern. "I'll go speak with him."

"Hello, Connor." She reached up to place a kiss on his cheek.

"And where have you been?" She could see him trying to rein in his temper.

"I had supper with Grace last night. It was late, so I stayed at her place in town. I'm sorry if it caused you to worry."

"And how is Grace?" Jericho walked up and gave Meggie a slight hug.

"Oh, she's wonderful. And the best thing, she's been asked to supper by a very dashing gentleman we met in town yesterday."

Connor choked on the coffee he'd been drinking.

"What man?" Connor ground out loud enough that all other conversation stopped.

Meggie glanced around the room realizing she shouldn't have said anything about Grace and her supper engagement.

"Mr. Chaz Yarbrough invited her to have dinner with him and she accepted."

"Chaz Yarbrough? Does anyone know this man?" Connor asked no one in particular.

"I haven't met him myself but believe he owns a drug store and a couple of other places in town. He's a friend of the new owner of the hotel," Niall offered. "Do we need to check him out?" he asked, only half joking.

"No! You'll do no such thing." Meggie's hands were on her hips as she addressed the rest of the MacLarens. "We met him today and he took us for ice cream sodas at his drug store. He walked us back to the boarding house where Grace lives and asked her to supper."

"When?" Connor's voice had turned hard.

"Tuesday. But I'm warning you, Connor, do not ruin this for her. You walked away from her, so let her move on. She deserves to meet new people and have fun." Meggie's face turned red as she confronted her oldest brother. He'd already hurt her closest friend through his stubborn pride and she'd do anything she could to prevent him from interfering in her new life.

So that was it, Alicia thought as she scanned the room seeing the looks on each person's face. She'd guessed something had gone on between Connor and Grace, yet neither had acknowledged a thing.

"Mr. Jericho," Alicia said to the man who stood a foot away. "I'd like a word with you, please."

Connor glared at Jericho, warning him not to say anything about Connor and Grace to his aunt.

"I'm not going to lie to her," Jericho said as he followed Alicia into the kitchen.

As soon as they were in the kitchen, Alicia turned to look up at the man who stood close to a foot taller than her. "I think I'd like to go to supper on Tuesday night, Mr. Jericho. Would you be free to accompany me?"

A giant grin broke out on Jericho's face. "Why, I'd be honored Mrs. MacLaren."

******

"Good evening. I'm Chaz Yarbrough, and I'm here to call on Miss Madison." Chaz had removed his hat and stood erect at the front door.

"Well, don't just stand there, come in. I'll get Grace for you." Maude closed the door behind him and walked to the foot of the stairs. "Grace, there's a gentleman here to see you."

Chaz heard a door open and close before he saw Grace descend the stairs. She looked beautiful in a simple cotton dress and shawl. She'd done her hair in ringlets at the back and wore a simple gold necklace.

She stopped in front of him. "Good evening, Mr. Yarbrough."

"Good evening, Miss Madison. You look stunning." He took another moment to appreciate the view then turned and offered his arm. "Shall we?"

She smiled up at him and his long, tedious day went from ordinary to brilliant in a split second.

He escorted her two blocks away to the restaurant in the hotel his friend had purchased from Anna and Hen Wright. Chaz had moved west to help run the operation for his friend who frequently traveled on business as well as open the other stores he'd shown Grace and Meggie.

"Have you been here before?" Chaz asked as he seated her at their corner table.

"No. I've only seen it from the outside, but I've heard it has a new owner."

"Yes, it does. He's been out of town but returned today. Perhaps he'll come down and I'll introduce you."

They'd just ordered their meal when Grace looked up to see Alicia MacLaren and Mr. Jericho enter the restaurant. Alicia spotted Grace and headed straight to her table.

"Hello, Grace. It's so good to see you." Alicia looked at the tall man who had stood when she approached the table.

"Mrs. MacLaren and Mr. Jericho, what a nice surprise. This is Mr. Chaz Yarbrough. Mr. Yarbrough, this is Meggie's aunt, Mrs. MacLaren and their family friend, Mr. Jericho."

"I believe the MacLarens have a connection to this hotel. Am I correct, Mrs. MacLaren?" Chaz asked.

"In a way. My nephew, Jamie MacLaren, is married to Victoria Wright."

"Ah, Mr. and Mrs. Wright's daughter." Chaz glanced at Grace, then back to the older couple. "Won't you join us?"

"That's very kind of you but we'll let you two young people enjoy your supper alone. Nice meeting you, Mr. Yarbrough."

Chaz watched them being escorted their table. "Do they dine out often?"

"I don't know them well, but no, I don't believe they do."

"Quite a coincidence, don't you think?"

It took Grace a minute to grasp his meaning before she laughed. "You don't think...?"

"I certainly do." Chaz smiled at her and relaxed in his chair, glad he'd asked this beautiful woman to supper.

******

"So what do you think of him?" Jericho asked after the waiter had taken their order.

"Seems like a nice man. Very proper, yet not stiff like many who come out here from the east. We'll see." Alicia picked up her glass of wine and took a sip. She wasn't much for drinking, yet she was enjoying the evening out. It had been years.

"Connor is outside you know, over in the courthouse square."

Alicia turned in her seat to look out the window. "Ah, I see him next to one of the larger trees. Do you think he'll cause trouble?"

"No. The lad wants to be sure she's safe, that's all."

"Well, you may think that's all, but I'm not so sure. I think he cares a great deal more about Grace than he lets on."

"Oh, you are right about that. The boy's in love with her, but too stubborn to see things from her point of view and not just his." Jericho sat back in the chair and focused on the woman across the table. He was glad she'd invited him to accompany her tonight.

"And what did happen, Mr. Jericho?"

He wouldn't betray Connor but felt an obligation to explain what he could. "There was a misunderstanding, you see. Connor didn't realize the lass was still married when he," Jericho paused, "well, when he decided she wasn't just someone passing through his life and how much he wanted to be with her."

"I see."

"He and your other nephews have much in common from what I can see. All take their obligations seriously, look out for the others in the family, and have strict codes of conduct that drive them. Until Grace, Connor's code had served him well. Now? I just don't know."

******

Meggie rode to Drew and Tessa's house wanting to visit and to speak with her brother, and to be sure he wasn't planning to ride into town.

"Hello, Meggie. Please, come in." Tess opened the door and stepped back. "We're sitting down to dinner and you'll join us, of course."

"Thank you, Tess, but I've already eaten. Actually, I came by to talk with Connor."

Tess looked to Drew who had joined them in the small foyer. Drew cleared his throat.

"He's not here. Rode out about an hour ago. Said he was headed to town."

"Oh, no," Meggie moaned and ran outside, mounting her horse, and taking off before either Tess or Drew could say another word.

Meggie rode non-stop, finally reining up in front of the hotel where she saw the MacLaren carriage. Sliding off her horse, she tried to dust off her dress and fix her hair—neither attempt did much good.

As she turned toward the hotel entrance she saw Connor standing across the street, watching but not approaching her or the hotel. He was relaxed, leaning against a large tree trunk, and pulling on a cheroot. She didn't remember him ever smoking and hadn't noticed it on the ride from Salt Lake. There was still much she didn't know about him.

Meggie looked into the restaurant to see Grace and Chaz engrossed in conversation. Grace laughed at something Chaz said then picked up her cup and took a sip. Meggie walked across the street to stand by her brother. "Nice night."

"Yes, it is." Connor ground out the last of his cheroot under his boot. "What are you doing here?"

"The same thing you are. Making sure Grace is safe. Is she?"

"Appears so. Guess I'd better head back. You coming?" Connor asked.

"Yes." As she turned to cross the street Meggie noticed a man walking into the restaurant. Something about him seemed familiar. The hair, his height, and the way he stood. She stared for a moment, her breath caught in her throat.

"No, it couldn't be," she whispered.

"What did you say?" Connor asked but Meggie didn't hear him.

Her legs moved on their own, up the steps to the hotel entrance, toward the restaurant, and toward Grace's table. She could feel her heart pounding in her chest.

Alicia and Jericho noticed the scene unfolding across the room but stayed in their seats.

"Meggie, wait up." Connor came up behind her and grasped her arm. She shook it loose. "What are you doing?"

"The man. The man walking toward Grace's table. I have to look at him." She kept moving until she stood no more than six feet away, and stared at a man she knew so well. Her stomach clenched as her breath caught.

"Dodge?" she said on a soft whisper.

The man turned, the shock on his face clear. He moved closer. "Meggie," he breathed out just before her eyes rolled back in her head and his arms wrapped around her to stop her fall.

******

"Who the hell are you?" Connor demanded as they waited in an upstairs hallway for Doc McCauley to check out Meggie.

Grace stood a few feet away, next to Chaz, and wanted to know the same thing as Connor. Alicia and Jericho had followed everyone upstairs and waited for the man's response.

"I'm Dodge Delaney. Who are you?"

Grace began to move toward the tall, handsome hotel owner.

"Connor MacLaren. Meggie's oldest brother. What just happened down there?"

"You're Dodge?" Grace asked. "The man who was to marry Meggie?"

Dodge looked at the woman he'd seen at the table with Chaz but had not met. "Yes."

Grace hauled back and landed a blow to his jaw that any man would've been proud of. "You despicable piece of trash." She moved toward him again, preparing for another blow. "You lying..."

She was stopped by Connor's strong arm around her waist pulling her back toward him. "Stop, Grace."

She kicked and tried to pull free of Connor's grasp. "You did this to her," she spit at Dodge. "All these years and you let her believe you were dead."

Alicia moved to help calm Grace as Jericho moved to within a few feet of Delaney, between Dodge and Chaz.

Dodge scrubbed a hand over his face. "I'll explain, if you'll let me." He paced to a chair, slumped into it, and stared at the floor. "I didn't die that night, although everyone thought I had."

Connor had no idea what his statement meant. "Grace, I'll let you go if you let Delaney speak. If you act up again, I'll haul you out of here, hand you over to Sheriff Browning, and come back so that I can learn what's going on. You understand?"

She let out a disgusted breath. "Yes, of course I understand. Let me go."

Connor dropped his grip and walked over to stand before Dodge. "I want to know everything before I'll let Meggie get anywhere near you again."

"God, Meggie. She's been alive all this time," Dodge mumbled, more to himself than to anyone else.

"Yes, she's alive but life's been hard. Very hard," Connor pulled up a chair in front of Dodge. "Now. Tell me why."

It took Dodge thirty minutes to give a short version of his life with Meggie, ending with what most thought was his death. "I was in a hospital for weeks. Meggie was gone. I had every one of my men looking for her. Hired a private detective. Nothing. She'd vanished. A few months after she disappeared I received a letter telling me Meggie was dead." He reached into his pocket and pulled out a chain with a small locket. "This came with the letter." He dropped the necklace into Connor's hand.

He stared at what most would consider to be nothing special. "It was our grandmother's. She gave it to Meggie on her fifth birthday."

"If she wasn't wearing it, she had it in a pocket. She was never without it." Dodge leaned back against the chair then stood and turned suddenly, slamming his palm into the nearby wall. "Damn it. The letter said she was dead."

Chaz had stood silent. He'd heard the story of Meggie many times and knew his friend had never stopped loving her. He'd never heard Dodge mention her last name, only Meggie. Until now, he hadn't connected her to his friend. Chaz had been in Europe for an extended stay and missed the death of his other good friend, Eugene Jackson, as well as Dodge's *almost* death. He'd arrived back in

Charleston in time to help nurse Dodge back to health, physically if not mentally. It had taken a couple of years before his friend was ready to face life again. This time without Meggie.

"Do you want me to check with the doctor?" Alicia asked. She turned to see Caleb McCauley walk out of the room.

"She's awake," Doc McCauley informed everyone. "Extremely disoriented and agitated." He looked to Alicia. "I want her to stay in town tonight. You may take her home in the morning." He shifted his gaze to Dodge. "She's asking for you, Mr. Delaney. Or, more accurately, saying your name."

Dodge pushed away from the wall. "All right." He walked through the door on shaky legs and closed it behind him. She was in one of the upscale guest rooms, in a huge bed with expensive linens. She looked like a child, laying on her side, facing away from him.

"Meggie?" he whispered as he got closer. "Can you hear me?"

She turned slowly and stared at him, accusation and pain on her face.

He pulled a heavy upholstered chair next to the bed and sat down, trying to calm his racing heart. He reached out to caress her cheek, pulling back when she flinched.

She licked her lips and shifted to her back, staring at the ceiling.

"Are you thirsty?" He grabbed a nearby pitcher, poured water into a glass, and held it out to her. She didn't move. He sat on the edge of the bed, glass in hand. When she didn't acknowledge his presence he set it on a table and leaned over her.

"I was told you were dead, Meggie. They sent me your grandmother's locket as proof."

Her eyes shifted to his. "I saw you die."

"One of the kitchen staff got away and went for help. They took me to the hospital, where I stayed for weeks. By then, you were gone." He searched her face, looking for any sign of forgiveness or understanding. "I looked for you until I received the letter and locket, then I believed you were truly lost to me." His voice broke.

She reached over and grabbed his hand, squeezing it tight. "I never stopped loving you." Her voice had the same soft lilt he remembered.

Dodger reached into a pocket to pull out the gold band he'd planned to give her that night. He opened her hand and pressed the ring into it. "Ah, Meggie, I'll always love you." He pulled her to him and held tight. "I'll never let anyone take you away from me again."

******

Connor insisted Meggie go back to the ranch with him. Dodge insisted she wasn't leaving. In the end, Grace suggested that Connor take a room at the hotel, with Meggie in a room next to him. Dodge took a room on the other side of Meggie. It wasn't ideal, but it was progress. Alicia and Jericho excused themselves to ride back to the ranch, wanting time to explain to the rest of the family what had happened.

Chaz waited while Grace said goodbye to Meggie. She closed the door to her friend's room and knocked on Connor's. He opened the door and stared at her, a question in his eyes.

"Did you want something, Grace?"

She hesitated. Her feelings for him hadn't changed. Not one bit, even though he wanted nothing more to do with her. She cleared her throat. "I just wanted to say that Meggie has loved Dodge for years. I doubt she'd have ever been with another man, not willingly. That's how much she still loves him." She turned to leave.

"Grace?"

She looked back. "Yes?"

He struggled for words. What he wanted to say was that he wanted to work it through with her, figure out a way to put the past behind them and move on. "Thanks for being such a good friend to Meggie."

"You don't understand. I'm the lucky one." This time she did walk up to Chaz and let him escort her home.

Chapter Twenty-Five

"Everything is beautiful, Torie. You and the others worked miracles to have our retirement party so soon." Anna Wright hugged her only child.

"What are your plans, Mother? Will you and Father travel?"

"We'd like to, as soon as everything is set with Mr. Delaney. He understands the hotel business quite well, and his friend, Mr. Yarbrough has experience in the mercantile trade. We hope to leave for New Orleans in a few weeks. I've always wanted to visit that city and now we have the chance."

Torie watched as her husband and her brother-in-law, Niall, talked to Pierce. She knew they wanted him to stay at the ranch. He was smart and a quick learner. Jamie had told her that he asked lots of questions, many of which caused the brothers to look at the way they operated and consider changes for improvement. She noticed that Jerrod Minton had joined the men.

"Tell me more about your background, Pierce. I understand you're an expert at several trades." Jerrod Minton handled everything from land issues to criminal charges.

"I wouldn't say I'm an expert, but I've had a variety of jobs. I started out apprenticing in a small tool shop. The reasons for the tools fascinated me.

Come to find out the owner had a side business—breaking into homes. It was more of a hobby than because he needed the money. I accompanied him several times, watched, and started doing it on my own."

"You were a thief?" Jerrod choked out.

"Let's just say I took from people who owed my employer money and refused to pay." Pierce sipped his beer and watched the reactions of the men who stood around. "You must understand, the docks around Red Hook were rough. It was hard to make a living. When someone contracted with the shop to make tools, then didn't pay, it affected a lot of people. They usually thought that because they came from money they could stiff the owner. He'd try to collect, but when nothing came, I'd help out, and became pretty good at it."

"You never got caught?" Jerrod was fascinated. Pierce's background was so opposite his own.

"Well, not exactly. At least, not by the law." Pierce thought back on the time Jericho had followed him. He'd caught Pierce as he left a home with a sack of jewelry. Made him return every piece. From then on, Pierce was more careful about being followed.

"You gave it up?" Niall asked, as curious as Jerrod was to learn about his cousin.

"No, not completely. Alex McCann had hired Connor to help with his investigation business. Alex hired me to gather information others couldn't get. By then I'd learned how to open safes, most anything that had a lock. I didn't steal, just found information and relayed it to Alex."

"Why'd you quit?" Jamie asked.

"I was offered a job working for a man who was a decoder during the war. He'd also become proficient at spotting counterfeit bills. He taught me all he knew about both. It's amazing how many coded messages are still used. People don't completely trust telegrams for important communications so they have the messages written in code. We coded and deciphered a lot for the government, private businesses, and wealthy individuals. Also helped a couple of government offices when they'd confiscated what they thought were counterfeit bills and needed someone to confirm if they were authentic or fake."

"Now you're ranching? Quite a change." Jerrod took note of all of Pierce's different skills. Skills that people Jerrod knew could put to use if Pierce was interested.

"Wouldn't say I'm ranching, not yet, but I'm learning."

"Yeah, he's learning to tear up his hands and grow callouses just fine. Good thing he already knew how to ride and handle a gun or we'd be in real trouble," Niall chided his cousin. He admired the younger man and his older brother. He and Connor had done it all on their own.

"Come see me this week, Pierce. I'd like to run some things by you, get your input." Jerrod had been contacted a few weeks before by a gentleman looking for specific skills. Pierce might be interested in what the man had to offer.

"Does this have anything to do with Delaney?" Pierce asked the attorney.

"What makes you ask?"

"Nothing. Just curious, that's all."

"In a roundabout way, yes. I'll explain it all when we meet."

"Works for me. Well, looks like the ladies are ready to serve up the food. Anybody else hungry?" Pierce eyed Jerrod, wondering what the attorney had going on that required his help. Guess he'd find out in a few days, but his gut told him it had something to do with the newest business owner in Fire Mountain.

Meggie and Dodge hadn't gotten more than five feet away from each other all day. She continued to finger the gold engagement band on her right hand, the one he'd carried all those years. They'd made plans to marry the following weekend. A simple ceremony at the ranch with her family, followed by supper at the hotel. She'd move into his suite at the hotel until he had time to build her a house. He wanted lots of children.

Now, Meggie watched Connor standing alone on the porch, his arms crossed, leaning against a wall, and watching Grace visiting with a group of women.

Meggie's heart ached for the two of them.

She knew Grace was putting up a brave front, pretending not to notice the way his eyes followed her everywhere, and acting as if it didn't bother her when another pretty woman tried to engage Connor in conversation. Meggie knew not one of them interested her brother. His eyes were fixed on Grace.

******

Connor tapped on the downstairs bedroom door the women were using.

"Who is it?" Torie asked.

"Connor."

"All right, come on in as long as Dodge isn't with you."

He turned the knob, pushed open the door, and stopped to take in the sight. "You look beautiful, Meggie."

She wore a magnificent cream and light gold colored silk wedding dress with pearls sewn across the bodice and down the skirt.

Meggie turned to flash a brilliant smile toward her brother. "You think he'll like it?"

"I think Dodge and everyone else will find you stunning."

"Come on, Meggie, turn back this way so that I can finish applying the last of the pearls," Amanda said as she gently placed her hands on her cousin's shoulders to turn Meggie toward her.

Kate and Tess walked into the room, preparing to make the final touches to Meggie's hair. The ceremony was to take place in the front room in thirty minutes and everyone was milling around outside.

"Where can she be?" Meggie asked no one in particular.

"Who?" Connor asked.

"Grace, of course. She's my maid of honor."

"She'll get here, don't worry. Stand still," Amanda chastised.

"She was supposed to ride out with Dodge and Chaz."

"Both just arrived, but without Grace. I'll go check with them," Connor said as he walked outside with brisk strides and down the front steps. Dodge was with Jamie, Drew, and Will, laughing about something one of them had said. "You know when Grace plans to arrive?" he asked Dodge without preamble.

"Isn't she here? Her landlady said she'd left quite a while before Chaz and I came to pick her up. Is something wrong?" Dodge asked.

Pierce and Niall walked up to join the men to catch the last of what Dodge had to say.

"She's not here. Meggie is worried."

Everyone turned at the sound of shouting as a rider, who was pushing his horse hard, came to a stop. "Fire, downtown. We need all the men we can get!"

"I'll go tell the women," Will said and dashed into the house.

The others ran to find their mounts, Drew grabbing Will's horse, Justice, and leading him to the front steps. Will bounded down the steps, jumped on Justice, and the two were off, following the other men to town.

The sky darkened as they rode closer. Big billows of black smoke appeared. They rode straight toward the center of town, where most of the smoke seemed to be coming from, and saw several buildings consumed by unrelenting flames. A wind from the southwest encouraged the fire, sending balls of flaming debris from one building to another.

Niall was the first to dismount and ran up to Sam Browning, the sheriff.

"Where do you want us?"

Sam held a damp bandana over his face and coughed before answering. "Our one fire wagon is on Curtis. Why don't you form a water brigade on Walker, the next street over? You won't have much support. All the other volunteers are doing what they can on the other streets."

The men dismounted and let their horses go, not wanting to keep them in the area of fast moving flames. Each dipped their bandanas in a nearby trough and tied them around their faces. It was two blocks to Walker Street and they took off at a fast pace, skirting other volunteers, grabbed anything that could be used as a bucket, and located water pumps.

They stopped in unison at the horror before them. Flames engulfed virtually every building on the street—it was hard to know where to begin. The sound of crashing timber and screams sent them back into action.

Chaz, with Dodge beside him, found Connor, grabbed his arm and pulled him around. "That's Grace's boarding house." He pointed to a building consumed in flames.

Connor didn't stop to talk but grabbed another bucket and made his way to the inferno that only minutes before had housed several young women. He filled the buckets, but knew his efforts were wasted. The structure was already destroyed. He threw the water onto the flames and ran around to the side of the building. The heat was unbearable and breathing was difficult. He was vaguely aware of other men around him, yelling at him.

"Grace! Grace, are you in there? Can you hear me?" His frantic attempts continued until his throat was parched and raw. He climbed over a burning pile of wood and continued his efforts, wiping a hand across his forehead, trying to see through the dense smoke.

He pulled his bandana tighter around his face and began to charge into what was left of the burning rubble when two sets of strong arms grabbed him from behind. He fought before two more men ran up and helped haul him away from the wreckage.

"Grace!" he screamed repeatedly as the four men physically lifted him and dashed to a safer location. They set him down but continued to restrain him.

"Connor, listen to me," Niall said in a quiet voice. "If she was in the building, there's nothing you can do. You'll only kill yourself. Better to wait and see if she made it to safety."

Connor looked at his older cousin, accepting that he was right, and hating it. He watched the flames turn to ash as the others ran to help form a break further up the street. He stared at the charred building, running both hands through his soot filled hair, not believing he'd lost her.

His dreams had become clear over the last couple of weeks. Watching his cousins and their wives he'd realized that was what he wanted—a stable life, a woman he loved, and children. No more coming up against those too mean to function in normal society. An end to the constant travel. A place to feel welcome without the need to look over his shoulder. To have it all—he needed Grace.

He'd planned to talk with her after the wedding, take her aside and try to work things out. She needed to understand how her lack of trust had affected him. He needed to know that she'd trust him in the future and not carry secrets.

Connor felt the presence of others near him. He looked to see Pierce and Jericho, both dirty with streaks of ash and soot across their faces. They stood next to him, coming to terms with the destruction and death around them.

"Sam Browning says that Dodge has opened the hotel for the injured to be treated. Doc McCauley and his new assistant are working non-stop," Pierce told him. "The women rode out from the ranch and are in there helping out. Mollie Jamison from the Desert Dove and a few other ladies are there also."

"And the dead?" Connor's voice was weary, ready to break.

Pierce indicated the large town square where some tents had been erected. "She's not there. Jericho and I already checked."

"She may have made it, laddie." Jericho wouldn't allow Connor to lose hope. It was hope that had driven the man for eight years and it could drive him now. At least until they knew about Grace.

An hour passed, two, then three, and before long the sun set and the winds calmed. The fire had been contained but wasn't out. Men still worked to water down the burning remains. Red embers glared against the black night and smoke hung thick above the town.

Connor stayed with the family, moving from one building to the next in an attempt to stop anything from reigniting. He refused to go look in the tents. Tess had told him she'd send word if Grace was brought in to the hotel. Dodge and Chaz made sure the doctors had everything needed to treat those who'd been brought to them. Burns, broken bones, cuts, lacerations, and smoke inhalation were being treated as rapidly as possible.

"Here, take this." Drew held out a glass of water to Connor, then drank his own. "What a mess. It'll take months to reconstruct everything." Drew looked behind him at a bench. Nothing on this side of the main street had been touched as if a wall had been erected to keep the flames away. He sat down and rested his muscled forearms on his knees. "Take a seat, Connor. We'll get back to it in a few minutes."

Connor sat down next to his cousin. Others were sitting or lying around them on the trampled grass area, arms over their eyes, trying to catch a few minutes of rest before starting again.

"Look," Will said and sat up straighter. "Who is that?"

Connor looked up at Will's question.

Several of the men stood and started to run toward the scene.

Drew nudged Connor. “Good Lord. Look over there,” he said and nodded with his head.

Connor’s eyes followed the direction Drew indicated to see a woman carrying another woman, stumbling, righting herself, and starting again.

“Grace?” Connor mumbled and stood. “Grace!” He ran to her, taking Grace in his arms as the others accepted the woman she’d been carrying. He picked her up, cradling her against his chest, and stepped over charred wood while making his way back to the bench.

“My God, Grace. I thought I’d lost you.” He pulled her tight, burying his head in her hair. He inched away to look at her. “I’m taking you to the hotel so Doc McCauley can look at you.”

“No, just hold me, Connor. Please?” Grace choked out and tightened her arms around his neck. She continued to cough, trying to clear smoke from her lungs.

He held her close another minute, then stood and walked to the make-shift hospital, needing to confirm that she was all right. Pierce followed behind, unwilling to let Connor wait through this alone.

“Doc, please help us,” Connor said as he walked into the dining room and set Grace on a table with sheets and a blanket.

“Grace!” Meggie saw Connor carefully lay Grace down and ran to stand by her friend. She threw her arms around Connor. “You found her.”

"More like she found us." Connor's voice choked on the emotion and he turned away in an attempt to compose himself.

Grace coughed, her eyes closing at times, then opening. She tried to shield her eyes from the bright lights.

Caleb McCauley walked up, several of the MacLaren women close behind him. "I appreciate your help and all, ladies, but you'll have to give me room to check out Miss Madison."

The MacLaren women backed away but kept their eyes and ears open, anxious to know how Grace was doing. Connor refused to leave and stood next to the table, holding Grace's hand and watching the doc's every move.

Pierce stepped back also. That's when he noticed Mollie Jamison had positioned herself beside him. For some reason his senses always went on alert when he was around Mollie. Tonight he needed to ignore them.

"How does she seem?" Mollie asked Pierce. She was as exhausted as everyone else yet had refused to leave the makeshift hospital.

"She's alive, that's all I know." Pierce placed a hand on her shoulder. "Thanks for all your help."

Mollie looked up at him, surprised. "This is where I live. I'm happy to help." Her eyes moved from his face to the table where the doctor continued his examination.

"What happened?" Caleb asked Connor as he moved his hands slowly over Grace's body, checking for any fractures or breaks.

"I don't know. We were taking a break and Will looked up to see Grace walking through the destruction, carrying another woman. Will and Drew took the other woman and I brought Grace to you."

"How is the other woman?" The doctor hadn't seen anyone else being brought in.

Connor just shook his head.

Grace coughed again and tried to speak, her voice was coarse and dry. "She was in the room next to me." She coughed again. "The stairs were on fire. We tried to jump from the window..." She coughed once more before the doctor put a hand on her wrist.

"It's all right, Grace. You can tell us everything later. Right now I'm going to have you sit up so you can breathe easier, and then I want you to rest." He turned to Connor. "I don't feel any breaks or fractures, some cuts and bruises are starting to form, but she's darn lucky to be here."

"Can I take her home?"

Meggie looked at Connor, knowing that Grace's home had gone down in the fire.

"Let her rest a while and I'll check her again. If all is okay, then yes, you can take her home." Caleb smiled and clapped Connor on the shoulder as he walked passed on his way to check another patient.

"Where will you take her?" Meggie asked.

"Where she belongs. With me."

Chapter Twenty-Six

"Hello, Mrs. MacLaren. I've come to see Grace, if she's accepting visitors." Chaz stood outside the main ranch house. He'd heard that Connor had brought Grace here as soon as the doc had given the okay.

"Come in, Mr. Yarbrough." Alicia stepped aside to let him enter. "She's doing much better than a few days ago and I'm sure she'd like some company. Most everyone goes back to town each day to help with the cleanup and plans to rebuild, so it's been pretty quiet around here. I'll be right back."

Alicia walked down the hall to the second room and knocked. "Grace, you have a visitor."

Doc McCauley had issued orders that she was to stay indoors and rest for a week, no exceptions. Grace felt like a prisoner even though she was grateful to be alive. Two other boarders had made it to safety. The rest, including Maude, had not been spared from the fast moving fire that destroyed three blocks of homes and businesses.

Grace opened the door, dressed, and ready to venture out of the solitary bedroom. "Who is it?"

"Chaz Yarbrough."

"Oh, how nice." Grace grabbed her shawl before making her way to the front room. "Mr. Yarbrough, it's so good of you to visit."

He walked up to her and took her hands. "You look wonderful." He leaned over and placed a kiss on each hand. "I heard you were doing well."

She carefully pulled her hands away and sat down. "To be truthful, I'm going crazy in this house. It's time I leave and find a new place, plus I must find work."

"Yes, you mentioned needing a job. I spoke to Dodge and we would be grateful if you'd consider working for us in the hotel dining room. We need a manager for breakfast and dinner clients. It would include a room and liberal food allowance."

Her smile grew wide as Chaz spoke. It was perfect and included a place to live.

"That is so generous of you and Mr. Delaney. Yes, I'll accept the offer."

Chaz watched the excitement on her face as he offered her what he knew she wanted. Now, he had to broach a more delicate subject.

"There is one condition. You must understand that neither Dodge nor I allow employees to court other employees. That would mean..."

Grace understood right away. "I see. So you and I..."

"Would remain friends. At least, that is what I hope."

"I would hope so, too."

"Will things work out for you and Connor?" It had been obvious to everyone that Connor had strong feelings for Grace.

Connor. He spent time with her each day, held her hands in his, yet hadn't voiced his desire to work through what happened or his feelings for her.

"I don't know what will happen with Connor." Her voice had softened, losing the exuberance of a few minutes before.

"Do you love him?"

Grace's gaze swung up to search Chaz's face. He'd become a good friend in a short period of time and she liked him. "Yes, I love him."

Chaz looked at his fingers as they worked the brim of his hat and stood. "Well then, it's time I take my leave. We'll expect you at the hotel, say, next week."

Grace walked Chaz outside. "Thanks so much for the job. You won't be disappointed." She stood on her toes to place a kiss on Chaz's cheek. "And thank you for being such a good friend."

Chaz picked up her hand and kissed it. "It's my pleasure to be your friend, Grace."

She watched him mount his horse and ride out, noticing for the first time that three riders were approaching. Pierce, Jericho, and Connor.

Jericho and Pierce had been speaking of plans for the construction of a new boarding house in town when they noticed Connor's attention had shifted to the house. He watched as Grace kissed Yarbrough and as Chaz returned her gesture with a kiss to her hand. The scene appeared intimate and not what Connor had expected to see when he returned to the house. Conversation stopped as the men rode the rest of the way.

They tipped their hats at Chaz as he rode past but didn't stop to chat. Pierce and Jericho continued to the barn while Connor rode straight to the front of the house and dismounted.

"Grace." He looped his reins around the post and stalked up the steps toward her.

"Hello, Connor."

"You're well enough to receive visitors?" He stood a few inches away, his eyes boring into hers.

She clasped her hands in front of her. "Yes."

"And do you always kiss men you don't know well?" His voice was hard. He watched her, deciding if it was time he said something.

"No." He saw the gleam in her eye, which should have warned him. "Sometimes I do more than kiss."

"Shit," he muttered and grabbed her hand, pulling her behind him into the house, and closed the office door behind them. "Have you?" he snarled.

"Have I what?" She was trying to keep her patience. He must have seen that all she'd done was give Chaz a harmless kiss on the cheek.

"Done more than kiss him?"

She walked to within a few inches of Connor. "That is none of your business."

"The hell it isn't," he hissed out.

"Don't swear," she threw back at him.

"I'll talk any damn way I want."

"Fine. Then you'll do it alone." She turned to leave.

Connor reached out and grabbed her arm, hauling her to him until their bodies touched. He could feel her warmth through his shirt as her soft, fast breaths fanned his face. His eyes locked with hers, hard and searching.

Grace stood motionless, glaring up at the man she loved. If only he'd give her a sign that he still wanted her. The beating of her heart was like a drum—fast, hard, and almost painful in its persistence. She wanted to push him away and, at the same time, wind her arms around his neck.

He loosened his grip, moving his hands from her arms to cup her face. He lowered his face to hers and captured her mouth.

She responded hungrily, without restraint, wrapping her arms around him and holding tight.

He slanted his mouth one way, then another before his lips traced her upper then lower lips, coaxing her to open for him. He plunged in, taking what he'd wanted for weeks. His hands drifted from her face to her back, and lower. He pulled her toward him, letting her feel his hardness.

She sighed. This is what she wanted, who she wanted. No one else, just Connor.

He stopped on a ragged breath, resting his forehead on hers.

"I won't accept anything except complete honesty."

"I know," Grace responded.

"No secrets, no lies, no manipulations."

"All right."

"I don't know yet how I'll make a living or where I'll live."

"I understand."

He took another deep breath. "Marry me."

"Yes."

A smile broke across his face and he pulled her in for another searing kiss. “I love you, Grace.”

“I believe I love you more, Connor MacLaren.”

Epilogue

Meggie and Dodge married two weeks after the fire. Today everyone gathered for Connor and Grace's wedding. Now all that had to happen was no emergencies or family crises until they'd said their vows.

Grace and Meggie had talked about getting married on the same day. In the end, they'd decided each deserved to have their own special date to celebrate, a day that belonged to them and no one else.

Now, Grace stood at the top of the stairs waiting for the cue to begin her walk. The sounds of the piano drifted through the air. Alicia nodded to Meggie, Grace's matron of honor, to start, then motioned for Grace to begin her descent down the stairs. She reached a middle step and stopped, seeing Connor's unwavering gaze fixed on her. His moss colored eyes were a deep green and his normally stoic face broke into a smile as she took the last step toward him.

Connor took her hand and pulled Grace to him for a kiss, ignoring the laughter and gasps behind him.

"Uh, Connor, you're supposed to wait until the end," the preacher said.

"Yes, sir. I can wait now." He smiled back at Grace whose eyes were filled with laughter.

An hour later they were man and wife. Although they'd included close friends and family for the wedding, many more were invited to celebrate afterward. The weather had threatened to turn sour earlier in the week, but today the sky was clear and the sun bright.

Nothing could be more perfect.

"Fifty cents," Drew said.

"I'll up it to a buck," Niall chimed in.

"What's going on?" Connor had left Grace's side long enough to visit a few of the men and finally made it to the circle of his cousins and brother.

"Betting how long you and Grace stay before disappearing to Drew's house for the night," Pierce laughed and slapped his brother on the back.

"Whoever bet another five minutes is the winner." Connor chuckled and accepted a glass of whiskey from Jamie.

"Here's to you and Grace. Long lives and lots of children," Niall raised his glass as did the others.

A few minutes later Connor excused himself and began his search for Grace.

Pierce joined him. "Got a minute?"

Connor looked at his brother. Something had been going on the last couple of weeks, but he'd been so busy helping at the ranch and getting ready for the wedding that he hadn't taken the time to ask Pierce.

"Of course," he gestured to a spot a few yards away. "What's going on?"

"I met with Jerrod Minton and another gentleman about a possible opportunity."

“A job?” Connor’s voice underscored his confusion. “I thought you liked it here and were ready to settle down.”

“This might allow me to do both.”

“Explain.”

“The man is in charge of finding a group of men with specific skills to join a government agency that investigates counterfeiting, fraud, and provides political intelligence. Jerrod thought I might have an interest.”

“Sounds like you do.” Connor wasn’t happy with this turn of events. He wanted to be close to his family now that they’d found Meggie.

“I need more information, but yes, I might be interested.”

“They want you to be a Secret Service Treasury Detective, right?”

“How’d you know?”

“Not hard to figure from what you told me. I don’t want you to go, but I understand how you’d be the perfect man for them. Where would you be?”

“Some of the work is right here in Arizona, some in California. They want to set me up with a partner for the first case. Some female they recruited a couple of years ago. I’ve been told she’s turned into one of their best detectives. She’s been snooping around Fire Mountain. With it being the territorial capital, they want to be sure everything’s clean here—apparently it’s not. I told them I’d be interested depending on who the partner is. I refuse to get stuck with some woman who can’t keep up her end.”

"You know this female?" Connor was intrigued.

"Jerrod and another man are bringing her here. They want it to appear social—hope that's all right."

"Hey, there you are." Connor and Pierce looked up to see Grace walking toward them. "Thought I'd already lost you." She looped her arm through her husband's.

"Not a chance," Connor responded and pulled her close. He turned his head at the sound of an approaching carriage. "Looks like that's Jerrod now."

The three waited as the carriage pulled to a stop near them.

"Hello, Jerrod. Thought you might not make it." Pierce extended his hand to the attorney when he jumped from the buggy.

Jerrod shook hands with Connor and kissed Grace on the cheek. "Congratulations. Wish I had been here for the ceremony."

"It was short. Now is the important part," Connor grinned, referring to the reception.

Pierce looked toward the carriage but couldn't see the face of the woman who sat inside with the other man who had his back to Pierce.

"I would guess you're anxious to meet your partner," Jerrod said.

"Possible partner," Pierce countered and waited for the other man to step down.

"Pierce, I'd like you to meet Noah Dodd. He's in charge of most of the western United States and its territories."

"Good to meet you, MacLaren. Heard great things about you."

"Thank you, sir."

Pierce's gaze swung back to the carriage, his curiosity stretching thin. The woman sat erect, her wide-brimmed hat pulled low, a parasol in her hand. She didn't appear tall, more medium height. Nothing else about her jumped out at Pierce.

Noah walked to the carriage and helped the woman down. He escorted her toward Pierce, all the while her face shielded.

"Mr. MacLaren, I'd like to introduce you to your partner."

That's when the woman finally raised her head and smiled.

Pierce stepped back, not believing who stood before him and already not liking this setup.

"Hello, Pierce." Mollie Jamison, held out her hand. "It's good to see you."

Thank you for taking time to read Deadlier than the Rest. If you enjoyed it, please consider telling your friends or posting a short review. Word of mouth is an author's best friend and much appreciated.

Please join my reader's group and sign up to be notified of my New Releases at www.shirleendavies.com.

About the Author

Shirleen Davies writes romance—historical, contemporary, and romantic suspense. She grew up in Southern California, attended Oregon State University, and has degrees from San Diego State University and the University of Maryland. During the day she provides consulting services to small and mid-sized businesses. But her real passion is writing emotionally charged stories of flawed people who find redemption through love and acceptance. She now lives with her husband in a beautiful town in northern Arizona.

Shirleen began her series, MacLarens of Fire Mountain, with Tougher than the Rest, the story of the oldest brother, Niall MacLaren. Other books in the series include, Faster than the Rest, Harder than the Rest, Stronger than the Rest, and Deadlier than the Rest. Book six, Wilder than the Rest, is due for release in early summer, 2014. Her contemporary romance series, MacLarens of Fire Mountain Contemporary, opened with book one, Second Summer. Book two, Hard Landing, released in April 2014, and Book three, One More day, is scheduled to release in midsummer, 2014. Book one of her newest historical western series, Redemption Mountain, will release in the fall of 2014.

Shirleen loves to hear from her readers.

Write to her at: shirleen@shirleendavies.com
Visit her website: http://www.shirleendavies.com
Comment on her blog:
http://www.shirleendavies.com/blog.html
Facebook Fan Page:
https://www.facebook.com/ShirleenDaviesAuthor
Twitter: http://twitter.com/shirleendavies
Google+: http://www.gplusid.com/shirleendavies
LinkedIn:
http://www.linkedin.com/in/shirleendaviesaut
hor

Other Books by Shirleen Davies

Tougher than the Rest – Book One
MacLarens of Fire Mountain Historical Western Romance Series

"A passionate, fast-paced story set in the untamed western frontier by an exciting new voice in historical romance."

Niall MacLaren is the oldest of four brothers, and the undisputed leader of the family. A widower, and single father, his focus is on building the MacLaren ranch into the largest and most successful in northern Arizona. He is serious about two things—his responsibility to the family and his future marriage to the wealthy, well-connected widow who will secure his place in the territory's destiny.

Katherine is determined to live the life she's dreamed about. With a job waiting for her in the growing town of Los Angeles, California, the young teacher from Philadelphia begins a journey across the United States with only a couple of trunks and her spinster companion. Life is perfect for this adventurous, beautiful young woman, until an accident throws her into the arms of the one man who can destroy it all.

Fighting his growing attraction and strong desire for the beautiful stranger, Niall is more determined than ever to push emotions aside to focus on his goals of wealth and political gain. But looking into the clear, blue eyes of the woman who could ruin everything, Niall discovers he will have to harden his heart and be tougher than he's ever been in his life...Tougher than the Rest.

Faster than the Rest – Book Two

MacLarens of Fire Mountain Historical Western Romance Series

"Headstrong, brash, confident, and complex, the MacLarens of Fire Mountain will captivate you with strong characters set in the wild and rugged western frontier."

Handsome, ruthless, young U.S. Marshal Jamie MacLaren had lost everything—his parents, his family connections, and his childhood sweetheart—but now he's back in Fire Mountain and ready for another chance. Just as he successfully reconnects with his family and starts to rebuild his life, he gets the unexpected and unwanted assignment of rescuing the woman who broke his heart.

Beautiful, wealthy Victoria Wicklin chose money and power over love, but is now fighting for her life—or is she? Who has she become in the seven years since she left Fire Mountain to take up her life in San Francisco? Is she really as innocent as she says?

Marshal MacLaren struggles to learn the truth and do his job, but the past and present lead him in different directions as his heart and brain wage battle. Is Victoria a victim or a villain? Is life offering him another chance, or just another heartbreak?

As Jamie and Victoria struggle to uncover past secrets and come to grips with their shared passion, another danger arises. A life-altering danger that is out of their control and threatens to destroy any chance for a shared future.

Harder than the Rest – Book Three
MacLarens of Fire Mountain Historical Western Romance Series

"They are men you want on your side. Hard, confident, and loyal, the MacLarens of Fire Mountain will seize your attention from the first page."

Will MacLaren is a hardened, plain-speaking bounty hunter. His life centers on finding men guilty of horrendous crimes and making sure justice is done. There is no place in his world for the carefree attitude he carried years before when a tragic event destroyed his dreams.

Amanda is the daughter of a successful Colorado rancher. Determined and proud, she works hard to prove she is as capable as any man and worthy to be her father's heir. When a stranger arrives, her independent nature collides with the strong pull toward the handsome ranch hand. But is he what he seems and could his secrets endanger her as well as her family?

The last thing Will needs is to feel passion for another woman. But Amanda elicits feelings he thought were long buried. Can Will's desire for her change him? Or will the vengeance he seeks against the one man he wants to destroy—a dangerous opponent without a conscious—continue to control his life?

Stronger than the Rest – Book Four

MacLarens of Fire Mountain Historical Western Romance Series

"Smart, tough, and capable, the MacLarens protect their own no matter the odds. Set against America's rugged frontier, the stories of the men from Fire Mountain are complex, fast-paced, and a must read for anyone who enjoys non-stop action and romance."

Drew MacLaren is focused and strong. He has achieved all of his goals except one—to return to the MacLaren ranch and build the best horse breeding program in the west. His successful career as an attorney is about to give way to his ranching roots when a bullet changes everything.

Tess Taylor is the quiet, serious daughter of a Colorado ranch family with dreams of her own. Her shy nature keeps her from developing friendships outside of her close-knit family until Drew enters her life. Their relationship grows. Then a bullet, meant for another, leaves him paralyzed and determined to distance himself from the one woman he's come to love.

Convinced he is no longer the man Tess needs, Drew focuses on regaining the use of his legs and recapturing a life he thought lost. But danger of another kind threatens those he cares about—including Tess—forcing him to rethink his future.

Can Drew overcome the barriers that stand between him, the safety of his friends and family, and a life with the woman he loves? To do it all, he has to be strong. Stronger than the Rest.

Deadlier than the Rest – Book Five

MacLarens of Fire Mountain Historical Western Romance Series

"A passionate, heartwarming story of the iconic MacLarens of Fire Mountain. This captivating historical western romance grabs your attention from the start with an engrossing story encompassing two romances set against the rugged backdrop of the burgeoning western frontier."

Connor MacLaren's search has already stolen eight years of his life. Now he is close to finding what he seeks—Meggie, his missing sister. His quest leads him to the growing city of Salt Lake and an encounter with the most captivating woman he has ever met.

Grace is the third wife of a Mormon farmer, forced into a life far different from what she'd have chosen. Her independent spirit longs for choices governed only by her own heart and mind. To achieve her dreams, she must hide behind secrets and half-truths, even as her heart pulls her towards the ruggedly handsome Connor.

Known as cool and uncompromising, Connor MacLaren lives by a few, firm rules that have served him well and kept him alive. However, danger stalks Connor, even to the front range of the beautiful Wasatch Mountains, threatening those he cares about and impacting his ability to find his sister.

Can Connor protect himself from those who seek his death? Will his eight-year search lead him to his sister while unlocking the secrets he knows are held tight within Grace, the woman who has captured his heart?

Read this heartening story of duty, honor, passion, and love in book five of the MacLarens of Fire Mountain series.

Wilder than the Rest – Book Six

MacLarens of Fire Mountain Historical Western Romance Series

"A captivating historical western romance set in the burgeoning and treacherous city of San Francisco. Go along for the ride in this gripping story that seizes your attention from the very first page."

"If you're a reader who wants to discover an entire family of characters you can fall in love with, this is the series for you." – Authors to Watch

Pierce is a rough man, but happy in his new life as a Special Agent. Tasked with defending the rights of the federal government, Pierce is a cunning gunslinger always ready to tackle the next job. That is, until he finds out that his new job involves Mollie Jamison.

Mollie can be a lot to handle. Headstrong and independent, Mollie has chosen a life of danger and intrigue guaranteed to prove her liquor-loving father wrong. She will make something of herself, and no one, not even arrogant Pierce MacLaren, will stand in her way.

A secret mission brings them together, but will their attraction to each other prove deadly in their hunt for justice? The payoff for success is high, much higher than any assignment either has taken before. But will the damage to their hearts and souls be too much to bear? Can Pierce and Mollie find a way to overcome their misgivings and work together as one?

Read Wilder than the Rest, another heartening story of duty, honor, passion, and love in book six of the MacLarens of Fire Mountain.

Second Summer – Book One
MacLarens of Fire Mountain Contemporary Romance Series

"In this passionate Contemporary Romance, author Shirleen Davies introduces her readers to the modern day MacLarens starting with Heath MacLaren, the head of the family."

The Chairman of both the MacLaren Cattle Co. and MacLaren Land Development, Heath MacLaren is a success professionally—his personal life is another matter.

Following a divorce after a long, loveless marriage, Heath spends his time with women who are beautiful and passionate, yet unable to provide what he longs for . . .

Heath has never experienced love even though he witnesses it every day between his younger brother, Jace, and wife, Caroline. He wants what they have, yet spends his time with women too young to understand what drives him and too focused on themselves to be true companions.

It's been two years since Annie's husband died, leaving her to build a new life. He was her soul mate and confidante. She has no desire to find a replacement, yet longs for male friendship.

Annie's closest friend in Fire Mountain, Caroline MacLaren, is determined to see Annie come out of her shell after almost two years of mourning. A chance meeting with Heath turns into an offer to be a part of the MacLaren Foundation Board and an opportunity for a life outside her home sanctuary which has also become her prison. The platonic friendship that builds between Annie and Heath points to a future where each may rely on the other without the bonds a romance would entail.

However, without consciously seeking it, each yearns for more . . .

The MacLaren Development Company is booming with Heath at the helm. His meetings at a partner company with the young, beautiful marketing director, who makes no secret of her desire for him, are a temptation. But is she the type of woman he truly wants?

Annie's acceptance of the deep, yet passionless, friendship with Heath sustains her, lulling her to believe it is all she needs. At least until Heath drops a bombshell, forcing Annie to realize that what she took for friendship is actually a deep, lasting love. One she doesn't want to lose.

Each must decide to settle—or fight for it all.

Hard Landing – Book Two
MacLarens of Fire Mountain Contemporary Romance Series

"The author really gets into the hearts and souls of her characters in this book, which is probably why I fell in love with the story the way I did. Wonderful, wonderful story." - Authors to Watch

Trey MacLaren is a confident, poised Navy pilot. He's focused, loyal, ethical, and a natural leader. He is also on his way to what he hopes will be a lasting relationship and marriage with fellow pilot, Jesse Evans.

Jesse has always been driven. Her graduation from the Naval Academy and acceptance into the pilot training program are all she thought she wanted—until she discovered love with Trey MacLaren

Trey and Jesse's lives are filled with fast flying, friends, and the demands of their military careers. Lives each has settled into with a passion. At least until the day Trey receives a letter that could change his and Jesse's lives forever.

It's been over two years since Trey has seen the woman in Pensacola. Her unexpected letter stuns him and pushes Jesse into a tailspin from which she might not pull back.

Each must make a choice. Will the choice Trey makes cause him to lose Jesse forever? Will she follow her heart or her head as she fights for a chance to save the love she's found? Will their independent decisions collide, forcing them to give up on a life together?

One More Day – Book Three
MacLarens of Fire Mountain Contemporary Romance Series

Watch for One More Day, Cameron and Lainey's story, in the summer of 2014.

For permission requests, contact the publisher.
Avalanche Ranch Press, LLC
PO Box 12618
Prescott, AZ 86304

Made in the USA
Las Vegas, NV
04 August 2021